KARMA'S
CHILDREN
DISCOVERY

MAVERICK MOSES

KARMA'S CHILDREN: DISCOVERY
Copyright © 2019 Maverick Moses

For information contact:
Mastermind Resource Group LLC
www.mastermindresourcegroup.com
Maverick Moses
www.maverickmoses.com

Editing by Melissa Frey
Cover design by Lisandra Gomez. Cover photos by
DepositPhotos.

ISBN: 9781733388306 (paperback)
9781733388313 (ebook)

First edition, 2019
Published by Mastermind Resource Group LLC

KARMA'S CHILDREN
DISCOVERY

MAVERICK MOSES

MASTERMIND
RESOURCE GROUP

*SIGN UP FOR THE
MONTHLY NEWSLETTER*
TO RECEIVE NEWS ABOUT UPCOMING RELEASES,
UPDATES FROM THE AUTHOR, SPECIAL OFFERS,
GIVEAWAYS, AND BONUS CONTENT:

WWW.MAVERICKMOSES.COM

Dedicated to my kind, loving, and wonderful mother. I think about you everyday and I hope you've found happiness in God's embrace. I love you.

CHAPTER 1

*I*N AND OUT, **KRISTA ATWOOD REMINDS** herself as she takes a deep breath then exhales slowly. Stepping out of the shower, one towel hiding her long black hair and another wrapped snugly around her body, she stops at the foggy bathroom mirror and looks at her clouded reflection. Butterflies erupt in her stomach as she thinks about the day to come, the first day of her senior year at Mirror Valley High School. The year she's been waiting for her whole life.

She can't wait.

In and out. She inhales again, closing her eyes and letting the world fall away as she remembers what her mother told her two short years ago, just after her father's sudden death: *Take care of your younger brothers, Krista. I may not be around much because of work, but promise me that you'll look after the two of them whenever I'm gone. Stick together, no matter what happens.*

Krista pictures her mother speaking those words to her fifteen-year-old self, remembering how scared she was back then. She's still scared now. But as she lifts her chin and pushes her shoulders back to stand just a little taller, she reminds herself again that she has no choice. Family comes first.

In and out, she breathes one last time. Opening her eyes, she takes a hand towel and wipes away the steam from the mirror, revealing her clear reflection. She looks deep into her own eyes, really stares, searching for that scared fifteen-year-old girl she's all but abolished. As always, she doesn't find her.

The makeshift knot holding the towel on her body suddenly comes loose, and the towel drops to the floor. She bends over to pick up the towel then straightens, catching a glimpse of her reflection in the mirror once again.

And something else.

At her side, a young girl stares back at her with a pair of haunting eyes; one eye is white, and the other is black. Krista jumps and whips around but only sees the white-paneled wall. She turns back around then and looks back in the mirror.

The strange girl is gone.

Damn, I'm more nervous about today than I thought, she thinks, rubbing her eyes. She shrugs as if to convince herself that nothing is wrong, reminding herself of the potentially wonderful day ahead.

Across the hall, alarms bray in Kevin's bedroom.

"Ugh," he moans as he wakes before he throws a pillow at the ringing alarm clock. *Thunk. Crash!* Kevin abruptly lifts his head then exclaims "oh, shoot!" when he realizes he has also just knocked over his table lamp—and his alarm is still going.

"Why does that work in the movies?" he asks himself as he quickly jumps out of bed to straighten up his nightstand and turn off his alarm.

Kevin sighs. *Well, this is probably an accurate representation of what my day will be like.*

Today is Kevin's first day at Mirror Valley High. Middle school is a thing of the past, and now it's hello to freshman year. *Freshman year,* he thinks to himself as he looks at his tired reflection in the mirror. *AKA, "fresh meat" year. How many times will I get beat up today? How many times will I be made fun of? How many times am I going to trip and drop all my books? Who knows?*

Kevin was only twelve when his father died, not even a teenager yet, and he finds himself missing him more and more as he gets older, wishing he could ask him questions, learn how to become a man. Yes, his older brother lives right down the hall, but they're two different people—and he doesn't really want to turn into his brother anyway.

As the youngest of the three, Kevin has always had to endure the torture wrought by his older brother. His sister, on the other hand, never really picked on him. Though they do have their arguments from time to time, as any siblings do, he has managed to keep his nose clean throughout the years. Afraid of turning into the kind of guy his brother is, he's always been the kindest of the three children. Some might call it passivity, but he prefers thinking of it as just being the best version of himself.

Making his way to his bedroom window, he squints at the rising sun peeking through the woods across from his house. A sense of peace comes over him as he gazes at the immense beauty of the trees. In the last two years, he's found comfort going out into the forest. He enjoys sitting on the massive boulder that not only marks the center of the forest but also, in turn, the center of the town around it. Every time he goes out there, he looks forward to experiencing the euphoria of being the center of his whole world and all he's ever known, even if just figuratively.

While sitting atop the rock, he frequently enjoys one of his favorite passions in life, one he's kept secret from his family: sketching. He'll draw the magnificent trees around him, and, every once in a while, he'll catch a glimpse of wildlife for more than a few seconds and sketch them as well. He hopes that school and the influx of homework won't keep him from practicing his art too much.

Kevin overhears his sister leave the bathroom, so he heads out of his room to get ready for school. "Morning," Kevin says as his sister walks past him on her way to her room to change.

"Morning, Kevin," Krista replies, smiling at her little brother.

Krista has her outfit all laid out and prepped in her closet. She's particularly proud of her find this year. Shopping trips with her brothers are always a struggle because they don't share her love of browsing around. And they especially hate hanging around the young women's section.

Because she is the only one with a driver's license, she had to take her brothers with her when they went back-to-school shopping this year. As the older sister and the responsible one, Krista doesn't allow them to get separated in the store. Klause, especially, doesn't like that. He'd much rather be looking at running shoes or sporting goods, or hitting on high school girls. So when Krista has to shop for clothes, she has to make it as quick as possible.

This year, by some miracle, she found a flirty yet conservative dress. Not too casual, but not too formal. Taking it out of the closet, she puts on the light blue dress with a skinny brown belt and selects a pair of suede boots to match. Finishing off her outfit with a silver necklace, she turns to face her bedroom window.

The red and orange glow of the sun shines over the tops of the trees across from her house. The gorgeous view is something she's always enjoyed about living near the center of Mirror Valley. The town had been built around this small, wooded circle, one only about two miles across. Although she's away from the main hub of the town, she knows she can always feel at home and at peace when she sits by her window and gazes out into the woods.

From the corner of her eye, she notices the time and breaks her trance to look back at herself in the mirror. She smiles as she looks at her fair skin, lightly tanned from summer, and her deep brown eyes, then she picks up a brush to start her makeup.

As Kevin steps out of the bathroom in just a pair of shorts, drying off his shaggy black hair, a woman's voice calls from downstairs. "Breakfast is ready!"

Krista exits her room, her face now adorned with black eyeliner, long eyelash extensions, and pink lip gloss then heads downstairs.

"Be right down, Mom!" Kevin calls, just before pushing his bedroom door closed.

"What do you think?" Krista asks as she strikes a pose at the bottom of the stairs, showing off her new outfit to her mother, Karmasha.

"You look so pretty," she replies. "You're definitely going to get Editor in Chief."

"Thanks, Mom!" Krista smiles. "But I hope I don't get it because of my looks. I'd better get it because I'm the right person for the job."

"I just meant . . . you know, like—"

"Don't worry. I know what you meant." Krista's smile widens.

"Is Klause up? I didn't hear him respond."

Krista puts her hands on her hips and just stares at her mother.

"Ugh. I should've known." Karmasha sighs as she rolls her eyes, then raises her voice. "Klause, get up!"

As she walks up the stairs to wake her eldest son, she thinks to herself, *If your father were here, you'd be getting an earful.*

Karmasha has been doing her best these last two years. She went from having help to being a single parent, and she knows that her work responsibilities aren't helping. With her constant travel, it's hard to keep up with everything. *I wish I didn't have to put so much pressure on her,* Karmasha laments. A tear forms and begins to roll down her cheek, but she quickly wipes it away at the sight of Kevin at the top of the stairs.

"Good morning, sweetie," Karmasha says with a smile as she eyes his combed, shaggy hair, clean-shaven face, and blue jeans with a white graphic T-shirt. "You look nice."

"Thanks." He nods, frowning, and Karmasha notices him rubbing his chin where his stubble would be if he could grow any. A smile pulls at the corner of her lips.

He heads downstairs as Karmasha continues up to Klause's room. Without hesitation, she opens his door, goes straight to the window, flings open the curtains, and lets the bright light of the now fully-risen sun into the room.

"Mmmm," Klause mumbles as the bright light hits his tightly-shut eyes.

Walking over to the bed, she snatches the pillows out from under Klause's head and throws back the covers. "Come on, it's time to get up."

"Engh . . ." Klause groans again, curling into a ball and covering his eyes with his hands.

"Fine, don't get up. Stay in bed. Miss school. Let that lead to detention, which will lead to getting kicked off the football team, which will lead to you picking a fight, which will lead to you getting suspended, which will lead to you losing all your motivation, which will lead to you getting fat and having no job."

Klause's eyes fly open, shooting daggers at his mother and her lame attempt at sarcasm.

"And no hot girl will ever want to be with you again."

Klause's eyes widen at "no hot girl" and he hurriedly jumps up and scurries to the bathroom.

Karmasha chuckles to herself. She knew that would work—the boy is just like how his father was before he met her. She isn't particularly fond of him being a stereotypical high school football player only concerned about getting with girls, but if she could use it to her advantage, why shouldn't she?

≪O≫

Downstairs, Kevin is pouring himself a glass of orange juice from the refrigerator. He takes a seat next to his sister at the dining room table.

"You want some?" Krista says teasingly to her brother as she holds her cup of coffee up to his nose.

"Ew, no," Kevin replies, softly pushing her hand away and scrunching up his nose. "I don't have a burning desire to get addicted to caffeine like you are."

"That's actually probably a smart move." Krista laughs. "Last week I started to get a headache because I had gone just two days without drinking any."

"That's called withdrawal," Kevin teases.

"Whatever," Krista replies, smiling. "You excited about your first day of high school?"

"Nope."

"Why not?"

"I don't think I'll fit in."

Krista's smile widens gently. "It's high school, Kevin—almost nobody thinks they're going to fit in on their first day."

"I vaguely remember Klause did."

"Well, it's disgustingly different for jocks, unfortunately—they already have their cliques."

"Disgustingly different?" Kevin asks.

"I stand by my word choice." Krista chuckles. "It's annoying how easy it is for them sometimes."

Kevin nods his head, looking down at his orange juice, a frown on his face.

"I'm sorry." Krista reaches over and tousles his hair. "Those weren't very good words of encouragement. I guess the best thing I can say is to just be yourself. You are probably the nicest guy I know, and you're so incredibly friendly it's ridiculous. You'll make friends, I'm sure of it. And remember, I'll be there, too. Even though I'll be hanging out with my friends most of the time, I will always be there for you if you need me. Okay?"

"Okay," replies Kevin as his eyes light up and a small smile turns up the corner of his mouth. He side-hugs his sister and briefly lays his head on her shoulder.

"Well, since Klause woke up so late and is still getting ready, I'll go ahead and serve breakfast," Karmasha calls out as she's coming down the stairs. "Don't want the food to get cold."

Unwrapping a foil-covered dish on the counter, Karmasha uncovers a stack of blueberry pancakes. She distributes them to three plates then delivers the plates to the table where the syrup and butter are already waiting.

"Smells great," Krista says. "Thank you, Mom."

Her mother smiles. "You're very welcome, sweetie."

"So, did you sell a lot of drugs on your last trip?" Krista asks her mom.

"Yes, it was a good trip, got a lot of bites." Karmasha laughs. "You know, one of these days someone is going to think I'm a drug dealer if you keep asking me like that."

Krista chuckles. "It's not like I say that in front of everyone; it's just funny. Besides, most people already know you're a pharmaceutical sales rep anyway."

Krista glances at the clock on the wall and turns to focus on her breakfast, nodding at Kevin to hurry as well. Kevin nods back and focuses on his plate.

"Klause, are you ready yet?" Karmasha calls out. "You have to leave soon."

"Coming! Coming!" Klause yells as he runs down the stairs two at a time.

"Now you're not going to have time to eat," says his mother.

"Yes, I will." Klause grabs a pancake and stuffs the whole thing in his mouth.

"Ugh." Krista rolls her eyes. "And that's my cue to leave," she says, getting up from the table and running upstairs to grab her backpack and purse from her room.

"Whatcha lookin' at?" Klause glares at his younger brother as Kevin just stares up at him.

"Nothing," Kevin replies, getting up from the table and taking Krista's and his dirty plates to the kitchen sink.

"Klause," Karmasha says sternly to her oldest son, scrunching her face at his attitude.

"I'm just messing with him," he replies, shrugging his shoulders.

Karmasha sighs. "And is that how you're going to school? You haven't even shaved, and your hair is a mess."

Klause is wearing his characteristic black, slim-fitting jeans and graphic muscle tank, showing off his athletic arms. "No, this is my look," he responds. His face is covered with a short, scruffy beard, and his hair is barely combed, but he somehow manages to look completely in style.

Karmasha shakes her head as she reaches for her purse and car keys. "Is everyone ready?"

"I love you, Mom," Krista responds, coming down the stairs with backpack and purse in hand, "but there's no way I'm arriving on the first day of school driven by my mother. I'll drive us there."

"Yeah, I figured." Her mother sighs. "I was just hoping to spend a little more time with the three of you before I leave for work."

"You're already leaving again?" Kevin asks, eyes drooping. "You've only been back a couple of days."

"I know," Karmasha says, frowning, "but duty calls."

The four of them walk outside, and Karmasha proceeds to give all three of them big—and long—goodbye hugs.

"'Bye, Mom!" Kevin calls out as they climb into Krista's silver SUV.

Karmasha remains standing outside for a few moments, waving and smiling as they drive away. Once they're out of sight, she sighs and lowers her arm. In that moment, all she hopes is that her children, whom she loves so much, will not have to deal with the one thing she never told them about her. Something that forces a special duty on her shoulders. Something she never wanted nor asked for but was bestowed upon her anyway. Something that has tormented her since childhood and can either bring her life incredible meaning or lead to tragedy.

While some might consider it a gift, to Karmasha it's really a curse, especially because it takes her away from her family so often. But this secret—this mystical blood running through her veins—is what makes her who she really is, a cross between an angel and something much more sinister.

CHAPTER 2

I N HER CAR, KRISTA TURNS UP THE RADIO and begins to sing along to some pop music, nodding her head in time with the rhythm. Klause, riding shotgun, reaches over and changes the channel to his favorite rap station.

"We're not listening to that, Klause," Krista says, reaching to turn the radio station back.

"Why not?"

"'Cause it sucks out my energy."

"Well, pop music sucks out *my* energy."

"Okay, how about a happy medium: alternative rock?"

"Fine," Klause says, crossing his arms and slouching back in his seat.

"Actually, what do *you* want, Kevin?" Krista glances in the rearview mirror at her little brother in the backseat. "You never get to pick."

"Whatever you want," Kevin murmurs as he stares out the window and watches the trees pass by. Krista knows he'd rather be out there, in the middle of nature, instead of on his way to his first day of freshman year. He'd probably rather be *anywhere* than on his way there.

But unfortunately for Kevin, they arrive at the high school in just a few minutes. "We're here!" Krista exclaims. Klause rolls his eyes.

As she finds a parking space, she sees Kevin looking out the window at the dozens of students rushing around. It reminds Krista of the images she's seen of Times Square, with so many people from every possible background imaginable. She imagines Kevin is feeling a bit intimidated right now, and her heart goes out to him.

After parking in a spot near the edge of the lot, the three siblings get out of the car and walk together across the parking lot through the crowd, Krista leading the group at the center. As they approach the building, they stop and face the front steps that lead up to the main entrance as one.

They stand there together, all three of them, for only a moment. But in that moment, the past two years of their lives since their father's death flash through their minds, as well as the years that are yet to come.

They recall the influence their father had on their lives and each is filled with sadness at first. But as they consider the school year ahead and how they all will fit in, each of them smile as they realize what the year ahead will really bring.

The three teens whisper to themselves, yet in unison: "I can't wait." And in that moment, a gust of wind encircles the three siblings, and a small vibration ripples through them. Each takes a step forward, bracing themselves, eager for the year to come. What each one anticipates is different, yet, unbeknownst to them all, right then the three become one, and their destinies intertwine. As they continue forward, they take their first steps on the path that will change their lives forever.

After ascending the small set of steps leading up to the entrance, the Atwood children enter the school.

Inside, their eyes are immediately drawn to a huge banner that reads *"Welcome to Mirror Valley High School"* printed in the school's black and red team colors and hanging above the central bulletin board.

The halls smell of fresh mint from the freshly-waxed linoleum tile floors and sounds of laughter, footsteps, and slamming locker doors echo around the siblings.

The first bell rings, and the three turn to look at each other briefly before going their separate ways.

Krista enters her assigned senior homeroom classroom and spots several of her friends. Some are actual friends, girls she's seen in the past week, while others are more like acquaintances, and she hasn't seen them all summer. Because it is senior year, however, Krista makes a goal for herself to make those acquaintances actual friends, so she can establish more connections for future professional opportunities. She's nothing if not practical.

"Hey, girl!" a curly-haired girl by a window across the classroom calls out. The natural rays of sunlight make her copper-brown skin glisten and her already white smile even brighter. Raising her hand in the air, she waves at Krista and signals for her to come over.

"Marsha!" Krista shouts back happily as she maneuvers her way through the desks and milling students to her best friend and embraces her, a giant smile on her face. "How was Connecticut?"

"Boring." Marsha sighs. "There was nothing to do, so I was stuck inside helping my grandma make jam the whole summer."

"Jam?" Krista laughs.

Marsha rolls her eyes. "Yeah. She grows berries in her garden and makes all these different kinds of jam to give as gifts throughout the year. That's all she gives out to family, so she likes to stock up during the summer."

"I bet you're sick of jam now."

"Definitely!" Marsha nods furiously.

RRINNG!!! sounds the second bell, signaling that it's time for homeroom to start.

"Take your seats," Mrs. Burbens calls, and Krista and Marsha head for two empty desks in the front row.

Down the hall, Kevin hears the same words from his homeroom teacher. He looks around, out of habit, for his only friend from middle school, David. But then he remembers that David moved across the country over the summer, so he slumps into a seat in the back corner, away from the main congregation of students.

"Welcome to Mirror Valley High School, students!" Miss Lavers says enthusiastically to the class. "Who's excited for school to start?" she ends with a wide, youthful smile that seems to brighten her already fair complexion.

A student's pen rolling off a desk and hitting the floor is the only sound to be heard as Miss Lavers looks at the class with a broad smile on her face and her arms outstretched.

"Okay . . ." her voice trails off, her excitement level audibly dropping from a ten to a three.

"Did everyone have a fun summer?" she tries again.

Silence.

"Any questions?" Her plump, rosy lips twist to the side.

More silence.

Miss Lavers' excitement falls the rest of the way down to zero, and her bright blue eyes seem to dull for a moment.

"Whatever," she quietly whispers to herself as she turns away from the class and brushes her long blonde hair behind her ears.

Then suddenly she spins around. "I know!" She exclaims to the students. "School sucks, right?"

Eyes widen—finally, a reaction.

"I promise you, I don't want to be here any more than you do. You know why? Because in four years, you all get to leave here and never look back. Meanwhile, I'll be stuck here for who-knows-how-long, thanks to my lowlife of an ex-husband who wiped out my bank account, which caused me to flee from my home in Michigan to avoid getting beaten up by his loan shark, and forced me to crash on my sister's best friend's cousin's couch and come back here to use that teaching certification I got four years ago only as a rock-bottom, last resort!"

Jaws drop in the classroom.

Miss Lavers reaches back over her desk to pick up a banana she had started to peel earlier and takes a bite. With her mouth full, she continues, "So go ahead and sit there and say nothing. Who knows? Maybe you'll get to be held back and have to relive freshman year over and over and never have to experience the absolute joy of adulthood where love and money never work in your favor. Maybe you'll even be lucky enough to turn out like me, staring at a classroom of freshman and just wishing you could throw this banana peel at the face of the ass you call your boss and hope he slips on it, falling and breaking the face he's so proud of, the face he thinks is the most beautiful face in the world. News flash: it isn't!"

No one in the room moves for a solid ten seconds. Then the entire classroom, including Kevin, erupts in riotous laughter.

Miss Lavers sighs and leans back against her desk, crossing her arms across her ample chest.

"Look around you," she says calmly after the laughter dies down. "No, really, do it. Look to your left, look to your right. You're all freshmen. Even me, in my own way. We're all new at this. We're all in this together. We're all just trying to survive, to get through each day and wake up to the beauty of the next. So who's with me? Who else wants to get past that 'fresh meat' stereotype? Who wants to join me and strive toward something more than what's confined within the walls of this school?"

Every hand in the room goes up, including Kevin's, and, in that moment, he realizes that he isn't *completely* alone. And he's even found his favorite teacher already.

After fifteen minutes of announcements and a solemn reciting of the pledge of allegiance, the bell rings and homeroom is done. The students disperse, heading off to their respective classrooms.

The morning continues uneventfully as Kevin experiences his first few high school classes, and Krista and Klause slowly get back into the swing of things. When the bell rings for lunch, the three siblings find each other in the cafeteria and stand next to each other in line.

Krista turns to Kevin. "So how are you liking it so far?"

Kevin shrugs. "It's not bad."

"Made any friends yet?"

Kevin thinks for a moment, figuring that if he tells the truth, his brother will give him a hard time. So he lies. "Yeah, a few."

"That's awesome! I knew you would," Krista exclaims. "What about you, Klause? How's your morning going?"

"One word: bitches."

"*Klause!*" Krista yells, eyes wide.

"What? It's true. All three of my teachers have already assigned me homework. They can't give us one day before we're thrust back into that awful *school* mindset?"

Krista just shakes her head.

Once they check out, Klause quickly walks off to the football jock table, his lunchtime family obligation behind him.

"Hey, hey, 'sup guys?" Klause shouts as he proceeds to put down his tray then high five, fist bump, and slap the backs of the other guys at the table.

Krista and Kevin stand and watch their brother for a moment, then Krista starts heading toward the yearbook staff table where Marsha and her other journalist friends are waiting for her.

"You're welcome to join us if you want," Krista tells her little brother.

Looking at the table full of senior girls, he knows that sitting there would make him an easy target. He doesn't want to let the bullies pick up his scent on the first day. "No, that's okay. I'll go sit with my new friends."

Krista smiles at him. "Okay! I guess I'll see you after school then."

As Krista walks away, she suddenly turns back to Kevin. "Oh, hey, after school lets out, go take a look at the bulletin board. Maybe you'll see some clubs or sports you'd like to try out. It would help you meet people with similar interests."

"Okay, I will." Kevin gives her his best smile. "See ya."

"Later!" Krista flips back around and is already heading to the tables before Kevin can even move.

Kevin stares out at the mass of tables, trying to find a place he belongs. When he doesn't find it, he hastily turns to leave the cafeteria to look for another place to eat his lunch and runs straight into another student. His lowered head smacks into the student's outthrust chest, and it's all he can do to keep his tray from tumbling to the ground.

"Hey!! Watch where you're going!" The voice is rough and unfriendly.

Kevin ducks and tries to run off, looking down at the ground while trying to hold on to his tray. "Sorry."

"'Sorry'?" the older student mocks as one of his friends steps forward to stop Kevin from running away. "Is that all you have to say?"

"I-I'm sorry," Kevin stammers as he tries to swerve away from his harasser again, but runs into the third member of the antagonist's crew.

"Where do you think you're going, kid?" the bully says louder as he grabs Kevin's arm.

"Nowhere," Kevin mumbles.

"Nowhere? What's your name, freshie?"

"Kevin," he replies softly, gulping deeply as he finally looks up at the dark-haired boy towering over him. His eyes are gray and angry, and he smells of sweat masked with an overabundance of musky cologne.

"Why you gotta act like such a little bitch, Kevin? Huh?"

Kevin doesn't respond. His entire body is shaking.

"'Cause that's what you are, a no-good little idiot. God, I can't wait to break you in. Welcome to Mirror Valley High. I'm Samson, but you can call me Sir. Do what I say and maybe you'll survive freshman year. Don't do what I say, and I'll smash your hands with a brick. Is that clear?"

Kevin nods vigorously, still trembling and trying to catch a breath.

"Good." Samson grins wickedly. "I see you got me a cookie and a soda, so I'll just take those." He grabs the items from Kevin's tray. "See ya later, freshie."

When Samson and his two goons finally let him go, Kevin runs out of the cafeteria and hides in a stall in the bathroom, eating the remainder of his lunch alone in silence, tears rolling down his cheeks.

Krista and Klause are oblivious to what is happening with Kevin. They sit at their friends' tables eating lunch, laughing and enjoying their first day back, not sensing that their youngest brother is in pain.

When the bell sounds to signify the end of lunch, Kevin summons up the courage to step out into the hallway again, but only after peeking his head out to look for Samson and his gang.

As he sits in his first class after lunch, he pulls out a notebook and starts sketching. Doing this calms his nerves. In his subsequent classes, he continues to draw, barely paying attention to the teachers as his mind is still absorbed by his run-in with his living nightmare, the thing he feared most about starting high school.

As he sits in his last class, still shaken with a seemingly permanent knot in his stomach, he starts drawing a tree. As he carefully sketches each limb of the tree, he slowly, stroke by stroke, lets go of his fear.

The trees he likes to draw mean a great deal to him. The roots symbolize his family and the strong ties of love that bind him to his truest self, while the branches represent those feelings of peace and happiness he longs for every day. In sketching the meticulously detailed tree, he realizes that this place—and all the pain and sadness he will experience here—are just the trunk of the tree, leading him, eventually, to the state of mind he really wants.

Engrossed in his artwork, Kevin barely notices as the bell rings for the last time. His first day of school is finally over. Per Krista's suggestion, he makes his way to the bulletin board in the main hall to see if anything catches his attention.

On the other side of the building, Krista makes her way to the newsroom after the final bell. Mirror Valley High is so small that the yearbook team doubles as the news team. The school focuses mainly on the end-of-term yearbook, but the team still likes to release a short weekly newsletter for the student body. At peak times, the newsroom can be a place of hustle and bustle, students rushing to not only tackle yearbook assignments but also news stories and events as well. It's a fast-paced environment that Krista loves.

In and out, Krista thinks to herself as she pauses outside the door to take a deep breath. This is the moment she's been waiting for all day, if not all summer: the moment when she will hopefully be voted the new editor in chief. It's a huge responsibility, but she's up for it—she knows it will be an awesome addition to her college applications.

Upon entering the room, she feels her tension dissolve away as her friends offer up warm, welcoming smiles.

"Krista, welcome back," comes a man's voice from across the room. "Take a seat. How was your summer?"

"It was great, Mr. Pippin, thank you."

"How many times do I have to tell you to call me Rick?"

Krista smiles and takes a seat. "That's right, sorry. Thank you, Rick."

Rick turns to the rest of the group. "Alright, we're still waiting on a few more students; then we'll get right into it."

"How's your brother doing?" Marsha whispers in her direction.

"Which one?" Krista whispers back to her best friend.

"The one who isn't talking about gross guy stuff in the locker room right now."

Krista chuckles. "Right, Kevin. I don't know, he says that he made some friends, but I'm getting a funny feeling, you know?"

Marsha isn't far from the truth about Klause, who at that moment is indeed in the locker room getting ready for football practice.

Klause is already buddies with all of the players on the team, their camaraderie having grown during their gruesome summer practices at the school.

"Dude, guess what?" asks Tyler, a fellow junior.

"You discovered a fourth nipple?" Klause quips.

"Ha, ha. Very funny."

"What?"

"So there's a new teacher who's actually really hot."

Klause makes a face. "Ew, are you really crushing on a teacher?"

"You'd understand if you saw her," he smirks as he cups imaginary balls in front of his chest. "She's my art teacher, Miss Lavers."

"Wait—you're taking art?" Klause's eyes narrow.

"What? Thought it would be an easy A so I can keep my GPA up and stay on the team."

"Congrats, Tyler, you're officially one of the art geeks," Klause says, slapping his hand on Tyler's shoulder.

"Whatever, man."

"Let's go, ladies!" A deep, scratchy voice yells from the doorway. "You're starting with five laps around the field."

"Yes, Coach!" The players shout back in unison as they make their way outside.

"Let's go! Let's go! Move!"

While Klause is getting an earful from his coach, back in the newsroom the last of the students arrive.

"Alright, everyone, welcome back to the yearbook team." Rick opens the meeting. "All of you will be at the front of every event and will get to know every single student in this school by the end of the year. As we go through the school year, you'll record everything you deem important. But before we get fully into it, let's start with the one thing I know several of you have been thinking about all summer." Krista and Marsha turn and smile at one another.

"Elections!" Rick grins. "Here's how this will work: for each position, I'll call for nominations. You cannot nominate yourself, so keep that in mind. After nominations, each person nominated will be given sixty seconds to state their reason why they should be selected for that position. After this, each person not running will write their choice on a piece of paper, fold it, and hand it to me."

He eyed the group. "We're doing it this way instead of showing hands like in past years because we don't want a repeat of the unfortunate happenings of last year." Krista nodded, remembering all too well the catfight that ensued in the staircase because one girl didn't vote for the other and the subsequent suspension. "This way, it's completely anonymous. I'll then count up the votes and reveal the winner. Everyone clear on the rules of the election?"

Scattered yeses float around the room.

"Let's start with the big one, then," Rick continues. "Editor in Chief. Any nominations?"

Marsha stands up and states, "I nominate Krista Atwood for Editor in Chief of the Mirror Valley High yearbook."

"Very well," says Rick, then he turns to Krista as Marsha returns to her seat. "Do you accept the nomination?"

Krista stands and replies, "I do."

"Are there any other nominations for the editor in chief?" Rick asks the room as Krista sits back down, unable to hide her smile.

No one responds, so Rick looks around and asks again. "Is there no one else deserving of the position?"

Another student stands, and Krista's heart skips a beat. But only for an instant, as the student says, "Honestly, Rick, I don't think anyone here wants to nominate an opponent, because we all believe that Krista is the perfect person for the job. Her dedication to the yearbook is beyond anyone else's in this room, and she's proven herself as a skilled writer and journalist throughout her time on the team."

Rick pauses for a moment, then smiles. "In that case," he replies, "congratulations, Krista; you're our new editor in chief!"

Krista beams as she stands up once more and thanks the team, shaking Rick's hand to make it official.

As elections continue and the yearbook team's first meeting is nearing its close, Kevin stands in the main hall looking up at the bulletin board.

Posted on the board is every kind of group activity imaginable. From chess to soccer, marching band to cheerleading, anything and everything is up there. Looking at the sports, Kevin is only able to picture himself falling on his face and running from the field, or court, with his two left feet.

Then a flyer catches his attention: *"Art Club: Unleash Your Creative Mind and Join Us for Monthly Field Trips to Scenic Locations Around Town to Sketch to Your Heart's Content."* As Kevin reaches up to unpin the flyer so he can look at it more closely, a strong hand suddenly comes from above and behind him and snatches it from his grasp.

"Art club, huh? You like to draw, freshie?" Samson says mockingly. His faithful sidekicks snicker.

"Give it back, please," Kevin responds, snatching at the flyer in Samson's grasp. In the process, he inadvertently touches his nemesis' hand, which Samson immediately uses to strike Kevin across the face.

"You dare touch me, you little bitch?" Samson shouts as Kevin falls to his knees, clutching the side of his now-swollen face.

Samson reaches down to grab Kevin's backpack off his shoulder. He opens it up and rummages through it, finally pulling out Kevin's sketchbook.

"What do we have here?" Samson antagonizes Kevin as he flips through the sketchbook and tears out each page one by one. "Stand him up," he orders his gang. They grab Kevin's arms and drag him to his feet in front of Samson.

"Alright, Kiddie Kevin—time to learn your lesson," Samson growls as his hand reaches back and his fingers wrap in a tight fist.

"Hey!" A loud, stern voice shouts at them from down the hall. Samson and his gang look up to see a girl storming toward them.

"What do you think you're doing?" snarls Krista.

"Hey, hey, we're just having some fun, sweetie," Samson says, raising his hands in mock surrender. "No need to get your panties in a bunch."

"*Excuse* me?" Krista crosses her arms as her eyes narrow, leaning toward him slightly.

Samson licks his lips and throws a self-satisfied grin in Krista's direction.

"You wouldn't hit a girl, would you?"

"Not unless one hits me first, sugar," he smirks.

"Good thing I don't need to hit you, then!" A smile erupts on her face as she grabs Samson's waistband, pulling down his gym shorts and boxers in one good yank. "As I expected. So tiny for such a big coward like you." She shakes her head as she looks down at the exposed area.

As his buddies laugh, Samson turns red, blushing at first, then squints his eyes and furls his brows. He bends over and jerks his shorts back up.

"You may have won this time, missy, but you can't protect him forever. Every time you're not there, I'll unleash a world of hurt on that little boy." Samson pivots and stalks away, snapping his fingers for his cohorts to follow him.

After watching the bullies turn the corner, Krista turns to check on her little brother. "Are you okay?" she asks.

"Yeah, I'll be fine." Kevin sighs. "Why did you do that? He's right—you can't protect me forever."

"Don't worry. I'm Editor in Chief now. I'll use my connections and see what I can do." She grins, but Kevin doesn't return her smile.

"You guys ready?" Klause shouts, coming down the hall toward them. He's still wearing his gym clothes from practice, but most of the sweat has dried already.

"Yeah," Krista responds.

"What happened to *you*?" Klause asks Kevin, eyeing the red mark under his brother's eye. "Actually, never mind, I don't wanna know—as long as you're okay."

Kevin blinks. It's been a while since Klause expressed any kind of concern for him at all. "I'm okay. Thanks."

Krista speaks up. "You guys go ahead and go to the car. I'll be right there. I just realized I forgot my purse."

Klause and Kevin nod and make their way outside as Krista runs back to the newsroom.

There you are, Krista says to her purse when she spots it under the desk she sat at during the meeting. As she looks through it to make sure everything is there, she hears a door slam outside in the hall followed by footsteps and muffled voices. While it's not uncommon to hear others this late in the day, Krista's intuition tells her something else is going on, and she shivers as the feeling deepens. She slowly creeps toward the door and opens it an inch, peering through the narrow opening out into the hallway.

She hears Samson's voice before she actually sees him. "That bitch thinks she's so tough. Wait until she sees that kid's mangled body and cracked skull in the school's dumpster tomorrow."

Tears form in Krista's eyes, her mind immediately thinking of her youngest brother, and she starts trembling. She watches, undetected, as Samson and his gang pass by.

Once she decides they're far enough away, she wipes under her eyes and quietly steps out of the newsroom, keeping an eye on the three as they continue down the hall in front of her.

Suddenly, pushing aside the fear, a darker thought creeps into Krista's mind, the darkest thought she's ever had in her life. "I'd like to see *your* big head cracked," she whispers, her eyes glaring at the back of Samson's head.

Then the unthinkable happens. Samson, as he passes by the main bulletin board, slips on the Art Club flyer he had seized from Kevin and discarded on the floor. He falls backward, fumbling first to regain his balance and then to break his fall, both to no avail.

Krista sees it happen as if in slow motion: first the ungainly fall, then the back of his head hitting the floor so hard she can hear the crack of it hitting the tiles from here.

Krista's purse drops to the floor. As items trickle out of her bag, so too does the blood from Samson's skull—and the life from his body.

In that moment, were she to look down, Krista would see a nightmarish reflection of herself in the shiny, waxed floors of the hallway. But she doesn't see how her left eye has become pure white and her right eye solid black. How neither pupils nor irises are to be seen. How her eyes have become only two contrasting orbs, hollow and soulless.

Unaware of her transformation, Krista just stands there, frozen, staring. Wondering. And all she can think is: *Was that me?*

CHAPTER 3

RINNG! **SOUNDS THE BELL AT MIRROR** Valley High School, and homeroom lets out, signaling the start of classes for the day.

Krista's mind hasn't settled since the incident on the first day of school. All she's been able to think about for the last two weeks is what happened to Samson.

"Chuck is so cute," Marsha is saying to Krista as they walk down the hall. "Yesterday, we ran into each other in the hall, and he gave me this super-charming smile that I literally couldn't say anything to. Seriously, like I was speechless. I really hope he asks me to homecoming. Who do you want to ask you?"

Only Krista isn't hearing anything her best friend is saying to her. All she can think about is Samson's death as she stares down the hall at the exact spot where he fell.

"Krista?"

Still deep in thought, Krista doesn't respond.

"Krista!" Marsha snaps at her, and Krista finally looks up.

"What?" she asks, still staring down the hall.

"Did you even hear anything I was saying?"

"Huh?"

Marsha gives an annoyed grunt. "I was talking about homecoming and how I want Chuck to ask me."

Krista finally snaps out of it when she hears the name. "Wait. Chuck *Malowska?*" She puts her hand on her friend's shoulder. "Marsha, I'm pretty sure he's a drug dealer."

"No, you're thinking of Chuck-*y* Malowska. I'm talking about Chuck *Bevins.* Captain of the track team."

"Oh, that's right. My fault."

"Are you okay?" Marsha inquires, her brow furrowing. "You always know everyone in the school. Plus, didn't you know Chuck from when you were on the team?"

"Yeah, I've just had a lot of things on my mind."

Marsha sighs. "Well, I guess I'll repeat my question then: who are you hoping to go with?"

"I don't know. Honestly, I don't think I'm even going to go. I have a lot of work to do." Krista has already fallen behind on her duties as editor in chief during the first two weeks of school because she's been distracted by the incident with Samson.

"What?" Marsha exclaims. "You *have* to go. It's our senior year!"

RRINNG!! The trill of the school bell indicates that class is about to start.

"We need to get to class, Marsha," Krista says, conveniently shutting down the topic. They walk swiftly down the hall and are about to enter their third period classroom when something catches Krista's eye. She jerks to a stop.

A few yards down the hallway stands Samson's locker. Since his death, students have been adding flowers and pictures to a memorial below the bank of black metal doors. A school picture of a semi-respectable-looking Samson is taped on the locker door.

The sight is enough to once again flood her mind with graphic memories of the accident. The small bouquet of red roses conjures up the image of Samson's blood oozing out of his head. And, just as the life slowly left his body, so too are the flowers now dying in the cold, austere hallway.

Her thoughts naturally progress to what happened that day, how Samson died in the same exact way she had been thinking at that moment, wishing even. The thing she can't get past, though, is how her thoughts could be connected to what actually happened. In fact, her last two weeks have been filled with the shock of *how* it happened, rather than what actually happened.

On top of that, every time Krista sees the locker memorial, she wants to feel bad, but no matter how hard she tries, she just isn't able to. She hasn't told a soul that she doesn't feel bad about him, that she actually thinks he got what was coming to him. She knew him as a bully to her little brother— all Krista can remember is the cruel face of the sadistic bully who threatened her youngest brother's life—and that's all he was to her. In her mind, he deserved what happened to him.

"Krista?" Marsha says, a little too harshly. "Come on, class is starting." She pulls Krista through the classroom door just ahead.

"Take your seats, girls," Mrs. Burbens calls out from her desk at the front of the classroom as they enter.

The two girls oblige, making their way to the front row seats they selected on the first day of school.

Meanwhile, on the other side of the school in a small, windowless room crammed with thirty small writing desks, Kevin is sitting in the back corner, just like he did on his first day of high school.

His history teacher is going on about something regarding the Revolutionary War, though Kevin is taking little notice. History is one of Kevin's least favorite subjects. In his mind, history class is just a textbook full of people hurting other people over and over to get what they want. Not exactly his thing.

So Kevin spends most of his time in class drawing in his notebook. He knows from his sister that Mr. Haney doesn't quiz or test over anything he says in class anyway. How could he, with all his rambling? It's a wonder he can even keep track of what he's saying half the time.

Kevin has been adjusting to high school better since Samson's death. Fear of bullying is one of the main things that has kept Kevin's expectations of high school low, and fortunately, since his nemesis' untimely death, no other bullies have come forward. Maybe the idea of someone reaping what he sows is enough to ward off would-be tormentors, at least for now.

But Kevin knows that it's only a matter of time until it all blows over, and Samson goes from tragic school accident to just another name in the yearbook. Especially since his posse quickly disbanded shortly after the accident—and one of the two who were in it fell into excessive drug use and is about to serve six months in juvenile detention.

So although Kevin is relieved about Samson's death, he actually feels bad for the big guy. Even after the way Samson treated him, he just can't bring himself to hate him. As much as he might want to.

A few doors down the hall, Klause sits in his literature class. He has a pen in one hand and his head comfortably resting in the other. A novel lies open on his desk, and he pretends to be taking notes. In reality, as his teacher goes on about the symbolism in Hester Prynne's experiences, his eyes are starting to get heavy. He remains conscious enough, though, to keep his head from falling off its perch and alerting his teacher.

"Psst," Tyler whispers to him from an adjacent desk.

Klause doesn't respond, so Tyler hisses at him again, this time reaching over to poke his shoulder.

Klause snorts and quickly looks forward to see if Miss Therou spotted him asleep. Nope, all good. He sighs, then resumes staring at his fake notes.

Not thirty seconds later, Klause hears another noise. He glares at Tyler just as his friend stretches out his hand toward him, closed fist angled down.

Klause quickly takes the offered note, a small sheet of notebook paper folded over twice to conceal the message, as he eyes Miss Therou.

Eyebrows scrunched together, he begins to unwrap the note until Tyler gestures for him to stop, pointing to the girl sitting on the other side of him. He smirks at his friend then passes the note to the girl.

She opens it then shoots a look at Klause until he points in Tyler's direction.

She looks down at the note again, then up at Tyler as she nods her head and mouths a quick "yes" before finishing it all up with a wink then turning back to the front.

Klause looks back at his friend and whispers "what just happened?" before he's interrupted.

"Attention, Mirror Valley High School students," a woman's voice suddenly comes over the loudspeaker. "I would like to announce this year's final list of nominees for homecoming king and queen."

The voice is full of static coming through the school's ancient PA system, but the woman's scratchy words are still recognizable as she reads the list in alphabetical order by last name.

Klause immediately tunes out the scratchy voice—that is, until he hears "Klause Atwood" amid the static. He freezes for a brief second then shakes it off, quickly perking up and grinning from ear to ear . . . until he hears the next name:

"Krista Atwood." His grin quickly fades as he cringes at the thought of being named king to his sister's queen.

Moments after the announcer finishes reading the list, the bell signals the end of class. Immediately sounds of closing books, backpack zippers, and homework reminders from the teacher fill the room.

Tyler stands up to high-five his best friend, draping his arm across Klause's shoulder as they exit the classroom.

Klause inquires about the mysterious goings-on between Tyler and the girl in class.

"Oh, I was asking her to homecoming."

"With a piece of paper?"

"Yeah, it's a classic."

"Very romantic," Klause responds with an eye roll.

"Hey, she said yes, didn't she?" Tyler defends. "Who are you asking? As the star receiver of the football team, I'm sure you could get any girl you want on your arm."

"I was thinking of Jessica Ray. She's definitely one of the hottest girls in the whole school."

"Nice!" Tyler leans back against a wall of lockers to look at his friend, then nods with a smirk on his face. "Senior girl."

"Yeah, man."

"You've definitely got a chance with her, especially now that you're nominated for homecoming king."

"Yep. I just hope Krista doesn't accept her nomination, 'cause that would be awkward standing next to her when I'm crowned on stage," he says.

Tyler is about to respond when he catches sight of a tall girl wearing a skin-tight, white minidress on the other side of the hall. She's looking at herself in the mirror she has attached to the inside of her locker door, checking her eye makeup and reapplying a coat of red lipstick to her puckered, plump lips. Her long blonde hair frames the beauty of her face as she flips it away from her shoulder, while her slim-fitting outfit accentuates her athletic, cheerleader figure.

"There she is," Tyler whispers to Klause, directing his eyes toward the gorgeous girl in front of them. "Now's your chance, future homecoming king."

Klause takes a deep breath, steps forward toward Jessica, and leans against the locker next to hers, catching a whiff of her sweet perfume that smells like fresh flowers.

"Hey, Jessica," he says, leaning back casually with a satisfied grin on his face.

Hearing his voice, she closes her locker door to look at him. "Oh, hey, Klause." A slightly flirtatious smile answers his own. "Congrats on the nomination."

"Yeah, about that . . ." Klause lays it on thick. "The thought of going to that dance without you makes me doubt I'll have any fun. A beautiful girl like you deserves to be treated like royalty, and, as king, I would definitely make that happen." He winks. "Would you like to join me so we can walk into that room and own the place?"

Jessica raises her eyebrows and laughs. "Why would I go with you? You're a junior. I've got my eyes on some way-better-looking senior guys. Right now, I see a wannabe kid who thinks he's the hottest and best thing to ever come into the world. And my new nose agrees. You reek of desperation, and you'll *never* win homecoming king."

Klause's stomach drops, and his jaw follows as he watches Jessica turn her back to him and walk away, the clicking from her stiletto heels on the tile floor amplified through the haze in his brain. He blinks once then starts cursing under his breath about Jessica and her "new nose."

He can feel his anger building as he clenches his fists, then, without his awareness, his eyes start to change. One eye becomes white and the other becomes black, just as Krista's did only weeks before. The change lasts only an instant, but it's enough.

Jessica, looking down at her phone to tell the world she was just asked out by a junior boy, doesn't notice the classroom door opening right in front of her. The door handle knocks the phone from her grasp a split second before the rest of the door smacks her in the face. Her nose starts bleeding as she crumples gracelessly to the floor.

Klause grins widely, chuckling at how such a popular girl is getting no comfort or help from the students passing by. Instead, they are staring and pointing, some even laughing hysterically at what they just witnessed.

Unable to stop himself, Klause eyes Jessica, whose white dress is now streaked with the blood dripping from what promises to be a broken nose, and shouts, "Good luck finding a date with that nose now!"

He continues to laugh as he turns and walks away, in no way suspecting that he had anything to do with the accident. Had it been more severe or resulted in death as Krista's episode did, he might perhaps examine his role in it. Instead, in his mind, this is just an accident that Jessica deservedly brought on herself.

CHAPTER 4

BACK ON THE OTHER SIDE OF THE school, Krista is changing out some books at her locker when Marsha skips up to her.

"Hello, Your Majesty," Marsha says to her with an impish smile, her eyes sparkling with mischief as she dips to curtsy to her friend.

Krista rolls her eyes. "Don't say that."

"Well, now that you're nominated, you'll *really* have to go to the dance now." Marsha nudges her in the shoulder.

"I'm going to turn down the nomination."

"What?!" Marsha shrieks. "But why?"

"Homecoming queen isn't exactly something I can put on my college and future job applications. I'd rather be on the front line, reporting about the concept of popularity that pervades the tradition—the very popularity that makes it nearly impossible for someone with actual intellect to win against the big-butt, big-boob, blonde girls after they tell their five-thousand-plus social media followers to vote for them. Thank goodness the school doesn't place any kind of responsibilities on the queen and king. We'd be doomed."

"Wow, such eloquence," Marsha comments on Krista's diatribe.

Krista rolls her eyes again as she grabs the last of her books and notepads for her next class.

"Are you just not going to go?"

"No, I'll probably go to the dance. I *am* Editor in Chief, after all, so I should be there to see it firsthand." She sighs. "Plus, my brother plays in the homecoming game, so, of course, I'll be at that, too."

Krista slams her locker shut, and the girls begin walking to their next class, AP History. Suddenly, two adults holding hands speed past them on their right and continue down the hallway, weaving in and out of the students in their path. Krista doesn't recognize them, so she knows they can't be teachers. *I wonder who they are?* She watches as the two enter the school office.

Marsha doesn't seem to notice the couple and keeps right on talking about the upcoming homecoming dance. But Krista, whose intuition is telling her something is up, can't relax. As they approach the office, she peers into the open doorway to get a better look at the two strangers.

Krista can't make out what the couple is saying, but it looks like they're reading the riot act—first to the office manager, then to the principal, who has come out of his office upon hearing the ruckus. Krista doesn't want to be too obvious by getting closer or stopping, so she just slows her pace a little and looks half-ahead, half-sideways as she continues to walk by with Marsha.

For the most part, the yelling is unintelligible to Krista, but a few key words strike both her eardrums and her heart.

"Accident . . . floors . . . fault . . . son . . . suing . . ."

With those five words, Krista knows exactly who the couple is and why they're here, and her stomach knots. *Should I tell Principal Withers what happened? What would I even say? It's not like I pushed him down—I wasn't even near him. He would just think I'm crazy or something. No, I can't . . . I can't say anything to anyone, not yet.*

Meanwhile, Kevin is also getting ready to go to his next class. After pulling some books and papers out of his locker, he shuts the door and turns to start down the hallway, still looking down at the paper on top of his stack.

"Watch it!" yells the student he clearly did not see. Kevin jumps back, losing hold of his stack of books and dropping them, papers flying everywhere. His heart is racing.

The student just walks on, so Kevin is left alone. With a deep sigh and his eyes trained on the ground, he bends over to pick up the scattered papers by himself.

While he's still on the floor, he starts to hear a staccato *click click, click click*. The clicking stays steady but grows louder and closer. It eventually stops right next to him, and Kevin looks over to see a pair of red, high-heeled shoes. Looking up slowly, he sees legs, a black, knee-length skirt, a white flowy blouse, and finally, blonde hair draping the shoulders of a fair-skinned young woman.

"Oh, hi, Miss Lavers."

"Let me help," she says with a smile as she squats down beside Kevin, reaching for the scattered papers he hasn't gotten to yet. "Wow, this is really good." She picks up a sheet of paper with pencil markings filling the white space around the printed material.

Kevin is motionless for an instant before snatching the paper from her hands and insisting that it's nothing.

Miss Lavers pays no heed to his overprotectiveness. "You know, we have an art club here that's really great. They go on field trips to different locations to draw and paint things."

"That's okay," Kevin mumbles as he continues to look down at the floor, avoiding eye contact. "It's kind of, just . . . *my* thing."

Miss Lavers stands up and watches as Kevin collects the rest of his papers and piles them into a disheveled stack. He picks up the stack and stands, turning away from his teacher.

"Kevin," Miss Lavers calls softly, her voice sweet and melodic, and Kevin stops. "I know high school can be a big transition, and I know that you may be going through some changes. But I want you to know I'm here for you if you need to talk about anything. I care about all of my students, but I see something in *you* in particular, something great, and I really hope you'll eventually become comfortable with confiding in me about any of your troubles. Okay?"

Kevin finally makes eye contact with her bright, caring eyes. Her irises are as blue as the sky and the whites of her eyes brighter and softer than clouds. He takes a deep breath.

"Okay," Kevin replies. "And thank you," he adds, allowing a small, subtle smile to emerge as he heads off to his next class. Miss Lavers remains where she is, smiling at her student. If Kevin had looked back, he would've seen a smile expressing more than just the respect and care of a teacher— he would have noticed loving concern, like that of a friend.

The hours pass, the school day comes to a close, and the three Atwood children proceed to their own particular after-school spots. Krista leads her yearbook team in a project, Klause digs in at football practice, and Kevin sequesters himself outside at a small wooden picnic table. Each is in his or her own domain, comfortable, not imagining that dark and mysterious events are once again heading their way.

When yearbook is over, Krista goes outside to find her little brother. "Hey, Kevin," she greets him as she approaches.

At the sound of her voice, Kevin jumps and hurries to hide whatever he's working on under some books. "Hey."

"How was school today?" Krista smiles at his attempt at subtlety.

"Fine," Kevin offers. "How are you?"

"I'm well," Krista responds tonelessly as she nods, avoiding eye contact as she attempts to disguise her true mood. After seeing Samson's parents that day, she really wants to talk to Kevin about the accident and the role she thinks she played, but she just can't find the right words to start. Even *she* questions her *own* sanity on the subject.

"Oh, hey." Kevin perks up. "Congrats on the homecoming queen nomination."

"Thanks, but I actually turned it down," Krista says as she takes a seat across from her brother. "Not my style."

"I figured you had." Kevin shrugs. "Are you still going to the dance on Saturday?"

"Yeah, I'll still go . . . yearbook, you know." Krista shrugs back, resigned that her responsibilities will force her to attend an event she's managed to avoid the last three years.

Though she's always tried to make it clear to her friends and family that her lack of desire to participate is based on her intelligence and thinking about college and her future, there's actually more to it. While her mind hates the idea of a dance and homecoming "royalty" because it's neither practical nor useful to her, the hidden issue—the real issue—is in her heart. Deep down, she isn't happy. Deep down, she feels like there's something missing in her life, despite being proud of where she is today.

She wonders if it's love she's been missing. She's never had a good track record with guys, though that's probably because of her first-and-foremost commitment to school and family. When she thinks about it, though, she doesn't think that the hole in her heart is due to her lack of a love life. It's something else. To her, it feels as if she isn't being her true self. Something is missing, but she's unable to pinpoint exactly what.

"Hey," Krista says aloud, trying to take her mind off her internal struggle. "I'd like to make some signs for the homecoming game tomorrow. You know, to cheer on Klause and the rest of the team. Will you help me with them? It can be some fun brother-sister bonding time."

"Sure," Kevin replies quickly.

"Cool!" Krista says, grinning. "We'll need to go to the craft store to pick up some supplies. I think Klause said that he was going to stay late today to put in some extra gym time, so we can leave now. We could go get craft supplies today, then tomorrow we'll work on the signs between school and the homecoming game."

"Sounds good," Kevin says as he gathers his things and stuffs them haphazardly into his backpack.

The two get up from the table and make their way to the parking lot, and Krista swings her arm up and around Kevin's shoulders to give him a loving squeeze.

CHAPTER 5

AS HIS SIBLINGS HEAD TO THE CRAFT store, Klause finishes up at football practice and makes his way to the school gym, which he usually has to himself at this time of day. He plugs his headphones into his phone, pulls up his favorite workout music—a mix of rap and hip hop—and starts with some push-ups before moving on to pull-ups.

He likes getting in some body-weight work before he lifts weights—his workout journal says it's arm and chest day, his favorite.

"Four . . . five . . . six . . ." He counts the repetitions out loud since he did turn out to be the only person in the gym. His music blasting in his ear, he murmurs words of encouragement to himself, trying to get just one more repetition in . . . then one more, then one more. Today he is spurred on by his homecoming rejection earlier. As he pulls himself up to the bar, his count flying past twenty, then twenty-five, he continues to laugh to himself about what happened. *She totally deserved that.*

Then suddenly, through his music, he hears a noise, a crash, coming from behind him, like two pieces of metal clanging against each other.

Stopping his pull-ups, he hops down from the bar, wiping sweat from his brow as he turns around to see what's going on.

No one is there. He's still alone. But for some reason, two dumbbell weights have fallen off the rack onto the gym's rubber-like floor.

"Is someone there?" he calls out.

No one responds.

His eyes searching the uninhabited space, he walks over to the fallen dumbbells. As he approaches, he notices that a joint in the structure of the rack is bent inward, causing the rack to tilt ever so slightly.

That must be the answer. That makes sense.

Since he's there, he decides to go ahead and do some work with the weights. He picks up the fallen dumbbells and carries them over to the bench.

Lying back, parallel to the floor, he grips the two dumbbells and presses them up above his chest. He lets his arms down perpendicular to his torso, then pushes them upward again. He repeats.

"Fourteen . . . fifteen . . . sixteen . . ." he says out loud, releasing a forceful breath with each exertion.

He stares up at the ceiling, the bright lights shining in his eyes. With no windows in the gym, the lack of natural light is made up for by harsh, artificial lighting illuminating the dank, sweat-stained gym.

He continues his lifting and his counting—until the lights above him suddenly go dark.

He drops the weights abruptly and jolts upright. He yanks his headphones out of his ears and listens intently while he looks around again.

He doesn't hear or see anything. The gym is silent and pitch black. He calls out, "Ha, ha. Very funny. Turn them back on."

Nothing.

"Guys?"

Still nothing, only darkness, and silence. Klause's heart begins to pump harder and faster. He knows this is silly, so why is he so scared?

He doesn't hear a thing except for his own heavy breathing.

Then, as if a backup generator has started up, the room fills with a soft buzzing sound as the lights begin to flicker back on.

Klause sighs, looking around for other students, but sees only a man, standing in the doorway of the gym. The man's eyes are two black orbs, as dark as the room just was.

Klause jumps up, nearly tripping himself on one of the bench's legs, and blinks harder than he ever thought he could. He looks up again, and the man's eyes are perfectly normal, with the usual complement of whites and irises.

"Accidentally short-circuited a power line while cleaning," the man, wearing a gray jumpsuit and holding a mop, says. His name tag reads "Levi." "Sorry about that. Everything okay?"

Klause blinks again and rubs his eyes. His pupils haven't fully adjusted to the sudden brightness of the lights after such inky blackness.

"You okay?" the school janitor says again in his deep, scratchy voice.

"Yeah, I'm fine . . ." Klause mumbles, still trying to figure out what just happened. As he stares at the janitor, what he said about the lights finally sinks in. Klause shakes it off, puts his headphones back on, and returns to his workout as the janitor leaves, closing the door behind him.

CHAPTER 6

A T THE CRAFT STORE, KRISTA AND Kevin wander down the aisles.

Krista wants to take her signs to the next level by drawing a wolf on them to match their mascot, so she searches for a stencil, unaware that her little brother would easily be able to sketch something.

"Should I get some red and black poster board, too, or just stick with white?" Krista asks her brother.

"Definitely get red and black, too. They're our school colors, after all."

"Yeah, but it'll be harder to write on those colors and have the words and images stand out."

"White paint markers should show up well on them," Kevin replies. "And I think it'll be well worth it."

"Sounds good!"

As the two focus on their shopping, they begin to hear yelling a few aisles over. They make their way toward the sound—purely out of curiosity.

Around the corner from the voices, they pause to listen.

"What was her name?" a teenage girl's voice barks out.

"Why does that matter?" a teenage boy's voice shoots back.

The girl screams, "I can't *believe* you would cheat on me!"

"Calm down!" he shouts back. "You're the one that's all 'I don't wanna get serious yet,'" he says in a high-pitched, whiny voice.

"Yeah, emphasis on *yet!*"

"Ugh, you're so selfish!"

"How am *I* the selfish one?" the girl counters. "You're the one out sleeping with other girls!"

"Because you don't let me have fun with whoever I want and sleep with whoever I want. You don't own me, you bitch!"

"*How does that even make sense to you?*" the girl shouts back in a wobbly voice as if about to cry.

The argument breaks down into further name-calling, at which point Krista decides that she's had enough and grabs Kevin by the shoulders to steer him away from the situation.

"Promise me you won't turn into a douche like that guy."

"Don't worry, I won't," Kevin responds calmly. "I don't get how anyone can treat someone like that."

After checking to make sure they have everything they need, the two make their way to the front of the store and check out, the fight still raging on behind them.

With their arms full of bags, the two leave the store and head to Krista's vehicle.

Krista opens a rear door and takes the bags from Kevin's hands. As she arranges the bags in the backseat, Kevin sees the quarreling couple emerge from the store.

While Krista focuses on her task, Kevin watches the couple continue their argument one row over from them.

Although he can't make out any actual words, their body language is very clear.

The girl seems to be crying but not actually saying anything at this point, while the boy is still yelling and now gesturing violently. He reaches out and grabs her shoulders, and, as he shakes her, his open mouth is releasing a torrent of anger right at her face. When he finishes, he brusquely lets go of her shoulders with a push and slaps her across the face, sending her falling off to the side and smacking into a parked car, then grasping at her face. Then the boy reaches out, grabs her hair, and yanks her head up, once more thrusting his face into hers.

Kevin watches in shock, but also in silence. He wants to go help the girl, but he knows that the bully would beat him down in a second. All he can do is hope that it ends, and quickly. As a pacifist, he first thinks only about protecting the girl, but, as his anxiety and agitation grow, darker thoughts creep in. He starts thinking about what would stop that vicious beast and what he deserves for treating his girlfriend like that. He knows it won't do any good, but he gives free reign to his dark fantasy as he glares at the boy.

Behind him, Krista shuts the rear door and turns to open Kevin's door for him when she sees that he hasn't done so himself yet.

Standing behind him as he glares across the parking lot, she doesn't see her brother's eyes change the same way hers did two weeks ago, one to white and the other to black. Even if she had, she still would not have been prepared for what she was about to witness.

The evil boyfriend, leaving the girl collapsed and shaking against the car, starts walking away from her—backward—as he continues to curse and shake his fists at her. He gets two steps out from between the parked cars when a car moving way too fast for a parking lot comes seemingly from out of nowhere and plows into him.

Krista and Kevin watch through the gaps between parked cars as his body flies up and hits the windshield, skids over the roof, lands face down on the asphalt, and rolls a few times before coming to a deadly halt.

Krista screams as Kevin's mouth drops. His eyes, no longer transformed, widen, and he feels like he might be sick. They both instinctively run forward as if to help, or perhaps to satisfy a morbid curiosity, but once they have a clear view, they stop short.

Blood is spattered on the car's windshield and seeping from all parts of the boy's body, which is sprawled unnaturally on the hard pavement with bones protruding from the skin of his awkwardly splayed arms and legs. The eyes, though open, are still and lifeless, never to register the light of day again.

Krista tries to shield her little brother from the sight by reaching out to cover his eyes with her hands and pulling him into a fierce embrace.

This lasts only a moment before she lets go enough to pull Kevin back with her, pushing him into their car and running around to get in herself. Without a word and without hesitation, Krista starts the car and drives away, not even looking back in her rear-view mirror.

CHAPTER 7

FOR KRISTA, THE NEXT DAY AT SCHOOL IS like a repeat of the day after Samson's death, only this time it seems a little less disturbing because she doesn't have the feeling that she had anything to do with this accident.

"It was crazy. He didn't see it coming," Krista whispers to her best friend in the newsroom after school, the first time she has opened up about the event to anyone all day.

Marsha hugs her. "Well, it seems to me that he got what was coming to him. Karma got him good."

"Karma?" Krista inquires.

"Yeah, you've never heard of karma?" Marsha blinks.

Krista shakes her head before Marsha explains. "It's supposedly some kind of force that gives good people good luck and bad people bad luck."

Krista looks at her, tilting her head.

"I don't know, it just came to mind. Don't really know if I believe in it or not. I think it's related to some religion or another, but I feel like a lot of people just use the term loosely." Marsha shrugs. "So did you tell Klause?"

Krista shakes her head. "No, he ended up staying at a friend's house last night, and I haven't seen him yet. But I'm not sure if I *should* tell him. It was a horrible sight, and I don't particularly want to relive it with him."

"Alright, everyone!" shouts Rick to the newsroom. Clapping his hands together a few times to get the students' attention, he continues, "The big homecoming game is tonight. Charles, you're our sports journalist, so you'll be on the front line reporting the game. Marsha, I expect you to direct the photographers throughout the game. I would really like to get some good shots of the players in action. I also think it would be cool for the school newsletter to feature the nominated homecoming kings and queens at the game, so I'm giving you a special assignment to take pictures of the nominees at the game. Krista, I know you'll be there tonight to support your brother, but feel free to direct the reporters in any way you see fit. After your photo op, of course." Rick grins.

The students nod their heads, and Rick continues, "We're going to break early today because there's a lot of prep work that I'm sure many of you still have to get done before tonight, so you're all released. Have fun at the game!"

While Krista packs up her things in the newsroom, Kevin sits outside at his usual picnic table. He has a pencil in his hand, but he can't seem to draw anything. His mind is still focused on the horrific accident the day before.

"Hi, Kevin," says a woman's soft voice.

Looking up from the blank paper, he responds flatly, "Hi, Miss Lavers."

"You're not sketching anything today. Is everything okay?"

He pauses for a moment. "Yeah," he replies quietly.

"I'm sensing some hesitation there." Miss Lavers sits down on the bench next to Kevin. "What's wrong?"

"I don't know."

"You can tell me anything," Miss Lavers says attentively.

"I don't know . . . I just—" Kevin takes a deep breath. "Something happened. Something bad. And I can't help but think that I caused it."

Miss Lavers' brows pull together. "What do you mean?"

Kevin shrugs his shoulders.

"Kevin, you're a very kind and innocent young man. It's hard for me to believe you'd be capable of purposely doing anything bad. Unless you're protecting somebody. And if that's the case, then it's not bad. If anything, it has goodness in it because you did it with good intentions."

Kevin looks at her, his eyes beginning to tear up.

"Look, I don't know what happened, and if you don't feel comfortable telling me, I won't force you. Just please keep in mind that you're a good person. I can only see you capable of good, kind things. So just try not to be hard on yourself. Okay?"

"Okay," Kevin breathes out. "Thanks." He looks at his teacher and smiles faintly.

"Oh, hi, Miss Lavers."

"Krista, so good to see you," Kevin's teacher says as she looks up at his sister, who has joined them at the picnic table.

"Everything okay?" Krista asks her, concerned that her brother might be in trouble.

"Of course," she responds. "We were just chatting." She gets up from the table and starts to walk toward the parking lot, but pauses to look back. "Kevin, please, always remember what I said. Okay?"

Kevin nods his head. "Okay. Thanks again."

Once Miss Lavers is out of earshot, Krista looks over at Kevin. "What was that about?"

"Nothing. Just chatting."

"Okay, well, are you ready to go? We gotta get those signs done before the game tonight."

"Yeah, let's go."

The drive home is devoid of conversation, with just the music coming from the radio filling space between them. Krista doesn't know what to talk about—and she certainly doesn't want to mention the accident—and Kevin is off in his own world.

When they get home, the two immediately begin work on the signs, sitting down at the kitchen table and spreading out all the supplies and tools.

They work in silence, still avoiding the subject that is consuming both of them.

Finally, Kevin breaks the silence. "You'll think I'm crazy, but I think I caused it."

"Caused what?" Krista stops her work, looking over at her brother. She has a feeling that she already knows, but she waits to hear him say it.

"The guy's death yesterday. The accident."

Krista becomes very still and waits a moment before asking him carefully, "What do you mean? How could you have caused it?"

"I mean, I didn't *directly* cause it. It's not like I pushed him. But for some reason, I have this feeling that I did that to him."

Krista's heart beats loudly in her chest as she stares expectantly at her little brother and waits for him to continue.

"You didn't see it, but the guy was hitting that girl in the parking lot. He was being really mean and just acting crazy, grabbing her hair and everything." Kevin chokes up. "When I saw that happen, I just wanted to protect her, to save her, and I wished that something would happen to him so she could be safe."

He stumbles on. "And something did happen to him. Something really bad. And I know that I didn't cause the accident, but I just can't shake this horrible feeling that I had something to do with it. That I hurt him. That I killed him."

Krista watches as her brother breaks down into tears, and she reaches over to touch his hand. Once he calms down a little, she gathers her courage, takes a deep breath, and begins to tell him what she has been hiding for the last two weeks.

She tells him what happened to Samson through her own eyes. All the blood, the sound of the thud on the floor, the way time seemed to stand still. And . . . that feeling that she had something to do with it.

Now she, too, begins to break down. "I've been so confused since then. I haven't told anyone about it. Not Mom, not Marsha. No one! I thought about telling the principal, but it's not like I touched Samson or was even near him. He would just think I'm going nuts." Krista sobs into her hands.

Kevin places his hand on her shoulder, and she looks up into his eyes. "I have a bad feeling about all this, Kevin." She pauses to think for a moment before continuing. "I can't explain it. But I think something is happening to us. I think we might have caused the accidents with our thoughts. I just have this . . . this bad feeling."

"I have a bad feeling, too." Kevin sighs. "Maybe that bad feeling is just from witnessing someone die right in front of us?"

"I don't think it's that simple though. Our thoughts were explicitly about harming the person in question, and somehow those thoughts came true in real life."

Kevin looks down at the table.

"And Kevin," Krista nudges him, "the bad feeling I got the moment Samson fell . . . I . . . I don't have that same feeling when it comes to the guy at the craft store. So these emotions that we're experiencing have to be linked to more than just witnessing death. After all, I witnessed both of them die, but I only feel responsible for Samson's death."

Krista eyes the confusion in Kevin's face and continues. "When we were facing this alone, we both had bad feelings about the deaths we think we caused, right?"

"Yeah," Kevin manages to choke out.

"But now that we know the other experienced something similar, do you agree that this bad feeling is about more than that now? That maybe there's something happening to us siblings?"

Kevin slowly nods his head. "B-but—" he stutters. "But what?"

"I don't know, Kevin," Krista shakes her head. "I don't know. But our instincts are definitely telling us there's more to the story. We just have to figure it out."

Kevin stops and thinks for a moment. "Do you think Klause has experienced anything like this?"

"Klause!" Krista exclaims. "Oh my gosh—what if this is happening to Klause, too? If you and I are causing these accidents somehow, then who's to say it's not happening to him as well? After all, we're family. We're one entity, you know? We have to talk to him. I'm worried now. What if it's happening to him, too? We have to warn him."

The two siblings get up quickly and rush out the door to drive to the school, leaving their unfinished signs on the table.

CHAPTER 8

I N THE CAR, KRISTA LOOKS AT THE CLOCK and realizes that the game has already started. Their talk sucked away more time than she realized.

"I have a bad feeling, Kevin."

"Yeah, me too."

At the high school, Krista takes the first parking spot she sees, and the two worried siblings jump out and start running toward the stadium.

They rush up to the entrance but are stopped by the ticket booth attendees. "Tickets?"

"Um," Krista mumbles as she reaches into her purse and rummages around. "Here, press pass, and he's with me," she says, holding up her credentials.

Inside, an impatiently-waiting Marsha catches sight of them and rushes over.

"Krista! There you are. I was getting worried. Hi, Kevin," Marsha says, leaning over to look at him standing behind his sister.

"Marsha, I need to talk to Klause."

"Well, good luck with that. He's killing it out there."

"Wait, who's he killing?" Krista says, her eyes wide.

"No one, silly," Marsha laughs. "He's just doing really good."

"It's important!"

"Well, I can't see us being able to do anything right now," Marsha replies. "Look, it's almost halftime—you can talk to him then. In the meantime, let's go sit over in the press section. It has a great view of the game."

The three of them make their way to the press booth. Krista doesn't take her eyes off the field once she spots number fourteen, her brother's number. Cheering and screaming are all around her, but she barely notices, focusing solely on her brother and the players around him. She worries not that something might happen to Klause, but that something might happen to another player because of him.

Out on the field, to the sounds of a stadium full of fans cheering, Klause catches a pass thrown to him and runs thirty yards down the field and into the end zone just before the whistle sounds for halftime.

Krista hurries down the steps toward the field, leaving Kevin behind to save their seats. Klause is just taking off his helmet when Krista rushes toward him. "Klause!"

"Krista?" Klause says, blinking. "What are you doing down here?"

"I need to ask you something."

"Well, spill."

"Has anything weird happened to you recently?"

"You mean like my sister running up to me halfway through a game for the first time in my life?"

"Klause, I'm serious. Has anything weird or unexplainable happened to you recently? Wait, let me reword that. Has anything weird happened around you, to other people? Has anybody gotten hurt around you?"

"What are you talking about? No, I don't think so. The only thing semi-weird was that the lights went out in the gym yesterday, but it turns out that the janitor just hit a wire or something."

"What?" Krista says. "That doesn't make sense."

"What doesn't make sense?" Klause says impatiently. "What's going on?"

"Yo, Klause, team meeting!" a player calls out behind him.

Looking back at his sister, he asks again. "I gotta go, what is it?"

"Um, I don't know. Something weird happened with me and Kevin and I wanted to see if something similar has happened to you. But I guess it hasn't." She shrugs. "I'll talk to you later."

Krista turns to walk back to the stands, shaking her head.

"What did he say?" Kevin asks when she returns to the seats.

"He said he hasn't experienced anything weird, but I still have a really bad feeling."

Kevin grabs his sister's hand. "We'll just talk to him after the game. Explain everything in more detail."

The game starts into the third quarter, and Klause continues his stellar performance on the field, making amazing runs and seemingly impossible catches.

At the beginning of the fourth quarter, the Mirror Valley quarterback drops back to throw the ball and, pressured by the opposing team, throws a short pass to Klause. With his face to the quarterback, and his back to the sideline, Klause catches the ball then turns to start running toward the goal. In that moment, he's taken down, and Krista's eyes widen as the blow and the fall both knock the wind out of him. And, as if that weren't enough, the opposing player gets up and starts mocking and taunting Klause, calling him names.

Krista jumps up to see if Klause is okay, and, to her relief, he stands up unassisted. Moments later, however, as he begins to walk back toward the huddle, he stumbles and falls forward. Players and coaches rush to his side and help him off the field.

Krista moves through the stands to get a better view and sees her brother limping along the sideline. It looks to her like his left leg was injured in the play.

With Klause now benched, a backup wide receiver runs onto the field to replace him as the next play gets ready to begin. The cornerback who tackled Klause is out on the field laughing and high-fiving his teammates, seemingly congratulating himself on having taken out Mirror Valley's best player.

At the snap of the football, the play starts. The cornerback watches the replacement receiver, and, when the receiver gets thrown the ball, pursues him. Just as the cornerback gains on him, the receiver jukes him. The cornerback tries to make the quick direction change, too, but instead trips over his own feet and falls spectacularly to the ground. His scream of pain pierces the air as the receiver continues running to the end zone for a touchdown.

Mirror Valley's celebration is short-lived, however, when the spectators notice that the fallen player has not gotten up. Then, when a stretcher is brought onto the field and the player is lifted up, those closer to the field, including Krista in the press box, can see that his shin bone has been snapped in half and is protruding from his leg.

From her vantage point, Krista can see the blood staining the player's uniform, and her already bad feeling gets worse, making her feel like she might even throw up. The player had broken his left leg—the same leg that he injured on Klause just moments earlier. A coincidence, maybe, but the exact kind of strange coincidence that had accompanied both Krista's and Kevin's experiences. And the person who got hurt had pretty much deserved what he got, which also fit the bill to a tee.

Krista looks back over at Kevin. They both run toward the field to talk to their brother, but with the game still going on, they're stopped by the coaches. Returning together to their seats, they wait for the game to end, both of them trying to deal with the unsettling feeling that Klause had something to do with the player's injury.

The game finally ends, with Mirror Valley winning for their homecoming. As the crowd cheers raucously, the players rush over to Klause on the bench, not forgetting that his efforts were what got them that win, even if he couldn't finish the game. They pick him up and put him on their shoulders as they chant his name in unison.

Krista and Kevin are finally able to make their way down to the field, but Klause has already been carried off.

"Klause! Klause!" Krista shouts, but he doesn't hear over the distance and noise.

Tyler's mother sees Krista and comes over, placing her hand on Krista's shoulder.

"Hi, Krista—don't worry about him. You go take care of your journalism stuff. The players are going to our house for a celebration party, and he's just going to stay the night there with Tyler. I'll take care of him in any way I can."

"But I have to talk to him about something."

"Well, he'll be at the homecoming dance tomorrow, I'm sure, so you can talk to him there. I'm going to drive him and Tyler to it."

"But—" Krista tries to object, but Tyler's mom interjects.

"Don't worry, I've got him," she says once more before she trots away toward the crowd of players.

Kevin grabs his sister's arm. "Come on, Krista, let's just go home. We'll talk to him tomorrow at the dance. It'll give us some time to think about this more first. Maybe we can figure out what's happening before then."

Krista pauses and bites her lip then shrugs, and they head for the parking lot.

On the drive home, Krista remembers something Marsha had mentioned to her, and she begins to formulate a theory.

"Have you ever heard of something called karma?" she asks Kevin.

"I think I've heard of it, but I don't know what it is."

"Marsha told me briefly about it. Some sort of force that dishes out good and bad luck to people."

"I'm not following."

"I don't know, Kevin," Krista says as she shakes her head contemplatively. "It's just that when she said it, something inside of me lit up, like it should mean something. Let's look it up when we get home."

Safely back at the house, Krista runs up to her room and boots up her laptop. She types "karma" in the search bar and thousands of results pop up.

"Okay, so karma means 'action, work, or deed,'" Krista reads aloud.

Kevin leans over and points at the screen. "It says here it's connected mainly with the concept of rebirth in several ancient religions of India and other parts of Asia."

"Look!" Krista exclaims, pointing at another article. "It says here that it's a principle of cause and effect where the actions of someone influence the future of that person, whether good or bad."

"Meaning if someone does something bad, something bad will later happen to them?"

"Yeah. But . . ." Krista's voice trails off.

". . . but it's not a *person* doing it," Kevin finishes her sentence. "It's just a mystical force."

"What if we have power over that mystical force?" Krista theorizes.

"What, like we're witches with magical powers over the force of karma?" he ponders out loud.

"I don't know," Krista shrugs. "Maybe? But you have to admit, this karma thing sounds similar to what we're experiencing."

"Okay, I know that all we've been wanting is some answers." Kevin stands up, shaking his head. "But this is all too weird."

"Weirder than the feelings we've been having?"

"Witches? Karma? Magical powers? This is all just insane."

"I know, Kevin! But we don't know for sure. It's still too early. We can't come to any conclusions yet. There's no proof."

"If it *is* the case that we can control this karma thing, *how* do we control it? I don't want to hurt anyone ever again, even if it's just my thoughts that are doing it."

"I don't know, Kevin. I really don't." Krista looks at her brother and takes hold of his hand. "But we'll figure it out together."

The two spend the night combing through all the material. Their research keeps them up well into the morning hours until they finally fall asleep in place, Krista's head lying on her desk and Kevin's head resting on her shoulders.

CHAPTER 9

BROTHER AND SISTER WAKE FROM their slumber to the sound of Krista's phone ringing.

Groaning, the two slowly raise their heads, grasping and cracking their necks, trying to get the cricks out after sleeping in such unnatural positions.

Squinting her eyes, Krista sees Marsha's name on her phone and answers.

"Mmm, hello?" she mumbles, still half-asleep.

"Krista, where are you? I thought you were coming over at four to do our hair and makeup together."

Krista quickly sits up straight and looks at the clock. Five fifteen. "Oh my gosh! I'm so sorry, I just woke up."

"Just woke up?" Marsha queries, almost yelling. "How late did you stay up?"

"Um, I don't know. Pretty sure the sun had already risen, though."

"Wow! Well, I've only done my hair, still gotta do my makeup. The dance is at seven—and remember, I have to get there a little early to take pictures of the venue and event setup before people start arriving. Do you just want to meet there, or do you still want to come over?"

"No, I'll come over," Krista replies. "I'll see you soon."

Krista turns to Kevin, who has laid his head on the desk, and shakes him fully awake. "Kevin, we have to get going. It's already five fifteen."

"What? How did that happen?"

"I guess when you stay up all night doing research, you sleep really late. We'll have to talk to Klause about what we've read and about what happened with that football player last night."

"Yeah, that karma thing is really weird. It fits, but at the same time it doesn't."

"I know," Krista replies as she stuffs some makeup in her bag and collects her dress and shoes. "Go get your homecoming dance outfit. We can change and get ready at Marsha's."

"Okay."

After gathering his clothes, Kevin and his sister leave the house and drive over to Marsha's.

Once there, the two drop the subject that had kept them up all night. Even though Marsha is her best friend, Krista doesn't want to say anything until she knows more and has proof.

After getting ready faster than she's ever gotten ready for a special occasion, Krista slips on her black high heels, grabs her clutch, and heads downstairs.

Kevin is already waiting by the front door, cleaned up nicely in a slim-fitting gray suit with a white collared shirt and black bow tie. He smiles as he looks at his sister. "You look really nice."

"Thanks, Kevin!" Krista responds, hugging him, but carefully so as not to wrinkle her sparkly silver dress.

Marsha comes in from the kitchen, putting on her earrings before picking up her keys and purse from the hall table.

The three leave the house together, Marsha driving them in her car. Excited about the dance and not noticing her friends' serious moods and tired faces, she turns the car stereo up and sings along loudly.

When they arrive at the school, the three enter the gymnasium where the dance will be held. The space is decked out in fancy decorations, and Marsha starts taking pictures to fulfill her press duties.

"Wow!" Krista exclaims, pointing up at the ceiling. "They were actually able to put in those big chandeliers after all. Those are impressive!"

"They're impressive all right, but they're also fake, as far as I know," Marsha responds matter-of-factly. "I was told that they just have battery-powered lights stuck in the metal fixtures. They're not hooked up to any kind of actual power source. But it did take three guys to hoist each one of 'em up there."

"It still looks really cool," Kevin says, looking around the room at the feathery table centerpieces and shiny serving dishes and drinkware.

Time passes quickly, and students begin to file in with their dates and friends. The gym is soon quite packed, the music starts up, and the homecoming dance commences.

Krista and Kevin stand together near the entrance, waiting for Klause to arrive. When he finally comes limping through the doorway, a buzz spreads throughout the gym until the space echoes with cheering and clapping for the hero of homecoming.

"Klause!" Krista shouts as she rushes over to embrace her brother in a big hug while Kevin hangs back, staying out of the spotlight.

Klause pushes his sister away from him. "Hey, c'mon, don't embarrass me."

"I'm sorry. I was just really worried. How's the leg?"

"Not bad. Turns out it was just a twisted ankle. Coach said I should be able to play again in a week or two."

Krista sighs then gets right to the point. "Can we talk to you about something? It's really important."

Somewhat annoyed, Klause looks around him for a reason to break away, but when he spots his little brother with a worried look on his face, he gives in. "Yeah, sure," Klause responds, beginning to get worried himself. He hopes nothing has happened to their mother.

The two join Kevin off to the side, where Krista tells Klause her Samson story and Kevin follows up with his craft store parking lot story. Klause listens in silence.

"Does any of that sound similar to anything that's happened to you recently?" Krista inquires.

After a moment's reflection, Klause's eyebrows lift. "Well . . . there was this one thing that happened a couple of days ago when I asked Jessica Ray to the dance. She turned me down, so I wished that something bad would happen to her nose, and, just seconds later, a door hit her in the face and broke her nose."

Krista takes a deep breath in and exchanges looks with Kevin.

"But it was just an accident," Klause insists. "It's not like I pushed her into the door."

"That seems to be the thing, though. They're all just 'freak accidents.' Accidents that people would never even think could happen." She pauses for a moment then continues. "Have you ever heard of something called karma?"

Klause shrugs his shoulders. "I've heard it mentioned here and there as part of a joke, but I don't know what it is exactly. What about it?"

"Well, it's some sort of mystical force of cause and effect that makes a person get what they deserve. And that's what has been happening with our incidents. The people involved either hurt us or somebody else in some way, and they got hurt or even killed for it."

"Whoa, there," Klause responds, putting his hands up. "They're all just coincidences. Crazy coincidences, but still. You sound like you're trying to make us out to be, I dunno, witches or psychics or psychos or something."

"I don't know, Klause. I don't know what's happening for sure. But don't you agree that there's something weird going on with us?"

"You talk about coincidences . . ." Kevin jumps in to back up his sister, ". . . well, here's another one. Why is all of this happening to *us*? Siblings! And all around the same time! It's like they're all connected somehow!"

Klause continues to protest the absurdity of it all until suddenly the three are interrupted by a slightly wobbly senior classman. The tall boy, a basketball player, awkwardly moves in close to Krista, who takes a step back when she realizes he's probably drunk.

"Hey, sexy, come dance with me," he says, his speech slurred and barely comprehensible.

"No," she responds firmly, completely turned off by his inebriated advances.

"Come on, babe, come dance."

"I said no, and don't call me babe," she says with more force then turns away from him.

Klause and Kevin stand up straight, on alert and ready to defend their sister should her harasser not get the message.

"Aw, come on, gorgeous." The boy lurches forward once more, this time grabbing her behind with one hand and her arm with the other and pulling her around to face him.

Her brothers are stepping forward and about to reach out to help her when Krista suddenly yells, "*NO!*" at the top of her lungs. Using all her strength, she pushes her attacker away from her.

He stumbles several steps backward and finally trips over his own feet, falling awkwardly onto his back and sending nearby dancegoers scattering. After he struggles for a moment, trying to get to his feet, a movement from above catches his eye, and he stops and looks up toward the ceiling. "Oh, sh—" he mumbles.

It's too late to get out of the way, and the heavy chandelier lands squarely on the boy, crushing his ribcage under its weight. Not one other person around him is harmed.

Screams and panic erupt in the gymnasium as students, staring wide-eyed at the other chandeliers, run for the doors. The teachers and chaperones work their way through the crazed mobs, trying to get to the boy under the fallen chandelier, but by the time they get there he is letting out his last breath.

When Krista turns to face her brothers, she sees Klause with his hands covering his wide-open mouth and Kevin standing frozen, his eyes wider than she's ever seen.

Krista runs over to her youngest brother, arms open to embrace him, but Kevin cowers away.

"What's wrong? Are you okay?" Krista searches her brother's face, then the rest of him, as she can't see if he's been injured in any way.

"Are *you*?" Kevin queries back in a low voice. His whole body is trembling, and tears are welling in his eyes.

Krista stares at him, her eyebrows scrunching together.

"Your eyes changed," Kevin whispers.

"What?" Her voice rises.

"Your eyes . . . they changed." Kevin's voice is shaky and quiet. "It was like you were a-a ghost—or worse . . . a demon."

CHAPTER 10

"SO HOW'S SCHOOL GOING?" KARMASHA says as she sits at the kitchen table with her three children on Monday morning. She arrived home late Saturday night but had only caught glimpses of them since then, when they emerged from their rooms to grab food and disappear again.

The siblings respond with a mixture of "fine"s, "good"s, and head nods.

Sensing an intentional vagueness in their responses, Karmasha gets suspicious, concerned that something bad may be going on. She tries to push the conversation forward. "Anything exciting happen during my last work trip?"

Krista, Klause, and Kevin briefly exchange side glances. "Not really," Krista speaks for the group. "Pretty boring—just school, you know?"

"'Just school'?" her mother inquires, raising her eyebrows. "But you of all people are always excited about school."

"Well, I mean, nothing out of the ordinary," Krista replies, glancing over at her brothers.

Karmasha looks at her sons to try to read their body language. She definitely gets some odd vibes from them as they avoid eye contact with her while casually eating their cereal.

She wonders what's going on, sensing something is wrong—but she can't seem to put her finger on it. Her children have always been forthcoming about their lives, especially Krista, so the awkward silences and vague answers she's been getting this morning are troubling.

She wonders if perhaps her children are finally acting like typical teenagers, no longer wanting to communicate with her or have her be so involved in their lives. *I guess this was inevitable*, she thinks to herself, her heart sinking at her offspring beginning to distance themselves from her for the first time in their lives.

Karmasha sighs and says aloud, "I'll be leaving again this afternoon." Her children look up in unison from their breakfast, wide-eyed. "I know, I've only been home for about a day. I was hoping that we could've done something together yesterday, but you all locked yourselves in your rooms all day."

Krista, Klause, and Kevin once again exchange looks, but while they don't want to tell their mother about what's been bothering them, they still don't want her to leave again so soon.

Karmasha continues, "So I probably won't be home when you get back from school." Looking at the kitchen clock, she sees that it's getting late. "Speaking of which, you'd better get going."

The three children get up and hug her goodbye as they gather their things and head for the door.

"Klause, make sure you take it easy on that ankle!" Karmasha calls out. "Use that crutch I got you yesterday."

"Will do, Mom!" Klause grabs his crutch and follows his siblings outside.

"I feel bad," Kevin says to his older siblings once they're in the car. "You can tell she's really sad and worried."

"We can't tell her," Klause says vehemently. "She'll think we're crazy!"

"We can't tell her *yet*," Krista adds. "Emphasis on the yet. We still don't really know what's happening to us and why. Without more proof, we can't tell anyone. Not even Mom."

Kevin sighs. "Then I think we'll have to learn how to do a better job of acting like everything is fine. Especially around Mom. She knows us too well."

"It's a good thing she's leaving town again, then," Krista responds. "Don't get me wrong; I'll miss her, but we need to figure out what's going on and try to get over the shock of last Saturday."

"Yeah," Klause speaks up. "Like why your eyes changed colors the way they did. I wonder if that happened during the incidents with me and Kevin, too."

"Ditto," Kevin chimes in. "That was freaky."

"Let's make a deal," Krista says firmly. "Completely open dialogue. If any of us gets any bad feelings or other suspicious accidents happen around us, we tell each other."

"Sounds like a plan," Klause agrees, but to Kevin he sounds less than enthusiastic about the idea of having to spend more time than he has to with his siblings.

Kevin draws in a deep breath, trying to calm his nerves and face reality. "I'm in, too. But we need to be more than just aware, we need to be *careful*. Whatever we're doing is hurting people. Killing people."

Krista takes her own deep, pensive breath in and out. "You're right, Kevin. We're in this together now," she says as she looks over at Klause in the passenger seat next to her. "We're connected in a way that's greater than just siblings. Please, be careful."

When they arrive at the school, Krista, Klause, and Kevin exchange one more glance then go their separate ways for the day.

CHAPTER 11

B ACK AT THE HOUSE, KARMASHA HEADS upstairs after cleaning up the kitchen.

At the top of the stairs, her attention is captured by a framed picture of her family taken four years ago. Her four loved ones stand together in a close-knit bundle of happiness, smiles on their faces, holding back laughter. Karmasha has one arm around the shoulders of Kevin, whom she towered over at the time, and her other arm is around her husband's waist. Klause, holding a football, is held in a playful headlock by his father, and Krista stands at Klause's other side, her hands reached over to support him in the mock wrestling match.

Karmasha continues to look at the photo, gazing upon the beautiful faces of her family. She stares into her husband's bright green eyes peeking through his black, rectangular glasses, which are sliding slightly down his nose like they always seemed to do.

Then a tear rolls down her face as her thoughts turn to the sudden death of the love of her life and the sorrow that resulted from it. On that fateful night, she'd lost more than just her husband; she'd also lost the essence of her family as she knew it. She's incredibly grateful and happy that what remains of her family is still together, but she knows it will never be the same as it used to be.

Karmasha turns away from the picture and walks down the hall to her children's rooms.

She opens Klause's door first. She considers searching his room to see if she can find clues as to why he and his siblings were acting odd this morning but decides against it. She doesn't want to be the kind of parent who goes snooping through her children's things.

Instead, she stands in the doorway and gazes into the room, not to look for something, but to take it in. She looks at his football trophies and the pictures of his friends and posters of famous football players and rock bands scattered on the walls. She looks over at his desk in the corner of the room, unable to see even a tiny patch of its birchwood finish under the mass of disheveled papers and books, half-drunk soda cans, and empty chip bags. Shaking her head, she remembers how she used to doggedly insist that he clean his room and how, after he'd turned sixteen, she'd stopped in the hopes that he would realize that he can't live his life in a pigsty.

Pulling the door shut, she proceeds down the hall to her daughter's room. Opening the door, she peers into the room, once again simply standing in the doorway and taking it in. Although she is presented with Krista's current minimalist style of decorating and her neatly organized desk, in her mind she also sees the way it used to be: bright pink walls overlaid with posters of boy bands and dolphins.

In the center of the room, the bed is now pushed back against the wall and neatly made up with solid gray sheets and black pillowcases. In the past, white sheets with pink polka dots were covered with a heaping mass of stuffed animals and dolls. She sees a vision of her daughter at seven years old, running into the room and diving onto her bed, then curling up under the covers with a paperback book and a grin.

She stays in her reminiscent trance as she leaves her daughter's room, continuing down the hall and passing the bathroom until she reaches the last bedroom at the far end of the hallway.

There she recalls sounds of playful screaming and laughter as she opens the door to what is now Kevin's room. Natural light from the morning sun radiates through the sheer white curtains of the window and shines onto her mind's image of young Klause and Kevin playing together. They race their toy cars and pretend that they're kings and knights of their castle, which is actually their bunk bed with the blankets hanging down to enclose the bottom bunk.

Karmasha smiles, but also sighs again as she thinks about how life used to be when her family was whole. She had been so happy, but now she feels like her happiness is being ripped away from her little by little. First, her husband was taken from her, and now her responsibilities have her traveling so much that she can't spend time with her children.

She thinks about how all of it is taking a toll on not only her but her children as well. She feels like they're drifting away from her, and there's nothing she can do to stop it. Once again her eyes mist up as she leaves the room and heads downstairs to pack for her trip.

In her own room, she goes straight to her closet and pulls out a large duffle bag from the top shelf. She stares at the bag, wondering how much she should pack—she doesn't know exactly how long she'll be gone. Looking through her closet, she sorts through multiple shirts, skirts, dresses, and shoes, and starts taking out possible selections.

As she continues to walk in and out of the closet, she thinks about the trip and worries what may transpire. Each trip is different, and each trip is accompanied by the fear of what she might have to do. The constant pressure of her duties is intense for her sometimes.

Going into the closet once again, she catches sight of a small, black box on the top shelf. It's usually hidden away in the back corner, but it must have gotten dragged forward when she pulled down the duffle bag. Standing on the tips of her toes, she reaches for the box, careful not to grab it in a way that would make her lose control and drop it. Bringing it down, she takes it to the bed, sits down on the edge, and opens it up. As she looks down at its contents, she once again revisits the past, this time back before she had Krista, Klause, and Kevin, before she was married, before she had even met her husband . . . all the way back to when she was a child taking care of her mother.

Rifling around in the box, she comes across some old photos of her mother and father. They're black and white, faded and wrinkled. Karmasha looks down at the pictures and then up at the mirror hanging on the wall opposite her. She is the spitting image of her mother back then. Dark-brown hair cascades in waves down her head, framing her light tan face that is reminiscent of her grandfather's bronze skin. Looking down at one of the pictures, she wonders what her mother's deep brown eyes looked like when they changed.

Karmasha sets the photos aside and rummages through the box some more. Digging under some other mementos, her fingertips feel a cold, hard surface. She grasps the object, knowing instantly what it is, and pulls out a pendant on a chain. The lights in the room reflect onto the silver frame around the centerpiece stone and gleam back into Karmasha's eyes. The necklace had belonged to Karmasha's mother, and to her mother's father before her. It's a wonder the pendant and chain are still shiny after all these years.

Nestled in the simple silver setting is a white stone with black slivers running through it. The marble-like stone shines bright, its glossy surface smooth to the touch. Looking at the necklace, Karmasha marvels at what it has witnessed over the years.

She remembers her mother wearing it as she tucked her into bed as a child. This family heirloom was passed down to her, and she thinks about when she will someday pass it down to Krista. She hopes that when she does, the necklace, and therefore Krista, will not see the kind of horrors that she, her mother, and her grandfather saw while wearing it.

Looking down at the necklace, she wonders how she has managed to forget about it for so long, hidden away in the closet. Even though the necklace has been a symbol of death in Karmasha's eyes, she reminds herself in this moment that it is also a symbol of life and hope. It has seen both the bad *and* the good, the hate *and* the love, the sorrow *and* the happiness. But so much more than that, it is also a remembrance of her mother. Karmasha decides to wear the necklace once again, and she vows never to take it off until she passes it down to her daughter.

The clasp has corroded shut over the years, but luckily the chain is long enough to slip on over her head. Looking at herself in the mirror, she admires the piece of old jewelry. Feeling the cool necklace against her skin, she's touched with a bit of hope and happiness.

Two fast beeps come from her phone, and her reverie is broken. She had set the alarm to remind her of when she needed to leave.

She carefully puts the photos back into the little black box and returns it to the top shelf of the closet, then quickly finishes packing, throwing an assortment of clothing and accessories into the duffle bag. After zipping it up, she carries it to the front door, turning off any lights on her way. In the doorway, she takes one more wistful look at her home and then smiles, closes the door behind her, and walks to her car.

On the long drive to her destination, Karmasha can't help but reflect further on the past. Unearthing the black box of photos and her mother's necklace unleashed a torrent of memories. Her mind takes her back to the very beginning, to her mother's story, the prelude to how Karmasha came into being and started her own journey to becoming the mystical being she is.

INTERLUDE

A YOUNG WOMAN RUSHES DOWN THE pothole-filled road through driving snow as strong winds chill her to the bone. She shivers, pressing her arms tightly to her body through her heavy coat. With each step, she sinks into the whiteness covering the ground, making staying upright a struggle. Though the storm is terrible, and the cold even worse, she doesn't have a choice.

Seeing a light ahead, she continues through the snow, fighting to pick up the pace. The wind howls in her ice-cold ears as she finally pushes open the heavy door with the little strength she has left.

In the small, rundown tavern just off the highway, she collapses and curls up into a ball on the floor, shivering uncontrollably.

Though there are a few people in the establishment, only one man steps forward to help the woman. The tavern is quite chilly, but the man kneels, takes off his own overgarments, and wraps the woman in them. Lifting her up in his strong arms, he carries her over to a corner near the fireplace. He holds her tight, contributing his own body heat to that of the fire to help warm the shivering woman.

"Do you have any hot coffee or tea?" the rescuer calls out to the man tending the bar, who seems to have already gone back to his own business along with the rest of the patrons in the small tavern.

"On your tab?" the bartender throws back.

"Yes, of course," the man growls, eyes narrowing.

The bartender brings over a cup of hot tea and hands it to the man. "Here, sip this," the gentleman says to the woman, still holding her close. "It'll help."

Taking the mug from his hands, she slowly lifts it up to her numb lips and takes a sip.

"I-I have money," the woman stammers. This kind man has helped enough.

"No, it's okay," replies the man, whose face is covered with a short and well-groomed beard. "It's my pleasure."

The woman smiles at her knight in shining armor and looks up into his eyes as he looks down into hers. He lacks the ability to see what happens next, but the color of her eyes changes from a beautiful brown to something else: one becomes black and the other becomes white. The change lasts only a second as she knows that it won't take much. In that second, while looking up at the man with her other eyes, she releases a special gift to him before changing them back to brown.

"My name is James."

Now warmed up significantly, thanks to his efforts, she replies softly with a genuine smile. "My name is Karmania."

Flash forward five years, and Karmania and James stand together under a white archway. The sun is setting beyond them on a warm spring afternoon. Colorful flowers and vibrant greenery surround them. Smiling faces crying tears of joy look up at the two standing together, holding hands and pledging their love and lives to each other.

"I now pronounce you man and wife," the minister before them says in a gentle yet cheerful voice. "You may kiss the bride."

The two embrace each other, then James lifts Karmania's white veil to reveal her lightly tanned face and kisses her plump pink lips. The two beam at each other, thinking of how the past five years have been the happiest of their lives, and that the best is yet to come. Karmania is grateful that her automobile broke down on that cold winter night, forcing her out into the snow to find shelter. Rather than finding shelter just for the night, she found shelter for life in the strong, safe arms of her now-husband.

Shortly after the night they met, James had received a wonderful promotion at his job, and, by saving up for a few years, he was able to buy a house for him and Karmania to start their life and family together.

After the wedding, James and Karmania travel the country, having adventures and enjoying their first year of marriage. The love they have for each other is true and strong and so unconditional that Karmania never has a lasting negative thought about her husband. She thinks the world of him, and, because of this, Karmania slacks in her other duties. Little does she know that this will haunt her for the rest of her life.

After just two years of marriage, James falls gravely ill. And though Karmania tries to help him heal, it seems that nothing can be done.

In what are to be his last remaining moments, she looks up toward the heavens and calls out in a loud voice, "Please! Let me help him!"

"No!" a deep voice echoes in her ears.

"Please!" she calls out again in desperation.

"You knew the consequences," another voice, this time a raspy one, grates in her ears. "Balance must be kept."

The exchange can be heard only by Karmania, and the voices continue to clamor in denial of Karmania's wish.

Tears stream down Karmania's face as she continues to beg the voices to let her do something, but they do not yield. James takes his final breath, and his life of love and adventure comes to an end.

Karmania is never the same after her beloved's death. She is once again alone. She has no family left, and the only reminder of her family comes from her father's necklace around her neck.

In a dream, Karmania speaks to the voices that forbade her from saving James.

"I can't do this anymore," Karmania says in a low voice. Her head droops as a tear rolls down her cheek.

"But it is your duty," a woman's voice counters.

"A duty I never asked for, nor wanted!" Karmania shouts, then bows slightly, backing up a half step. "Please. I've lost so much; I don't have the strength to continue this responsibility. It's too much."

The voices murmur, indiscernible to Karmania, but her heart starts racing anyway.

"Very well," the deep voice once again speaks up. "We will ease up on you a little, but the bloodline must be passed on to someone else, someone who will inherit your abilities."

"But my husband is dead," Karmania sobs, feeling the wounds reopen once again.

"We shall grant you a miracle. A miracle that hasn't occurred in two thousand years."

"What miracle?" Karmania asks through her tears, hoping they might bring James back to life.

"We shall grant you a child. A child you must bear within you, as this is the only way the bloodline will pass on."

Karmania looks up at the twelve thrones that seat the twelve spirits who are speaking to her, her mind racing, her spirit conflicted. She's always wanted a child, but her heart sinks when she realizes that it won't be the family she had envisioned with James.

Despite the heartache she slowly learns to live with, nine months pass quickly, and Karmania gives birth to a baby girl. Looking down into the eyes of the small bundle in her arms, she smiles lovingly. And, carrying on the tradition of her family, she names the baby Karmasha.

CHAPTER 12

K ARMASHA HAS MADE GOOD progress on her drive to Richmond, Virginia. Finally, however, she grows hungry and decides to take the exit for a small town just off the highway. Driving down the main, two-lane street, she looks around at her surroundings for a good place to stop and eat.

As the car ahead of her nears an intersecting side street, Karmasha notices that a school bus on the side street is approaching the intersection a little too fast to be able to stop in time.

She immediately honks her horn at the car in front of her, but she quickly realizes that the driver has run out of time to react. She braces herself for what she sees is about to happen.

The school bus runs the stop sign, and the driver in front of her slams on his brakes, trying to swerve to the right and avoid a collision, but it's too late. He hits the bus almost head-on at nearly full speed.

The car's hood crumples in, and the driver's head hits the steering wheel just before the airbags go off in his face.

Karmasha reacts quickly, pulling over to see if she can do anything to help. She rushes up to the car, and, with the help of other good Samaritans—passersby who have also stopped to help—she pulls the driver out of the car to examine his injuries. The man is conscious, but he has a large gash across his forehead. Karmasha sits on the ground, lays his head in her lap, and puts pressure on his forehead to stop the bleeding. The man is breathing heavily, and his whole body is shaking.

"Is everyone okay? Is anyone hurt? Were there children on the bus? Are the children all right?" the man pleads feverishly.

"Shh," Karmasha says softly to him. "It's okay—it'll all be okay."

Looking up at the bus, she sees that it retained little damage from the collision. Then she sees the children, followed by the bus driver, coming around the vehicles to look at them. The children appear to be fine, more curious than anything else.

"They're okay, see?" Karmasha says to the man who hasn't stopped babbling since he started.

The bus driver, however, strides angrily up to Karmasha and the driver. "Look what you did, you stupid son of a bitch!" he shouts.

Karmasha responds in defense of the injured man. "Please, Sir, stop this. It wasn't his fault. You ran the stop sign."

"You shut up, bitch!" the bus driver bellows back at her. The children scurry away and get back inside the bus.

Karmasha, her blood pressure soaring, feels a familiar feeling rise up in her body, and she makes a decision right there. Undetectable to the onlookers, her eyes make the change—just for a moment—as she focuses on the bus driver to invoke his retribution. Then they return to normal.

Ignoring the bus driver now and turning her attention to the injured driver, Karmasha's eyes change once more. This time, in recognition of the concern he expressed toward the children over his own well-being, she grants a reward. In this moment, Karmasha lives her true self, reveling in her magical powers.

The moment her eyes change back to brown, the sound of sirens pierces the air. In a few more seconds, emergency vehicles round the corner and surround the scene. The bus driver panics, looks around, and starts to run away, but he is quickly cut off and apprehended by the authorities and first responders emerging from their police cars, ambulances, and fire trucks.

The EMS personnel rush over to Karmasha and examine the man. She tells them what she knows of his injuries then watches as they load him into the ambulance and drive away.

Her work done, Karmasha's stomach suddenly rumbles, and she remembers why she turned in to this town to begin with. Getting into her car and taking a deep breath, she resumes her search for a place to eat.

Spotting a small diner, she parks and goes inside, placing her order right away. She stares out the window by her booth as she reflects on the happenings of the day, grateful she was able to help that compassionate driver. But then she remembers how she wasn't able to help her loved ones in the past, and feels an all-too-familiar prick in her heart. And that reminds her of her childhood, of the anguish and sadness she suffered. Especially when she first learned about her powers.

INTERLUDE

"**M**OMMY!" **CALLS OUT A LITTLE SEVEN**-year-old girl to Karmania, who is sitting on a rocking chair on the porch of her house.

"Hey, there, my little Karmasha," she replies to her young daughter just before she lets out a deep, scratchy cough.

"Mommy, are you okay?"

Karmania has actually been quite sick for the last few months, but, not wishing to worry her daughter now sitting on her lap, she avoids the question and speaks softly back to her. "My sweet baby, would you like to hear a story?"

Karmasha nods her head eagerly, looking up at her mother with a wide smile.

"Once upon a time, there was a beautiful young princess—"

"Ooh, a princess!" Karmasha interrupts her, clapping her hands in delight.

"Yes, a princess," Karmania chuckles, pausing until her daughter quiets down. "Once upon a time, there was a beautiful young princess who lived in a castle. It was a great big castle up in the sky. She loved flying through the air with the birds and running through the fluffy, white clouds. Her father, the ruler of the entire kingdom, was a kind and generous man. But he was also fair. So fair, in fact, that many called him the Fair King. When a subject of the kingdom did a kind, selfless thing for another, he would reward them greatly. But if someone did something bad and hurt someone, then that person would suffer a harsh punishment."

Karmasha's eyes widen.

Continuing, her mother says, "The Fair King was the eldest of thirteen. He had six younger brothers and six younger sisters."

"Wow, that's a big family!" Karmasha exclaims.

"Yes, it is!" Karmania continues. "The Fair King had a lot of different responsibilities, so he relied on his brothers and sisters to control his power to reward good behavior and punish bad. The kingdom lived happily for thousands of years like this. The Fair King never had to worry about that particular duty of his because his siblings upheld it so well.

"Over time, however, the twelve siblings began to argue over the power and over who should receive what reward or punishment. Half of the twelve favored hope, love, peace, and life over punishments, while the other half favored misery, hate, war, and death over rewards. A great battle began between the divided siblings, and the kingdom fell into chaos. Good people began to feel the horror and sadness of undeserved punishments while the evil began to receive undeserved rewards."

"Oh, no!" Karmasha cries out, covering her eyes as if to shield herself from these dark and evil images.

Her mother once again calms her down then continues. "The conflict not only took a toll on the people of the kingdom, but also on the twelve siblings themselves, as their appearances began to reflect their own inner souls. Their own unique powers then became corrupted, and they soon became symbols and idols of specific traits, like darkness, strength, or peace. The fighting continued until the Fair King finally stepped in. He thought about banishing the twelve from the kingdom, but they were still his family, and they possessed thousands of years of knowledge that he couldn't ignore.

"So the Fair King instead decided to take the power from his siblings and bestow it on his only daughter. The twelve tried to argue with the Fair King, insisting that all that power was too much for any one person to handle without becoming corrupted and favoring one side over the other.

"The Fair King, however, insisted. For his daughter was so special and unique that she possessed both good and bad qualities, both good and bad thoughts and intentions. Because of this, she would be able to keep the balance between good and evil, hope and sorrow, love and hate, peace and war, and life and death.

"And just in case it became too much for her, or she had trouble making important decisions, the Fair King created a special council of his twelve brothers and sisters. The twelve siblings would advise the young princess and allow her to hear and see both sides equally."

"What happened next, Mommy?" Karmasha inquires.

Her mother smiles. "Well, the young princess was beautiful, and she met a man, fell in love, and had a blessed child. You see, over her mortal lifetime she gained amazing wisdom. And even when she died, she still lived on in the spirit world and passed on the power and legacy to her own child. And that child passed it on to their child and so on, forever and ever.

"The name of the Fair King's daughter, the princess, was Karma, and thus the legend of Karma began. Over the years, the story of Karma got lost and found and lost and found, so much so that almost no one knows the true story anymore. But I do, and now you do, too. And do you know why?"

Karmasha shakes her head.

"Because, my little princess, the hundreds of generations of Karma have led to you. That's why your name is Karmasha, named after Karma herself. You're a beautiful young princess just like her, and I can't wait to see you develop in wisdom, love, and respect just like she did."

Over the next three years, Karmania's illness worsens. She has become bedridden, forced to lie helpless, unable to care for her child the way she wishes. The doctors couldn't figure out what the problem was exactly and tried everything they could think of. But, if anything, the treatment just made her sicker and weaker.

"Mommy?" Karmasha says one day to her mother, who is lying in bed with a miserable frown on her face.

"Yes, Princess?" she replies quietly.

"Are you going to die?" Karmasha asks, her voice quivering, and her eyes beginning to tear up.

Karmania pats the bed at her side and waits for her daughter to sit. "My sweet girl. There's no way for me to say no to that question. Because one day, yes, I am going to die. It might be tomorrow or it might be years from now. But even though I know you'll be really sad that I'm gone, I don't want you to dwell on it too long. Death is a very sad thing, especially when it comes to the people you love, but there are always elements of hope and happiness, too."

"Why would I be happy?" Karmasha protests.

"You'll be sad that I won't be in your life anymore, but you can find hope and joy when you think about how I will always be with you in spirit, looking down at you. I'll be returning to the Fair King's kingdom, a place of light and happiness. And I'll get to see your father again, whom I miss so much."

Karmasha silently begins to weep, tears rolling down her cheeks and dripping down onto the bed sheets.

Karmania raises her head, reaches around the back of her neck, and unhooks the clasp of a chain. "Take this," she says to her daughter, handing her the necklace. "That stone has been carried and worn by many of Karma's descendants. It's not the source of our power, but by wearing it you'll always be able to feel the guidance of all the Karmas that came before you, including me."

Karmasha takes the necklace and holds the white stone in her small hands, looking down at the beauty of the pendant.

"I don't know when you will grow into your destiny, but I have faith that you'll be strong in love and fairness. Let your heart be your guide, and you'll never be wrong. Do you understand me?"

Little Karmasha nods her head, refusing to look her mother in the eye so her mother won't see her tears.

Karmania brushes her hand through Karmasha's hair. She guides her daughter's chin up to look at her face and wipes away a large tear that has formed at the corner of her eye. Then she leans forward and places her forehead against Karmasha's and says, "I love you so much."

"I love you, too, Mommy."

And with those words, Karmania's eyes slowly close, and her head relaxes onto her pillow. With a faint smile on her face, she releases her last breath.

CHAPTER 13

LOOKING DOWN AT HER EMPTY PLATE, Karmasha begins to tear up as thoughts of her mother take her over. Then she feels the cool metal and stone from her mother's necklace on the skin of her chest and smiles. She reaches up and fingers the necklace, knowing that her mother will always be with her.

"Miss?" a young woman's voice speaks from Karmasha's left.

Karmasha blinks and looks up at the waitress.

"I just wanted to let you know that we're closing soon," the waitress says softly.

Karmasha's eyebrows furrow for a moment before she perks up and responds, "Oh!" She hurries to close out her check.

When she steps out of the diner, she feels a cool breeze. The sun is all the way down now, and she's surrounded by the combined luminescence of the street lamps and the nearly full moon high above. Spying a small hotel down the street, she decides to stay in town for the night and continue her journey tomorrow.

Once she's gotten settled in her room, she eagerly changes into her lounging clothes and gets comfortable, sitting up in the queen-size bed, pillows propped up behind her and the comforter covering her legs. She picks up the remote control lying on the bedside table, turns on the small flat-screen TV, and tunes it to the local news, hoping to admire her handiwork today.

The first thing she hears is a newswoman saying, ". . . so the next time you get a fish, make sure you put it in water."

"What?" Karmasha says out loud, cocking her head to one side.

"And in other news . . ." the newswoman continues. "Today, the town witnessed a vehicle collision of rare proportions for the area, and from it arose both a small scandal and a small miracle. A school bus carrying several young children ran a stop sign and pulled out in front of a young man's car. Witnesses say the driver of the car, Jack Singell, swerved and slammed on his brakes, but the impact was unavoidable. No one on the bus was injured, but Singell suffered a concussion and is now in the hospital. He is expected to make a full recovery.

"And now for the rest of the story. Police have discovered that the driver of the bus, first identified as Thomas Langal, is actually wanted felon Satchel Clemmens, who has been a fugitive from the law for the past three years. Clemmens illegally obtained a new identity that allowed him to get a job as a bus driver for our local elementary school. School officials have admitted to not running a full background check on the driver because of budget cuts and time constraints.

"Because of this negligence, city government is already discussing the settlements they will make with the injured driver. Mr. Singell is expected to receive approximately two hundred and fifty thousand dollars in addition to coverage of his medical bills. An insider close to Mr. Singell told us that the money is a true miracle, as he has been taking care of his sick mother for the last few years and was recently laid off from his job due to downsizing. And that is how this unfortunate accident has not only exposed a disturbing scandal but also created a miracle in disguise for a citizen in need."

Karmasha smiles and nods her head. She likes seeing how things turn out for all parties, those deserving of both good and bad.

Satisfied, Karmasha turns off the television, places the remote back on the bedside table, and turns off the lamp to go to sleep.

After her long day, she falls almost immediately into a deep slumber, and, in this slumber, her spirit is transported to another world.

She awakens in a hazy, dream-like place. Light surrounds her, coming from every direction and nowhere all at once. She feels an overall feeling of comfort, as if she has arrived at a second home.

In fact, she has arrived at her real place of work, the In Between.

The ground is soft and fluffy as if she were standing on a cloud, and wisps of fog puff up out of the ground surrounding her feet and reaching up almost to her knees. There are no walls nor other objects as far as the eye can see except directly in front of her. There, a few dozen feet ahead, stands a raised ledge where twelve thrones are erected in a semicircle.

Each of the thrones holds a person, but these beings are far from normal humans. Each seems to be only partially materialized and appears slightly transparent, like a ghost, though their forms are still fully present. Split down the middle, the six spirits on her left have luminous, bright white eyes. Looking into those eyes, Karmasha feels hope and peace, and she sees beauty and light. However, looking into the eyes of the six spirits on her right, she experiences the opposite. She feels sorrow and death and sees only darkness. These six spirits have pitch-black eyes—not merely black orbs or dark orifices displaying depth, but rather mysterious openings into nothingness.

"The Council welcomes you back to the spirit world, Karma," a deep voice comes from the sixth chair from the left.

"How many times do I have to tell you, Abraxos? Call me Karmasha," she says with easy self-assurance. "It's the name my mother gave me, and I prefer my name to my title."

The speaker Abraxos responds, "It may be just a title to you, but it is who you are."

Karmasha is about to roll her eyes when a man's scratchy voice cuts in from the fourth chair from the right. "Was two hundred and fifty thousand dollars really necessary?" the voice says angrily.

Karmasha shrugs her shoulders. "I don't control the numbers, only the chances and ideas."

"She was only doing her job, Abaddon, lay off," Abraxos snaps back.

The woman in the third chair from the left jumps in. "Guys, can we please calm down and start the requests?"

"Yes, let's move," Abraxos turns to her and replies. "Thank you, Zuriel." Looking forward again at Karmasha, he continues. "Sablo, I believe you had a request."

The spirit in the fourth chair from the left stands up to make his petition. "There is a doctor in Richmond who has done a very generous deed but with some pretty iffy intentions. She did a pro-bono surgery for a disabled veteran, but a major reason she did it was to get good press. What do you think should happen?"

As the Karma, Karmasha must investigate requests made by the Council in order to decide if someone deserves good or bad karma. She must weigh the differences between intentions and actions and determine which is more prominent.

"I'd have to see how much of a sacrifice it was for her to do the free surgery and how she feels about it now that it's all over," Karmasha responds. "If she didn't sacrifice much, and she doesn't feel genuinely glad about helping him, then I may have to bestow some bad karma for her selfish act."

Sablo nods his head and takes his seat, replaced on the floor by Rachmiel right beside him, who is now standing up from the fifth chair on the left.

"Today in Richmond, a young woman was walking home from work when she saw a little boy run out into the street to chase a ball. Long story short, she pushed the child out of the way of a taxi coming right at him. She saved the boy's life, but she unfortunately did not come out unscathed. She's currently in the hospital with critical injuries, and it doesn't look too good."

"That sounds more like you need a miracle, not an investigation," Karmasha remarks.

"Indeed." Abraxos nods his head.

Karmasha catches his meaning. "So you already held the vote?"

"Yes," Zuriel nods. "Miracle approved," she says as a smile lights up her face.

"For the record, I was against it," a woman with a high-pitched, whiny voice pipes up from the farthest chair on the right.

"But of course, Lillith," Zuriel responds, rolling her eyes.

Another deep voice speaks up, this one from the sixth chair from the right. It sounds like a foghorn, or as if it were being projected from deep within a cave, with a chill echoing through each word. "If that's the end of the light's need to investigate a good deed done with bad intentions, I would like to announce my request for a bad deed done with good intentions."

"Go ahead, Bernael," Karmasha responds to the council member, looking calmly up at his pitch-black, scaly skin which appears like that of a snake.

"Very well. I have a request that could bring down a corrupt politician. This city council member has been stealing city funds for his own benefit, and he has been cheating on his wife while sexually assaulting his assistant," Bernael growls. "But," he sighs, "he just donated the funds he stole to a charitable organization, and now I'm not sure how to proceed."

"Hmm. As far as the theft goes, I would have to look into whether he made the donation because of a true change of heart or because he felt guilty and wanted to make himself feel better," Karmasha says. "As for the cheating and sexual assault, you can go ahead and give him bad karma."

"Very well," Bernael says, bowing his head slightly.

Karmasha looks around the council to see if anyone else is going to speak up. "Are there no more requests?"

The council members shake their heads and voice scattered nos.

"See you tomorrow, Karma," Abraxos speaks one last time.

Karmasha nods her head and the Council vanishes from view. The vast, white space fades away, and the fog at her feet now rises up to eye level as she leaves the spirit world. Back in the mortal world, she goes on to sleep and dream like normal people do for the remainder of the night.

Hours later, Karmasha wakes to the sun shining through her hotel room windows. Squinting her eyes until she adjusts to the bright light, she gets out of bed and goes into the bathroom. When she looks in the mirror, she smiles at the sight of her mother's necklace hanging around her neck.

Now fully awake, she hurries to shower and dress so she can check out and get back on the road. Her detour yesterday put her back a few hours, and she needs to get to Richmond so she can begin her karma investigations.

With the road stretching out in front of her, Karmasha thinks about her children. She thinks about the crazy life she's hiding from them and prays that they won't have to go through what she's gone through. Although she hopes that they won't inherit her powers and become Karma like her, she knows it's a wish that probably won't come true. Someone has to take on this important responsibility.

She has thought about telling them, giving them a warning or something, but in the end she keeps putting it off. She didn't inherit her powers until her mother died, so, as far as she knows, that's what activated them. Hope keeps her from telling her children, hope that it will be many years before they start experiencing the karmic abilities, and thus hope that she will be alive for many more years to be with them. This hope has been especially strong since her husband died. She has no wish of leaving her children alone.

Once again, she is led to reflect on her past, on the moment she realized her life had changed forever.

INTERLUDE

"**M**OMMY! MOMMY!" **KARMASHA CRIES** out as she tries to rouse her mother, her mother who has just closed her eyes and released her last breath. Karmasha knows what has happened, she knows that her mother has died, but she continues to shake her mother's shoulders and call out to her anyway. Hot, wet, heart-breaking tears begin to well up in her eyes, and she finally collapses, sobbing, over her mother's lifeless body.

Suddenly, a blinding white light flashes. The light seems to have come from Karmania's body, and it throws Karmasha back, away from her mother, off the bed and against the wall with such force that she slides down and blacks out.

Somewhere within her subconscious, Karmasha's eyes open to another bright white light, but this time the light isn't coming from one concentrated locality, nor is it forceful and intense in any way. The light surrounds her in every direction, and it gives her a sense of calm and serenity. Mouth and eyes wide, she stands up in the infinite space of white. She looks down at her legs and sees wisps of fog licking at them. Looking around, there are no landmarks or structures of any kind as far as her eyes can see.

"Hello?" she calls out, her voice shaking.

No one answers her call. She's completely alone in this cloud of endless space. She starts to think about what could possibly be happening. Is she dreaming? Did she herself die and go to heaven? Or is something else going on?

Thoughts continue to swirl around in her mind as she stands there looking around and calling out for someone, anyone, to answer her.

After what seems like hours, she decides to walk. She doesn't know where to go, but she just can't stand around waiting anymore. She picks a direction and walks straight ahead, unwavering from her path.

She must have walked for miles, or at least it feels that way. With no markings in any direction, it's hard to keep track. She continues to walk, tears streaming down her face, until what seems like a miracle occurs: she sees something out in the distance ahead of her, a black speck.

Karmasha's stomach first drops then starts fluttering as her heart speeds up. As she gets closer to the speck, it gets bigger, becoming an enormous black hole of nothingness once she finally reaches it. Peering into the blackness, she suddenly understands that it's just like the stretch of endless light that has been surrounding her, only this is an endless void of . . . nothing. There is only darkness, blacker and darker than night, with not even the light behind her shining in. It's as if she were standing face to face with a solid-black wall, standing on the edge of a cliff, and staring into space all at once.

Looking down, she sees that the fog earlier shrouding her feet has dispersed, as if the darkness were eating it up. At the edge of the white, the tips of her toes are mere inches away from the black in front of her.

She stands there for a few moments, contemplating what to do. She's too scared to enter the darkness, but she's also too scared to stay where she is. So she decides to take a leap of faith—or at least a halfway jump. Turning to her left so that the light is to her left and the blackness is to her right, she lifts up her right leg and moves it slowly toward the line.

The instant her leg crosses into the black, the darkness consumes it and hides it from her sight. Although she's not in pain, she begins to tremble, her heart pumping harder than it ever has before. Yet she decides to continue, committing to immersing herself halfway into the darkness.

Putting her right leg down on ground she cannot see, she slowly shifts her weight onto it until the entire right side of her body—except for her head, which she warily holds back—is in the darkness. She takes a deep breath, worried that the darkness might keep her from breathing normally, and slowly starts leaning her head in. Once half of her head is immersed in blackness, she freezes.

For a split second, Karmasha sees only light in her left eye and only darkness in her right, but the effect quickly dissipates as she suddenly screams.

The scream sounds like a hundred other voices screaming at once: bloodcurdling, chilling, terrifying—as if something within her is trying to get out. She sees flashes of memories, only they aren't her memories. She sees memories that she realizes are her mother's, then memories of her grandfather, and then memories of hundreds of other men and women throughout time. In her left eye, she sees the happy times, the peace, the joy, the love. But in her right eye, she sees the times of anguish, of pain, of sorrow and war and death.

The flashes continue until they end with the image of a young girl not much older than she is. The girl is dressed in a lovely white dress with a tiara atop her head, looking like a princess. Karmasha no sooner registers this vision than it feels as if her essence is transferring over and into the young princess.

Then, looking out through the princess's eyes, she sees a semicircle of twelve chairs in front of her. Upon the six chairs to the left sit an equal number of men and women, all similar in magnificence with pure white eyes, yet differing with unique and distinct appearances. Upon the six chairs to the right sit three more men and three more women, these beings much more terrifying with eyes of pure darkness. Each has his or her own disturbing physical characteristics, what Karmasha recognizes as sinister omens of their specific natures.

The twelve men and women speak to the princess and therefore to Karmasha. They speak all at once, a range of voices chanting together in complete unison.

"We are the Council of Twelve. By the power of the Fair King, we bestow onto you our combined power. With these abilities you shall determine, using complete objectivity and fairness in deference to the Fair King, the rewards and punishments of humans throughout their world. You shall live with them, mortal and perishable, in order to greater understand their motives, thoughts, and actions. This power will not die with you, however, as your descendants will inherit the power, generation after generation. All worlds shall know your name, O Great and Powerful Karma."

With those words, Karmasha opens her eyes, once again on the floor of her mother's bedroom. Slowly getting up, she grasps her head, wincing, then blinks her eyes as she adjusts back to the physical realm.

She looks over at her mother, who lies lifeless on the bed, then realizes that she's still holding her mother's necklace after everything that just happened. She opens her hand and looks at the white stone. This time, the black lines passing through it are moving, swimming through the stone like snakes through snow. Then she sees her mother, her grandfather, and all of her ancestors in quick flashes—and finally Princess Karma herself.

Karmasha fastens the chain carefully, puts the necklace over her head, and walks over to the bedroom vanity. Upon gazing into the mirror, she jumps back, her breath catching. Her left eye has turned pure white and her right eye has become completely black.

She can't explain it, but in that moment she knows who she really is. She is no longer just Karmasha, daughter of Karmania. She is the descendant of the original Karma, and she must now step into her responsibilities as the new Karma of the universe.

CHAPTER 14

A CAR HORN BLARES RIGHT NEXT TO her, and Karmasha is torn from her flashback and catapulted to the present. She whips her head to the right and sees a black sports car weaving in front of the sedan right next to her, the sedan whose horn first jolted her from her reverie. In the next instant, the driver of the sports car jerks his vehicle right in front of her, its tail end barely missing her front bumper.

Karmasha growls as she swerves slightly and rams the brakes then lets her eyes change to activate her karmic power. The black sports car is several cars ahead of her now, near misses and blaring horns following in its wake. Suddenly, the car rapidly loses speed, and the man heads over to the shoulder as his engine sputters and stalls out, smoke coming from under the hood. As Karmasha drives past, she sees him pounding his fists on the steering wheel, his face beet red and his mouth spewing what has to be a stream of profanities toward the sky. She chuckles, shaking her head.

Only a few minutes later, Karmasha spies the first exit sign for Richmond. Subconsciously sensing where to go, she lets her spiritual abilities guide her to her first karmic investigation.

She ends up heading to the hospital first, where she hopes to take care of two investigations at the same time. As she nears the imposing building, she fights back a grin. She's eagerly looking forward to performing the miracle, assuming everything checks out. It's not every day that she's granted permission to perform one.

In the hospital's parking garage, she chooses a spot away from the other cars and gets out. After a deep, calming breath in and out and a quick glance at her surroundings to make sure no one else is around, she transforms from her physical being into a transparent spirit. This form allows her to enter the spirit realm of the mortal world and go anywhere without being seen—by the average human, anyway. As this spirit, she can pass through locked doors and go straight through solid walls as if they weren't even there. She's also able to know, without any conscious intervention, where to go and who to watch, thanks to her karmic instincts.

Karmasha decides to give the doctor a little bit of good karma, as the impact of the deed outweighed her intentions just slightly. Then she performs a healing miracle on the woman who sacrificed herself to save the little boy.

Although she won't be able to stick around long enough to see the results, she can't help but smile as she makes her way back to the garage, still unseen by human eyes, glad that she has been able to save that deserving woman's life. Once at the car, she looks around to make sure she's alone, then instantaneously morphs back into her physical self. With one last, quick look around—just to make sure—she opens the door to her car and climbs in.

She drives further into town, stopping in a quaint shopping area for a very late lunch. Since her day started late because of her overnight detour, it's already half past four, and there's hardly anyone around.

As she gets out of her car and starts to walk toward the restaurant, she decides to call Krista, figuring she should be done with school and yearbook for the day. She reaches for her phone, pulling up her contacts and scrolling quickly through the list, when suddenly a strange feeling stops her mid-stride and mid-scroll.

She shivers and pockets her phone as she feels a cold gust of wind come from behind her. She freezes as it hits her skin, her eyes wide as a dark presence permeates her surroundings. She cries out as the darkness rips through her, making her insides feel as though death itself has just passed through her body. The feeling lasts only for a moment, but it's long enough for her to know she never wants to feel that way ever again.

She blinks and looks up.

Standing before her is Lahash, one of the evil spirits of the Council. His skin is charcoal gray, textured like molten rock that has cooled. His jawline seems chiseled from the rough stone of his head. The ruggedness continues up his face and into a small and jagged peak at the top of his head, which appears like a crown of spikes and crags. He looks back at her, his solid-black eyes piercing through the afternoon light and into Karmasha's very soul.

Jumping back, she quickly leaps into action. Using her entire body, she pulls together the spiritual energy of her powers of karma and drives forward a sudden burst of energy from her outthrust hands. The energy comes out like a stream of light, white with serpents of black penetrating it like veins. The powerful expulsion pushes the evil spirit back, throwing him thirty feet away.

Lahash looks up from the ground, glowering at her with dark and sinister eyes. Yet his face is stern and emotionless with neither a smile nor a frown.

"What are you doing here?" Karmasha yells at him. She's never seen a spirit of the Council in the mortal world, only spoken to them in her dreams—and because he's an evil spirit, she can only assume that he's up to no good.

Lahash says nothing as he lies on the ground. Never taking his gaze off Karmasha, he waves a hand in front of his face and chest. As wisps of black smoke surround his body, he dissipates into the air, vanishing.

Karmasha stands there breathing heavily, frozen in place once again, thoughts swirling in her head. *What just happened?*

Lahash materializes back in the spirit world, but it's not the neutral realm Karmasha usually experiences in her dreams. This is the dark realm, a foreboding place forever consumed in eternal night. Lahash is standing in a forest thick with a fog barely penetrable by the full moon above. His dark skin and black robe make him almost invisible among the dark shadows from the trunks of the trees towering above him.

"She suspects nothing," he speaks out to seemingly no one. "But now she'll be wondering why I was in the mortal world."

"It had to be done," comes a woman's raspy voice from the shadows in front of him. The woman herself then emerges partially into view, enough to display her tall and muscular body.

"Uzza is right," says another woman as she comes into view as well. Her slender body seems to flow with the wisps of black fog surrounding her. Her body is an image of pure beauty—that is until she opens her mouth and displays her forked tongue and the two sharp teeth protruding from the upper regions of her mouth like those of a serpent.

One more woman and one more man also emerge from the darkness, stepping into the faint glow of the moon above, and the five spirits come together in an incomplete circle.

Lahash continues, eyes narrowing. "What will we tell her tonight at the council meeting?"

"Let me handle that," a deep and powerful voice speaks out from behind him. The voice sounds like a hundred voices at once and echoes through the dense woods.

"Bernael!" Belial, the second woman spirit, exclaims. "Or should I say 'Levi'?"

Bernael steps into the glimmer of the moonlight with the others, completing the circle. From his back hangs a pair of large black wings. Their structure is bony, and their webbed linings are a thin, cartilage-like skin covered in more of the characteristic black scales that cover the rest of his body. He rolls his eyes at the group. "Ugh, never call me that again. I hate mortal names. My only comfort is that I used the letters of the greatest power and force in the universe."

The six spirits laugh maniacally at his joke.

"I have great expectations for the middle one. Maybe the eldest, too, but the youngest will definitely take some coaxing," Bernael continues, serious again. He puts his hands together in a steeple in front of his lips, which curl into a sinister smile as he broodingly taps his fingertips against each other. "Lahash, continue to keep an eye on Karma, but keep your distance. After today's incident, we can't afford her seeing one of us in the mortal world again."

Lahash nods his head.

Bernael looks at the third man in the circle. "Abaddon, I need you to try to keep an eye out for the good spirits. We can't have them finding out what we're up to."

"Yes, Brother," Abaddon agrees, and he breathes out a dark stream of smoke from his nostrils that flows through the black ring piercing his septum like a bull's. The round piercing matches his large, round face and makes his hairless dome that much more pronounced.

"Uzza," Bernael continues. "You are my left-hand woman. You shall continue to watch over all of us from the spirit world and help me understand the entirety of the game board, for we shall make our greatest plans together."

"It is my honor, Brother," Uzza replies, nodding her head in obeisance.

"Let's not screw up this exquisite opportunity, Brothers and Sisters," Bernael cautions them after taking a deep breath in and out. "Tread carefully."

CHAPTER 15

A S THE SIX EVIL SPIRITS OF THE COUNCIL continue their meeting in the dark forest, the six good spirits of the Council are about to hold their daily meeting in the light realm of the spirit world.

Four of the six spirits lie on the white sandy beach of a tropical island under the endless rays of sunlight radiating from above. Surrounding them are scores of friendly, beautiful creatures roaming through the brightly colored flowers and trees blanketing the island. Around the island flow blue waters so clear and bright that the spirits can see the wonderful creatures swimming below the surface. Though the sun is beating down on them, it's never hot nor cold—just the perfect temperature for every person for all time. In the light realm, no shadows are cast, for there's never to be any kind of darkness.

"Is Dina still out?" queries a spirit lying back on a light-blue blanket on the soft white sand. She reclines propped up on her elbows, and her slender lightly-tanned, bikini-clad body glistens in the sun. Her short blonde hair drapes down to her shoulders.

"Yes, Zuriel," replies a spirit called Abraxos as he emerges from the water and comes jogging toward her. His muscular body is glistening, and his wavy sun-bleached blond hair is damp from his swim. His deep, strong voice is pleasant, and he speaks with poise. "Her assignment is taking a lot of her time and attention."

"Ah, Abraxos," says a second woman lying on the sand. "Are there any other plans in the making?"

Before Abraxos can respond, the good spirits hear a sudden loud gasp come from one of the two men lying on the beach.

"Paschar!" Abraxos calls out to him, panic evident in his tone. "What is it?"

"I saw a vision," Paschar replies in a rush, sitting up and opening his three eyelids to reveal three solid white eyes. Two of the eyes are in a normal position, like those of his brothers and sisters, and a third eye is centered on his forehead. His short silver hair and metallic skin sparkle in the bright daylight. Speaking quickly with his usually tempered and soothing voice, he recounts what he has seen. "It has already happened . . . but one of our evil brothers or sisters has initiated contact with Karma in the mortal world by passing through her body."

"Why are you only just now seeing it?" inquires the third male spirit, Sablo, who sits up on the sand between Paschar and Zuriel. His light-brown hair, long and curly, stands up voluminously, and his white garments set off his golden-brown skin. Standing up, his light-brown, feathery wings shake off the sand and majestically settle and relax on his back like an eagle's wings. His imposing, toned arms are the counterbalance to the size and strength of his wings.

Paschar shakes his head. "I don't know. Lahash must have been blocking me. He's the only one who has the power to interrupt my visions."

"They're trying to get to them!" exclaims the second woman, Rachmiel, her voice likewise shaken from its usual calm softness. Her solid white skin is unaffected by the rays of the sun, and her long white hair shines brightly, matching the light of her eyes.

Abraxos shakes his head, and, putting one hand on his hip, he reaches up with the other hand to rub his forehead.

"Brother," Rachmiel says, getting up, rushing over to Abraxos, and placing a hand on his shoulder.

"Rachmiel," he responds. "Call Dina. She needs to be here."

Nodding her head, Rachmiel turns to the trees, eyeing their stone and straw huts through the foliage. After taking a breath, she begins to sing a mesmerizing, four-note melody. Her mezzo-soprano voice is light and agile. She starts at a note in the middle of the scale; then, in one breath, she transitions to an octave higher, then higher again, then ends with a low note just below her first one.

Moments later, a woman clothed in a long white dress slowly emerges from the trees, her bare feet stepping softly onto the white sand. As she steps forward, her long blonde hair flows elegantly in the gentle breeze, and a smile lights up her face at the sight of her brothers and sisters.

"Dina," Abraxos immediately addresses the fair-skinned young woman, "we believe our evil brothers and sisters are plotting something in regard to the children. Lahash tried to block Paschar from seeing one of them in the mortal world with Karma."

"Wait," Dina quickly responds. "Does Karma know of the experiences of the children?"

"No," Paschar speaks up. "I don't think so, but our evil brothers and sisters clearly wanted to check it out for themselves."

"Sister," Zuriel interrupts, "what has been happening in the mortal world?"

Dina replies to her sister, her brow furrowed. "The children have begun to experience their powers, but they don't seem to understand what's happening. I'm getting close to the youngest, and he seems genuinely frightened. I get only good vibes from his aura, but we all know how tempting the darkness can be."

"What of the other two?" inquires Abraxos.

"I really don't know. I can't keep an eye on all of them at once without arousing suspicion," says Dina. She looks around at the other five good spirits. "I need more help down there."

Abraxos shakes his head. "If the evil spirits are already infiltrating their lives, we won't be able to effectively introduce new guides into their lives quickly enough. Trust takes a while, as I'm sure you're noticing."

"Indeed," Dina agrees, sighing.

"What about possession?" Sablo inserts himself.

"The Council forbids the act," Zuriel says. "You know that."

"But if it's the only way . . ." Sablo hesitates before pushing his point. "Look, we can't expect the dark spirits to play fairly. If we choose hosts that are already inherently good and are trustful guides in the lives of the children, then I think it's worth the risk. Yes, the effect possession has on the human host can never be predicted, but, I say again, it's worth the risk. If darkness consumes even just one of the three, there's no telling what death and destruction will come to the mortal world."

Abraxos sighs. "I believe Sablo is right. We all need to be down there."

"Very well, Brother," Paschar assents. "But, as Dina has been experiencing, once down in the mortal world, our attention will have to be extremely focused. I shall remain in the spirit world, as my power of vision will help you more if I'm up here watching over the five of you. I'll also be able to keep an eye on Karma."

"Speaking of her," Abraxos says, "she'll have a lot to say tonight about seeing an evil spirit in the mortal world."

"We must not let her learn of the children," Paschar puts forward. "That's probably the one thing the entire council would agree on."

Rachmiel speaks up. "Paschar is right. This is the first time the powers are developing before the current Karma dies, so we don't know how she might influence them. She can't know of the development. This is our chance to bring goodness to the world."

The resounding tone of a gong suddenly fills the ears of the six spirits.

Looking upward toward the sound, Zuriel sighs and says, "Well, it's time for the council meeting. Let the misdirects begin."

The spirits form a circle and join hands. Closing their eyes, they hum a note in unison. When they reopen their eyes, they shine radiantly. Then a bright light beams upward from the center of the circle and transports them to the In Between, where they materialize in front of their thrones in the cloudy-white atmosphere of the Council realm.

The good spirits exchange glances with their evil siblings who have just arrived as well.

Abraxos whispers to his kindred brothers and sisters, "Act surprised when Karma mentions the incident. Let the others try to explain it and, if she tries asking us, redirect the question. Our dark brothers and sisters don't know we're on to them, so that's our advantage, and we, of course, can't allow Karma to discover the truth."

The twelve spirits of the Council take their seats—Dina, Paschar, Zuriel, Sablo, Rachmiel, and Abraxos, spirits of the light, sit on the thrones to the left, while Bernael, Uzza, Abaddon, Belial, Lahash, and Lillith sit on their own thrones on the right as the spirits of darkness—and proceed to summon the presence of Karmasha. Once she materializes, the council meeting comes to order.

"Spirits of the Council," Karmasha says, immediately addressing the twelve. "An incident occurred today that deeply troubles me, as it's an act that I've never witnessed and always thought of as forbidden."

"What is it?" Dina speaks up.

"This afternoon, Lahash, member of the dark spirits of the Council, passed through me in the physical realm of the mortal world. Not only did I experience a horrible sensation when he did, but I was also filled with a terrible feeling that he was there to do something dark. So I acted in self-defense and forced him to leave the mortal world."

"I wasn't up to anything!" Lahash insists.

"Hmph," Karmasha snorts, crossing her arms. "I highly doubt that."

"Oh, yeah?" Lahash rebuts. "Well, *you* shouldn't have used pan—"

"Enough!" Bernael interrupts Lahash then turns to Karmasha. "While I can't speak to the idiocy and utter ridiculousness of the thought of him passing through you, I think I can speak for all the spirits in that we do, from time to time, walk among the living of the mortal world. It can get boring in the spirit world at times. But I assure you, there were no ulterior motives in him being in the physical realm."

The entire council seems to hold their collective breath.

Karmasha looks into Bernael's eyes as if to gauge whether or not he's lying, but, of course, all she sees in them is darkness and anguish. Finally breaking the gaze, she nods her head. "Very well. But don't ever pass through me like that again. None of you. It caught me off guard."

The twelve spirits nod their heads in unison.

The council meeting continues as usual, with both sides of the Council making their karmic investigation requests. And, apart from the typical bickering that takes place in their meetings, no further issue is made of the spirits walking in the mortal world.

When the meeting is over, Karmasha dematerializes, returning to a deep slumber back in her hotel room in Richmond.

Abraxos considers confronting Bernael about Lahash's interaction with Karmasha in the mortal world, but, in the end, he decides against it, hoping secrecy will give the good spirits the upper hand in the situation.

Before the council members part ways, the two leaders pull their fellow spirits aside for a brief follow-up meeting. Abraxos calls on his kindred spirits and Bernael on his dark brothers and sisters. These informal meetings are typically meant for the leaders to assign areas in the mortal world to watch for possible karmic investigations, as well as for informing those spirits which part of the mortal world they will carry out those assignments in.

This time, however, both leaders have a different agenda. On this night, they talk about the karmic powers of the children and walk through what needs to be done at this time to ensure their best possible future. Of course, the visions for that future are wildly different for the two sides of the Council.

"All right, everyone," Abraxos says to his five good siblings in a low voice. "We need to look thoroughly into the possibility of possession. We'll visit the children through the cloak of invisibility of the spirit realm and watch to determine who they might be able to accept as wise and kind guides.

We'll have to choose those hosts wisely, for we'll probably only have one chance at this. Dina, continue in your role; you're clearly making some headway. Paschar, remain in the spirit world to watch over us. If you see anything, don't hesitate to reach out to us. Zuriel, Rachmiel, Sablo—let's head down to the mortal world. Time to get to work."

On the other side, Bernael is giving a similar pep talk and a similar set of orders. "We need to step up our game, Brothers and Sisters. I have a suspicion that our brothers and sisters of the light may be on to us. Uzza, you will remain in the spirit world watching over us. Belial, Abaddon, and Lillith, you will join me in the mortal world. I have my part already, but we need to find hosts for you as well."

"Possession?" Lillith blurts out in her high-pitched, witch-like voice which matches her jagged teeth and pointed nose. Her skin is white like death and covered with dark, hideous scars.

"Hush, woman!" Bernael snaps harshly before confirming in a lowered voice. "But yes, that is what I had in mind."

Lillith cackles when she hears these words then rubs her hands together, displaying her long, sharp, talon-like nails.

"Shh," Bernael whispers. "Lahash, continue to keep an eye on Karma, but keep your distance; we don't want her suspicions to return. She must not find out our true intentions. These children are our chance to take over this council. They're not only experiencing their powers early, but there are three of them—three chances to raise an evil Karma who will finally stomp out the light and hope of the mortal world and bring darkness, suffering, and death."

CHAPTER 16

BEEP! BEEP! BEEP! **SOUND THE ALARMS** of the Atwood siblings as a new day shines its light upon them. Although it's Klause's first alarm, it's Krista's backup alarm. After staying up late to study the night before, she accidentally slept through her first one.

Brother and sister rush out of their rooms and toward the bathroom, arriving at the bathroom door at the same time.

"I woke up so late," Krista insists as she tries pushing her brother out of the way so she can get in first.

"Hey!" Klause pushes back. "You woke up late, so you missed your chance. You can go after me."

"But you have the knack of just taking a quick shower when I'm done, and I need to wash my hair today," Krista shoots back.

"Just go downstairs to Mom's bathroom."

Krista huffs. "You know I don't like doing that. Why don't *you* go down there?"

"Because I—"

"Guys!" Kevin interrupts as he approaches the two of them. "What's going on?"

Klause is breathing hard. "We can't figure out who gets the bathroom first."

"What are your arguments?" Kevin inquires.

While making their cases, Krista and Klause manage to calm down a little, and they let Kevin try to mediate the argument.

However, just as Kevin opens his mouth to issue his ruling, Krista sees her opportunity and quickly slips into the bathroom, locking the door behind her.

"Krista!" Klause shouts, banging on the door.

Kevin puts his hand on his brother's shoulder, but Klause shrugs it away and storms off to his room.

Once he gets to his door, Klause slams it as hard as he can. As he walks past the full-length mirror hanging by his door, something catches his eye, and he turns to look at himself. For just a moment, Klause gets a glimpse of himself with two unusual and contrasting eyes . . . one black and the other white. Then, just as quickly, the disturbing image is gone.

He steps back, blinking hard and breathing deep, suddenly recalling the incident at the homecoming dance. He feels a pit forming in his stomach as he remembers how Krista's eyes changed when she pushed her harasser away, and how, just moments later, a chandelier fell on top of him and killed him.

Pacing around the room, he wrestles with the implications of his own eyes changing. Were his emotions heightened from arguing with Krista? Is it possible he had just used this strange new mental power on Krista? This disturbing thought stops him short—he listens intently for any cries for help, but the quiet that greets him worries him even more. Unable to stand the suspense, he opens his door and goes out into the hallway.

Just as he reaches up to knock on the bathroom door, Krista opens it, a towel wrapped snugly around her body.

"Whoa!" Krista shouts, jerking to a stop.

"Krista!" Klause exclaims then exhales. Although he doesn't know exactly what he was expecting, he's still surprised to see her unharmed—no blood running down her face, no broken bones sticking out anywhere. He's probably wrong about how it all works.

"Hey, sorry, Klause," Krista murmurs. "I felt really bad when I got in there, so I cut my shower short and didn't wash my hair. Can you forgive me?"

Krista barely finishes her sentence before Klause pulls her into a hug. After he releases her, Krista looks at her brother wide-eyed.

Klause shifts his weight. "See you in a little—I'm gonna shower now." Klause shrugs as he walks into the bathroom leaving Krista standing there, blinking.

"Oh, by the way," she calls out as he's shutting the door, "there wasn't any warm water for some reason. It was cold the whole time. Just wanted to give you a heads-up."

Cold water? Klause shrugs his shoulders as he gets in the shower and turns on the water . . . and then almost trips in his hasty jump back out. The water is scalding. Klause stands on the bathmat, jolted at first, then lost in thought. Did his anger toward Krista backfire on him? Was she angry earlier and did this to him? *Maybe this is how it works after all,* he thinks to himself.

Afraid to try the shower again, Klause opts for just washing his face in the sink and heads to his room to change. He debates whether or not he should tell Krista what happened to him—it was only a couple of days ago, after all, that they had all agreed to share any strange incidents. But he decides against it; he wouldn't want Krista thinking he might want to harm her.

The siblings finish getting ready and load themselves into Krista's car. They exchange small talk on the way to school, but Klause keeps his mouth shut about what happened earlier that morning.

CHAPTER 17

"THANK YOU, HENRY," MISS LAVERS SAYS to the student who just led the Pledge of Allegiance before turning to the rest of the class. "You may all be seated."

At his desk at the back of the room, Kevin leans back and relaxes as he watches his favorite teacher start the day's announcements.

In the middle of Miss Lavers' address, the classroom door opens, and a young girl appears in the doorway. Dressed in skinny blue jeans, a dark green sweater, and a brown beanie, the girl steps forward hesitantly as she stares at the class. Almost immediately, Kevin's eyes meet hers, and the two gaze at each other briefly. Kevin feels a small smile come to his lips as he sees the glimmer of a smile on hers.

"Ah, you must be Belladonna!" Miss Lavers calls to the young girl, waving her to the front of the classroom. "Come on up here."

The girl slowly steps forward, lowering her head and clutching her elbow with her other hand.

"Students, I'd like to introduce you to our new student, Belladonna," Miss Lavers addresses the class. "She just moved here from Maryland. Say hello to the class, Belladonna."

The young girl faintly mumbles, "Hey."

As the new student makes her way down the aisle, Miss Lavers softly reassures her, "It's okay, sweetie," and reaches out her hand to lightly touch the girl's shoulder.

"Oh," Miss Lavers breathes in suddenly, jerking her hand back. She can't identify the strange sensation she just felt—perhaps it was just static electricity?

Teacher and student look at each other silently for a moment. Then Miss Lavers gestures toward an empty chair on the outer edge of the rows of desks. "There's an open seat right over there."

Once Belladonna sits down, Miss Lavers finishes up the announcements, and soon the bell rings to signal the end of homeroom. The students scoop up their bags and backpacks and head out into the hallway.

At his locker, Kevin takes some time to organize since he knows he has plenty of time to get to his next class. Once satisfied, he pulls out his math books, notebooks, and the folders holding the pages of his homework. His arms and hands precariously full, he carefully swings his locker door shut by nudging it with his shoulder.

As he turns to head down the hallway to class, however, he promptly runs into someone and loses his grip on his books. "Augh!" Kevin exclaims, but then stops short when he sees that that someone is the new girl, Belladonna.

"I'm so sorry!" the two say simultaneously as they drop down into a squat to pick up the scattered books and papers.

"It's my fault," Belladonna says hurriedly. "I was looking around at room numbers, trying to find my class, and wasn't looking where I was going."

"No, it's my fault," Kevin insists. "I wasn't paying attention. It happens to me a lot."

Just then, Kevin reaches for a disheveled stack of papers just as Belladonna does. His hand brushes her fingers, and his eyes flash to hers. As Kevin looks into Belladonna's beautiful hazel eyes, his heart skips a beat. She smiles back at him and quickly pulls her hand back.

She clears her throat. "Let's just say it was *that* guy's fault." Belladonna chuckles as she points to a random student down the hall.

"Okay," Kevin laughs. "You're the new student, right?"

"Yes. My name is Belladonna, but I go by Bella. I had to transfer here after my parents divorced." She drops her gaze down toward the floor and sighs.

"Oh," Kevin whispers, "I'm sorry." He stands up, and Bella follows suit.

"Thanks," she says softly as she runs her fingers through her long black hair, pulling the strays away from her face and tucking them back under her beanie. She smiles as she looks at Kevin, lingering for a moment. Kevin's heart leaps in his chest.

RRINNG!! the bell sounds again.

"Time for class . . ." Kevin mutters. "I guess I'll see you around?"

"Yeah," Bella says with a smile as Kevin begins to walk away. "Oh, wait!" Kevin turns back around eagerly. "Can you tell me where room thirty-seven is? That's where my first class is."

Kevin can't help grinning as he replies, "Yeah! Algebra, right? That's my first-period class, too."

"Awesome!" Bella grins back.

"Come on," Kevin says, holding his arm out in invitation. "I think there's even an open desk next to me."

As the day goes on, Kevin's lightning-fast crush grows deeper as the two spend more time together. It doesn't hurt that every one of Bella's classes matches up with Kevin's.

"I guess this is goodbye," Kevin says as they step outside together at the end of their last class.

"I guess so," she sighs. "'Bye, Kevin."

The two stand in the school courtyard facing each other, each waiting for the other to walk away. After several awkward moments pass, Kevin starts wondering if she's expecting something else. This is the first time he's ever had a crush on a girl, and he wonders if she's expecting a hug, or a handshake, or maybe even for him to ask her out. Rocking back and forth on his feet, trying to figure it all out, Kevin finally takes a breath to say something.

To his relief, Bella speaks first. "Don't you have to go to the bus?"

"Oh!" Kevin replies, finally realizing what's happening. "No, I wait for my sister and brother out here. My sister is the editor in chief of the yearbook, and my brother is on the football team, so they both have after-school activities. I ride with them, so I usually just sit out here until they're done."

"Oh, cool," Bella says, shoving her hands in her pockets. "My mom said she would pick me up an hour or so after school, so I was just going to wait here, too."

"Do you want to wait together?"

"Sure!"

Kevin can't hide his grin. "Let me take you to my newly-found favorite spot," he says as he leads Bella through the courtyard toward a slightly wooded area nearby. "It's this really big, beautiful tree with a great view of the school pathway. I like sitting under it and, um . . ." He hesitates.

"And what?"

Kevin stops walking and looks down, contemplating whether or not he should share his secret with someone he just met.

"I won't tell anyone if that's what you're afraid of," Bella says in a low voice, as if she had read his mind.

Kevin unslings then unzips his backpack, pulls out his sketchbook, and hands it to Bella. "Here."

Bella opens it up and looks through Kevin's sketches as they resume their walk over to the tree. "Wow, these are really good," she says with genuine admiration. "Why were you embarrassed about them?"

Kevin shrugs. "I don't know, I guess just because I feel like I'll get teased a lot for it. I'm already a popular target for bullies—I just don't want to give them another thing to tease me about."

Bella places her hand on Kevin's shoulder. "I know what you mean. Sometimes I feel embarrassed about my art, too. But I feel like it's mainly because I don't think they're that good."

"You draw, too?"

"Sort of. I actually like working with watercolor. I carry these watercolor pens with me everywhere," she says as she opens her bag to reveal an assortment of watercolor pens, markers, pencils, and her artbook.

"Wow! That's really cool," Kevin responds. "You think you can teach me sometime?"

"Absolutely!" Bella replies with a wide smile.

The two reach the large oak and take a seat on the ground at its base, beneath its widespread branches. They sit shoulder to shoulder and smile at each other, both of their hearts palpitating as the sparks between them ignite.

CHAPTER 18

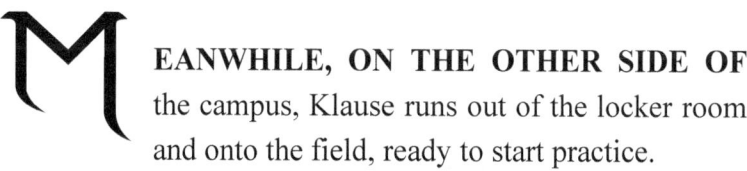EANWHILE, ON THE OTHER SIDE OF the campus, Klause runs out of the locker room and onto the field, ready to start practice.

After his twisted ankle almost a week prior, the pain has pretty much faded away. He's still just a little sore, but he's used to that by now from all the running he does in practice.

The coach yells out to the team, and they start doing speed drills. Waiting in line for his turn to go, a pat on his shoulder makes Klause turn around to face a senior linebacker towering over him. Stooping down to Klause's level, the senior boy whispers in Klause's ear, "I heard you got turned down by Jessica Ray for homecoming."

Klause shrugs his shoulders. "Yeah, so?"

"So . . ." the linebacker continues. "I thought it was hilarious. Little Junior Klause asking the hottest girl in school out. Ha!"

"Why is that hilarious?" Klause says through his teeth as his fists involuntarily start clenching.

"Just that a wuss like you thinks you would even have a chance with a girl like her."

"Who are you calling a wuss?" Klause shouts as he thrusts his face into the other player's.

"Hey, it's nothing to be ashamed of," the senior replies with mock concern. "Just maybe stick to your level of girl. You know—small . . . stupid . . . irrelevant."

"Well, I guess that leaves your mom then," Klause snaps back.

With a loud growl, the infuriated linebacker shoves Klause to the ground, and Klause's face hits the dirt. Klause leaps to his feet, punching the linebacker in the stomach before jabbing a well-placed heel in the side of his knee. The linebacker howls.

"Atwood!" the head coach yells when he sees the fight. Running over, the coach grabs the back of Klause's jersey at his neck, yanking him away from the other player.

"But, Coach . . ." Klause tries to defend himself. "He started it!"

"Sure he did," the coach responds, rolling his eyes. "Go run laps the rest of practice, Atwood!"

Klause huffs out his frustration but says nothing further, and, after shooting an angry glance at his antagonist, he takes off for the track.

While he runs his laps, Klause mutters angrily under his breath. "That miserable excuse for a linebacker started it. And then that bastard makes me run laps," he says, turning his anger toward the coach. "I'd like to see you get what you deserve."

As he says this, he is suddenly reminded of how, according to his brother and sister, he caused Jessica to fall and break her nose and the player who tackled him in the homecoming game to break his leg. If that's really his new power, dealing out this so-called "karma," why not try to have some fun with it? After all, the coach *does* deserve to be punished for not believing him.

As he runs around the field, Klause fixes his gaze intently on the coach, who's on the sidelines shouting at the other players. With his eyes glued on the coach, he begins to focus his mind. Lap after lap, his focus intensifies, and his anger grows.

Finally, his efforts pay off; Klause's eyes mutate into a perfect match to his sister's transformed eyes a week ago. Although he can't see this happen, he feels something deep inside when the power activates. It's a dark feeling that wrenches his gut and claws at his heart.

In the next moment, he notices a flock of birds flying over the field, and something makes him stop running. As he watches, four of the birds, one after the other, eject their waste . . . which lands smack dab on top of the coach's head.

Laughter erupts among the football players when they see the expression on their coach's face once he realizes what has happened.

Jamming his whistle into his mouth, the coach blows frenziedly while he waves his arms to signal the end of practice. Before the players even have time to clear the field, the coach sprints toward the locker room as the droppings run down his face.

Klause watches the scene, laughing hysterically at both his handiwork and his newfound power. At the same time, he's relieved that he didn't kill his coach and thinks that maybe he has more control over the power than his siblings. Unlike Krista and Kevin, *he's* never caused death, after all. The thought of being superior to his siblings in this way makes him smile and gives him a rush unlike that any drug could have provided. What he doesn't realize is that the rush is actually evil, seeping into his heart and soul and introducing a sliver of darkness in an otherwise innocent young man.

CHAPTER 19

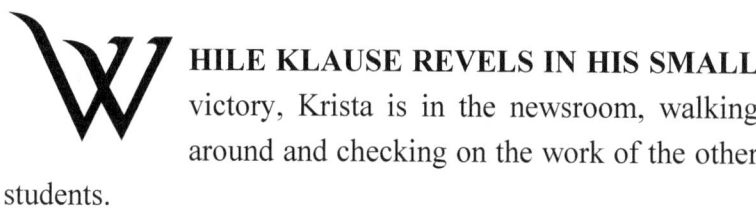 HILE KLAUSE REVELS IN HIS SMALL victory, Krista is in the newsroom, walking around and checking on the work of the other students.

"Jimmy, make sure you pick group photos where everyone looks at least semi-decent," she says as she leans over his shoulder and looks down at his layout for the yearbook's band page.

"Krista?" Marsha calls out from across the room.

"Coming," Krista says as she heads over to the main photography desk.

Watching her from a corner of the newsroom, invisible to the mortal world, are Abraxos and Sablo.

"That's her, right?" Sablo asks Abraxos, his voice undetectable by the mortals in the room.

"Yes," Abraxos replies as he watches Krista resume walking around the room and offering feedback to her fellow reporters.

"She seems like a great leader," says Sablo.

"Well, she *is* a descendant of Princess Karma, the most amazing leader we've ever encountered."

They stand there silent for a few moments.

"So what are we doing here again? Are we just going to watch Krista from the corner like a couple of creeps?" Sablo asks his older brother.

Abraxos frowns. "We're not creeps. Besides, it's not like she can see us anyway."

"I think that's what *makes* us creeps," Sablo says.

Abraxos sighs. "Dina mentioned someone by the name of Rick Pippin as a possible host. She said that he's a big part of Krista's life."

Their ears suddenly prick up when they hear a female student say, "Rick, can you come here?"

"Ah," Abraxos says as he observes a tall, lanky man walking over to the student. "I guess that's him."

"Rick," says the student, "can you please tell Heather that this article is dumb?"

"It's not dumb, Karen!" Heather defends. "It's *different.*"

"Dumb . . . different . . . what's the difference? Both could describe your outfit today," Karen says.

"My mom made me this dress!" Heather yells back, and her eyes begin to tear up.

"Ladies!" Rick steps in, his hands in the air between the fighting pair. "That's enough," he says sternly. Looking over at Heather, he inquires further. "What's the article idea?"

"The effect of slushies on your habits," Heather replies.

"Hmm . . ." Rick's voice trails off as he digests her unexpectedly off-the-wall answer.

"See?" Karen chimes in again. "Even *he* thinks it's dumb."

"No!" Rick quickly announces. "It's not a dumb idea. But I do think we can improve it to make it into a really awesome article."

"How?" Karen responds, crossing her arms.

"I am looking at two intelligent young ladies. Instead of tearing each other down, how about you work together to find a common ground that you can both agree on."

"What about . . ." Heather pauses. "What about the effect of slushies on your *study* habits?"

"Good," Rick says, nodding his head, a smile playing at the corner of his lips.

"Why limit it to slushies?" Karen turns toward her classmate. "Why not focus on all sugary drinks? Slushies, lemonade, sodas, and more!"

"Very good!" Rick says proudly, stepping away from the two girls now working together with gusto on their article.

"Wow," Abraxos says to Sablo. "Dina's feeling about him was right. He does seem like a wise and kind man. Did you see him mediate that argument?"

"Indeed," Sablo replies, taking a breath. "So are you taking this one?"

"No, you are. This Rick Pippin looks to be a very gracious man. That's right up your alley."

"Thank you, Brother."

Maintaining his invisibility, Sablo steps forward toward Rick.

"Krista," Rick calls out to her and points to his desk at the other end of the newsroom. "Can I talk to you for a moment?" Krista nods, and they both head over to his desk.

Just as Rick is about to sit down, Sablo steps up next to him. When he puts his hand out to touch Rick, the veil between the spirit and physical realm lifts for a split second. That's when Sablo converges with Rick and steps into his shoes, fully immersing himself in Rick's body, possessing him.

≪ O ≫

Rick's body shivers with an odd convulsion, then he stops short and shuts his eyes. This does not go unnoticed by Krista, whose eyes widen.

"Are you okay?" she asks in a concerned voice.

Rick lets out a deep breath and opens his eyes. Which, for a brief instant, are solid white, cloudy yet bright.

Krista gasps and steps back just as Rick's eyes return to normal. Then she just stands there, frozen in place.

"Krista?" Sablo says from within Rick's body, using Rick's voice. Seeing her reaction, he is worried about what she might have seen. After all, Krista and her siblings are the first descendants of Karma to possess their powers before the spirits of the Council have been revealed to them, and the extent of their abilities is still unknown.

Hoping that she didn't see anything, Sablo plays his new role as Rick Pippin and tries to comfort her by reaching out his hand to touch her shoulder. "What's wrong?"

Krista steps back instinctively. "Your eyes turned white," she says in a shaky voice.

"Oh, um . . ." Sablo thinks fast. "It's a vision problem I have. It just sometimes happens with my eyes. Nothing to worry about though, I'm seeing an eye doctor," he says casually as Rick as he nods his head and smiles at her.

"Oh . . . o-okay," Krista stutters. Then she blinks and a genuine smile spreads across her face. "So what did you want to talk to me about?"

CHAPTER 20

BACK OUTSIDE, KEVIN AND BELLA SIT under the large oak, laughing, talking, drawing, and having a good time getting to know each other.

"I can't believe you were asked once to be a taster at the movie theater," Bella says, laughing.

"What can I say, I'm a popcorn connoisseur," Kevin quips, shrugging his shoulders.

Bella continues to laugh as she places her hand on Kevin's leg and softly squeezes. Kevin's heart skips a beat as he stares at her hand. On his leg.

Suddenly their happy tête-à-tête is interrupted by two older boys who approach their tree. "Well, what do we have here? The weird loner kid found a weird loner girlfriend."

Kevin and Bella silently look up at the two jocks towering over them, their broad, muscular shoulders filling out their red and black letterman jackets.

"Oh, you're art geeks!" one of them exclaims as he reaches down and snatches Bella's artbook out of her hands.

In the past, Kevin wouldn't have done anything to defend himself. But when he sees Bella's head drop down to her chest, he decides that he has to try to be strong and do something.

"Hey!" he shouts as he jumps up. "Give that back!"

The two bullies chuckle and look at each other, their eyes lighting up. Kevin knows that look, and it's not good. He braces himself for what is certain to come next.

One of them grabs Kevin's shirt and pushes him up against the tree. His back hits hard, and his head follows, the knock making him disoriented. When the boy lets go, Kevin stumbles forward and swings his arms out to try to hit someone, but instead the other boy grabs his hair, pulling his head back, while the first one punches him in the stomach. Kevin falls to the ground, coughing and choking.

After seeing Kevin stand up for her, Bella leaps to her feet to defend him. "Stop it!" she yells as she grabs one of the boys' arms. The move backfires when the boy uses his other hand to slap her hard across the face.

Bella screams and falls, landing on her hands and knees on the earth and panting heavily.

Kevin, angered at the bully attacking a girl—and Bella especially—dives at the legs of the boy who hit her. The boy falls on his back, and Kevin crawls on top of him and starts punching him in the face.

As the other bully comes to pull Kevin off his friend, Bella, now risen, jumps in front of him and kicks him in the crotch.

The jock doubles over in pain, clutching at his groin as he struggles to breathe.

"Kevin!" Bella exclaims, pulling him up off the bully and taking hold of his hand. "Come on! Let's go!"

Without letting go of each other, they grab their bags from under the tree and sprint at full speed toward the back of the school building.

"Let's go in there!" Kevin points to the first door they come to behind the school.

Fortunately, the door is unlocked, and Kevin and Bella go inside and look around in the relative darkness for a place to hide.

"It looks abandoned," Bella says, looking around the hall and into the dark classrooms with dusty chairs and desks and covered windows. "Are we allowed in here?"

"No." Kevin knows from his sister that the area is currently an unused section of classrooms that has virtually become a dumping ground for extra storage and therefore has been barred from students. "But it's our only chance. There are no more places to hide."

"There!" Bella gestures down the hallway at a table with black sheeting hanging down over the sides.

They run to the table and quickly crawl under it then reposition the sheeting as best they can. Not a moment later, their pursuers come clambering in from the outside. The door slams shut loudly behind them, then a few seconds' silence follows.

Kevin's heart races as he tries to quiet his breathing.

"Oh, geeks, come on out . . ." one of the bullies says in a whiny, singsong voice. "You can run, but you can't hide!"

"Psst," the other one whispers. Kevin's eyes grow wide.

The two boys' footsteps start again as they continue their calls to Kevin and Bella. Kevin thinks they might be getting closer.

Under the table, Kevin draws in a deep breath and holds it. His emotions are running wild, and he feels strongly, insistently, that he must do something. Suddenly, he remembers that day in the craft store parking lot, where all he wanted to do was protect the girl being victimized by her boyfriend. Then he thinks about the research he and Krista did and the idea of karma as a possible power that he and his siblings might be able to control.

Remaining completely still, Kevin stares intently at the black tablecloth through which he hears footsteps approaching and focuses his energy on the approaching bullies, concentrating harder than he ever has before.

Although he can't see his eyes change colors, he feels something deep within him brush up against his soul and embrace his heart. The sensation sweeps away his swirling emotions and replaces them with a feeling of relief and safety.

At that moment, with the two jocks so close Kevin can see their shoes, a man's voice shouts from down the hall. "Hey! What are you two doing back here?"

"Mr. Vice Principal!" the boys blurt out in unison as they jump back.

"You two are in a world of trouble," the vice principal says sternly. "Come with me!"

"But—" they start to protest.

"But nothing." The vice principal cuts them off. "Come with me now. And not another word from either of you or it's suspension."

The jocks follow him to the office, and the sound of their fading footsteps is punctuated by the slamming of a distant door.

Kevin and Bella breathe a sigh of relief, but they remain quiet under the table for a few more minutes just in case.

Kevin isn't sure what exactly just went down, but he has a strong feeling that he had something to do with it. He's grateful that he was able to save Bella from trouble on her first day, and that, this time, no one died because of his thoughts.

Kevin and Bella turn to look at each other. Although their eyes have gotten used to the dark, they still have to look hard to discern each other's face under the black-draped table. Their hearts, having calmed down a little after all the adrenaline, begin beating harder again as they gaze into each other's eyes. Unconsciously, they start to lean toward each other, their faces getting closer and closer. With only an inch separating them, Kevin suddenly jumps when the phone in his pocket vibrates.

"It's my sister," he says after awkwardly fishing the phone out. "She and my brother are in the courtyard looking for me."

Bella sighs quietly, then lifts the sheeting up a few inches and looks out. "No one is around. Let's go now before he comes back," she whispers.

"Okay," Kevin reluctantly whispers back. He grabs his bag and follows her out from under the table.

They make it out of the back building without being seen and head to the front of the school.

"There you are," Krista says when Kevin gets close enough. "Who's your friend?"

"Oh, this is Bella," Kevin replies, then introduces his siblings to her. "Bella just transferred here from another school."

"Nice to meet you, Bella," Krista says kindly. "What are you still doing here? Do you have a ride home?"

"Oh, um . . ." Bella's voice trails off as she pulls out her phone and looks down at it. "I don't know. My mom told me she would be here by four, but I guess that didn't happen." She sighs.

"What about your dad?" Krista asks.

"Oh, my parents are divorced," Bella replies matter-of-factly. "My mom has been really depressed since the divorce, so she probably forgot. I'll just walk home."

"Nonsense!" Krista says earnestly. "You can ride with us."

"Oh!" Bella blinks, then smiles. "No, I couldn't ask you to do that. It's okay."

"Seriously, Bella," Krista insists, "let me give you a ride home."

"Well, okay." Bella perks up. "Thank you!"

In the car, both Kevin's embarrassed and Klause's antisocial silence prompt Krista to break the ice with Bella by politely showering her with questions. She can already tell that her little brother has a crush on the girl, so she tries to learn what she can—which isn't much in the short drive.

After a few short minutes, Bella sits up and points. "Oh, that's my house," she says, referring to a quaint, one-story house just ahead on the right.

"Oh, wow, our house is just down the block from yours," Krista says as she peeks at the rearview mirror to see Kevin's reaction. She isn't disappointed.

Kevin, after spending the entire car ride hugging his backpack and staring down at the seatback pocket in front of him, lifts his head up and looks over at Bella, then at her house, then back at Bella, and smiles.

"Really? That's awesome," Bella says as Krista pulls over to the curb. "Thank you for the ride. It was nice meeting you."

"No problem," Krista says with a smile. "Anytime."

After opening her door, Bella turns to Kevin. "I guess I'll see you at school tomorrow?"

"Yeah, definitely." He smiles. "Have a good night."

"'Night," she responds warmly, smiling at him once more as she stares into his eyes. To Kevin, it's as if she's looking deep within him, and the look and her voice convey a message: she likes him, too.

She gets out and shuts the door, and Kevin sits back in his seat, still hugging his backpack but now looking ahead with a smile on his face.

After pulling up to their own house, the three communicate enough to order a pizza and then get to work on their homework. Without saying a word about their long and interesting days, each one turns in fairly early, exhausted.

That night, the lives of the children intertwine as mysterious and strange occurrences plague the moonlit darkness.

CHAPTER 21

I N THE MIDDLE OF THE NIGHT, WITH THE moon at its peak, a peculiar feeling wakes Krista, Klause, and Kevin. The feeling makes their hearts beat faster and their hair stand on end.

In her room, Krista opens her eyes suddenly, as if waking from a nightmare. She sits up in bed and looks around, crossing her arms for warmth as she begins to shiver. Then the whispers begin. Though barely intelligible, she makes out one word in the murmurs: "Krista."

Thinking that one of her brothers might be outside her door trying to get her attention, Krista gets out of bed and walks across the room. When she opens the door, the whispers cease immediately. She pokes her head out and looks around, but no one is there.

As she walks slowly back toward her bed, she decides instead to go to the window to look at the full moon. Pulling back the curtain, her eyes are immediately drawn to five dark shadows standing down below, across the street from the Atwood home, at the edge of the forest.

Krista gasps—the dark figures appear to be looking directly back at her. She freezes, too frightened to move or even breathe, her heart pounding in her chest. The terrifying moment lasts only a few seconds until the dark shadows turn swiftly around and scatter into the woods, disappearing from view.

Krista breathes deeply, but it shakes coming out. Who—and what—were those things? She frowns as she turns away from the window and walks back to bed. Were her eyes playing tricks on her, or was something more creepy going on?

Meanwhile, concurrently, the strange feeling forces Klause's eyes open, and he sits up straight in bed.

Although he has no idea what's going on, he acts on the inexplicable urge to get out of bed and go downstairs. As he does so, he hears scattered whispers in his mind. As he reaches the bottom of the stairs, he heads to the living room window that looks out onto the front yard. He moves as if sleepwalking, not fully in control of his body, but not resisting either.

Peering out the window, Klause sees five dark figures standing at the edge of the forest across from the house, facing the house. The figures are human in shape, but they have no distinctive markings or characteristics that could identify them as anyone or anything in particular.

Klause just stands there, wide-eyed and open-mouthed, staring at the shadowy figures. His breathing is steady as he watches the shadows suddenly spin around and rush into the forest, disappearing into the darkness.

The eerie whispers continue in his subconscious and now urge him to follow the dark shadows. Still in a trance-like state, Klause walks to the front door, opens it, and steps outside, leaving the door ajar behind him.

Kevin, awakening at the same time as his older siblings, tries to ignore the strange feeling and go back to sleep. After a few long, unsuccessful moments, he decides to get up and go downstairs to get a drink of water. As he descends the stairs, he notices the front door is slightly open and walks over to investigate. He grabs the knob, pulling the door open fully, and sees his brother walking across the street toward the forest, wearing nothing but his sleeping shorts and tee.

Watching as his brother reaches the sidewalk on the opposite side of the street, Kevin cocks his head to the side as he stares. What could Klause be up to?

For Klause, the whispers in his head are getting louder and more intense with each step closer to the edge of the forest. Unaware that he's being watched, Klause continues in his trance, reaching the forest and stepping into the darkness as if being pulled by someone or something.

"Klause?" Kevin calls out from behind him.

"Huh?" Klause stops short as he wakes from his hypnotic state. He blinks his eyes and slowly shuffles around to look at his brother, who is standing at the front door with a concerned look on his face.

"Are you okay?" Kevin calls.

"Um . . ." Klause looks around, confused. "Yeah, I'm fine."

He slowly begins to head back home, stepping out of the forest and into the street, the full moon lighting his way. Unseen behind him, five shadowy pairs of hands reach out from the edge of the darkness in the forest, grasping at him. Failing to hold onto their prey, the hands retract and disappear into the blackness.

"Klause, what's going on?" Kevin inquires.

"I'm not sure," Klause replies, shaking his head. "I think I was sleepwalking."

"Sleepwalking? Have you ever done that before?"

"Um, no," Klause says before cutting the conversation short. "I'm gonna go back to bed. Thanks for um . . . waking me up, I guess. I don't know where I was going."

"Yeah, sure . . ." Kevin's reply trails off as his brother runs into the house and up the stairs.

Quietly shutting the door behind him, Klause leans back on his bedroom door and sinks down until he's sitting on the floor. His breathing is shallow, and the feeling he had when he awakened is actually getting stronger. He now feels the dark presence that he felt yesterday on the football field clawing at his heart, and he senses that a sinister presence is growing inside of him. That presence, or entity, seems desperate for something, but Klause has no idea what that would be.

Suddenly, however, he has a strange sense that this new darkness will somehow keep him safe. Comforted by the feeling, he gets up off the floor and goes to bed, sleeping the rest of the night without disturbance.

When the sun comes up the next morning, the three siblings wake once again, this time for more mundane reasons. As they get ready for school, not a word is mentioned about their strange, late-night experiences.

CHAPTER 22

I N THE CAR DRIVING TO SCHOOL, KRISTA is torn over telling her brothers what she saw through the window last night, but in the end she decides against it. She felt a terror she's never experienced before when she saw those dark figures, and she doesn't want them to be scared as well. She hasn't forgotten about their agreement to share possible incidences of karma, but she tells herself that seeing the five shadows didn't fit that bill. So she remains quiet, lost in thought.

Klause also considers telling his siblings what happened to him last night—and about his conscious testing of his newfound power yesterday—but the dark feeling in his heart urges him to keep both things a secret. On top of that, he doesn't want his siblings to think that something else might be happening to him beyond the already worrisome occurrences the three of them have in common. He rides along silently, wondering if the dark feeling inside of him is there because he intentionally caused something bad to happen. Even worse, he wonders if the dark feeling will ever go away.

In the backseat, Kevin contemplates bringing up Klause's sleepwalking adventure, but since Klause hasn't mentioned it himself yet, perhaps he is embarrassed about it. Deciding not to betray his brother's trust or embarrass him, Kevin too stays silent, instead focusing on his own experience from last night. He now recalls how he was awakened in the first place—by an unexplainable feeling that made his skin tingle. Could it have been some kind of brotherly instinct that forced him awake at just the right moment to catch Klause sleepwalking? Or was there something more mysterious going on, maybe something connected with the crazy coincidences of the past few weeks? *No*, he thinks to himself. *It can't be.*

"Are you okay, Kevin?" Bella asks after an uneventful morning as the two sit down for lunch.

"Yeah," Kevin mutters. "I just have some stuff on my mind."

"Well, you've been really quiet today. You haven't been yourself."

"'Myself'?" Kevin chuckles. "Funny how you say that— but we only just met yesterday."

Bella smiles as she shrugs her shoulders. "Yeah," she says as she lightly places her hand on Kevin's forearm. "But when I'm with you, I feel like I've known you longer."

Kevin looks into the hazel eyes shining back at him as she continues. "I don't know. It's like I've been waiting for you my whole life or something."

His arm tingles from Bella's soft touch, and Kevin's cheeks light up with a rosy glow as he blushes. He doesn't know what to do as his heartbeat pulses in his chest and the hair on the back of his neck raises ever so slightly. As he lives the moment in Bella's presence, he contemplates what he's feeling. It's a rush of sensations that are joyful, yet scary. *Could this be love?* He's never felt like this about anyone before, let alone someone he's only just met.

"I like you, Kevin," Bella announces suddenly.

There it is. Kevin's heart pumps even harder, and he freezes, a whirlwind of thoughts swirling in his head. *She likes me? Why me? What do I say? Why do I feel like I'm going to throw up? Oh, shoot!*

"Excuse me," Kevin says hastily as he jumps up and scurries off to the restroom. Safely inside, he bends over the trash can and vomits, as if all his bottled-up stress over his crush on Bella is suddenly being released.

Straightening up after the unexpected exodus of his lunch from his body, Kevin stands in front of the sink and looks at himself in the mirror. He wonders what Bella could possibly see in him. He's used to seeing girls hang all over his brother, but that had never happened to him. His eyes quiver as he thinks about what she may think of him now. She just openly confessed to liking him, and he ran out of the room without saying anything back. *I'm an idiot*, he berates himself. *What am I supposed to do now? Go back in there? And what do I say?*

Then it comes to him: Krista will know what to do.

He pulls out his cell phone and messages his sister about the whole situation. His hands are shaking so much that the message is full of typos.

Krista takes a couple of minutes to respond. *Kevin, just tell her how you feel. Obviously, you like her back, and every moment you're waiting you're just making her doubt herself. She's probably thinking that you don't feel the same about her.*

This is new to me, Krista, Kevin responds.

Krista replies with just one word: *Breathe.*

Taking his sister's advice, Kevin looks up at himself in the mirror and takes a deep breath in and out before heading back to the cafeteria.

Kevin takes another deep breath before sliding back onto the bench next to her. "I like you, too," Kevin says, his voice soft. "I'm sorry I ran out, I was just caught off guard and I—"

"Shh," Bella interrupts him. "It's okay. You make me really happy, Kevin, and I'm so glad to have met you yesterday."

Across the room, Krista grins as she watches the two give each other a hug then resume eating.

CHAPTER 23

AFTER SCHOOL, KEVIN AND BELLA SIT under the large oak in the courtyard, talking and drawing. Although they were hesitant to go back after their adverse encounter there yesterday, they liked the spot too much to let it go.

"Can you show me some things with your watercolor pens?" Kevin asks eagerly.

"Yeah, for sure!" Bella exclaims. Picking up one of her pens, she dampens the brush tip in a small water tray and dips it in a light-red paint. "Here, hold this," she says as she hands the watercolor pen to Kevin. "So, just like with a pencil, the amount you press down determines the harshness of the stroke. Except with watercolor, the lighter you press, the thinner the stroke."

"Like this?" Kevin says as he draws a line down the page.

"No, like this." Bella leans in close and holds the back of his drawing hand to guide his stroke on the page.

Still not used to such close contact, Kevin's hand starts getting sweaty. When his phone suddenly rings, his arm jerks, and the pen slips out of his hand.

"Oh!" Bella jumps then chuckles. "Are you okay?"

"Yeah," Kevin says with a timid half-smile, looking down at his phone. "My sister just messaged me. She's ready out front." Then he has a thought. "Hey, do you need a ride again today?"

"Uh, no," Bella replies shakily. "I'm good—my mom is actually on her way."

"I can stay with you until she gets here," Kevin suggests.

"No!" Bella snaps back. "I mean, that's okay. Your sister is waiting. It shouldn't be long."

"Okay," Kevin says as he feels his face fall. "Well, do you want to hang out later, after you get home?"

Bella's eyes light up. "Yeah, sounds like fun! I'll meet you at your house after I get home."

Kevin grins as he gathers his belongings together and stuffs them unceremoniously into his backpack before getting up and heading to the front steps. "Awesome! See ya then!" he says after a quick wave goodbye.

"See ya," Bella calls, smiling back. She waves and watches him run off, then quickly grabs her own things and stuffs them into her bag. Getting up, she turns and walks briskly toward some bushes a dozen yards away.

Suddenly realizing he took Bella's watercolor pen, Kevin turns around and rushes back over to the tree to return it to her.

As he gets closer, he sees Bella speed-walking away. "Bella!" he calls out as he rushes to catch up with her. As he comes around the bushes, he expects to see her, but there's nothing there but the shadow cast by the shrubbery.

"Huh," he says, biting his lower lip. *I guess I'll just give it to her later,* he tells himself as he starts heading back to the front of the school to meet up with his siblings.

During the ride home, Krista keeps glancing back at Kevin in the rearview mirror with a smile on her face. She doesn't mention anything, though—she knows Klause would give him a hard time.

Once home, Klause immediately goes up to his room, and Krista and Kevin hang back downstairs in the kitchen.

"Thanks for not mentioning anything about Bella in front of Klause," Kevin says as he pulls out a can of soda from the fridge.

"No problem," Krista chuckles. "I figured you wouldn't want him to know. At least not yet."

"She's the first girl I've ever felt this cool connection with, and I don't know what to do. She's only known me for like two days. What if she discovers more about me and doesn't like it?"

Krista shrugs. "Then it wasn't meant to be." Putting her hand on Kevin's shoulder, she adds, "Just don't change for her, okay? Always be yourself."

"Thanks," Kevin says, nodding.

"What are sisters for?" She grins as she turns to open a kitchen cupboard. "Aw, man, we're out of coffee. I forgot that I used up the rest of it this morning."

"Do you really need it?" Kevin responds, narrowing his eyes.

"Well, I have a big test tomorrow that I need to study for. Might have an all-nighter ahead of me." She sighs. "I wish Mom were here—she would've reminded me."

"She probably would've just gotten it for you. She knows how much you love coffee."

"Yeah," Krista chuckles once before frowning. "You know, even though Mom has been going out of town like this for a while, I don't think I'll ever be one-hundred-percent used to it. I miss her every day," Krista says as she frowns, her head drooping.

"I miss her, too," Kevin sighs. "Especially with Dad gone."

Then Krista perks up. "Hey, I think I'm going to go study at the coffee shop for a little bit. It might help studying in a different environment, you know? Get out of the house. And I can get some more coffee while I'm there. Will you and Klause be alright?"

"Something tells me Klause will be stuffed in his room all night, and, um . . ." Kevin's voice trails off.

"What?"

Kevin stuffs his hands in his pockets. "Well, Bella was going to come over later, and we were going to hang out."

"What were your plans?"

"I don't know yet," Kevin shrugs. "Probably just hang out outside, so Klause doesn't see us."

"Okay," Krista says, smiling. "Don't go too far, and if you need anything, just text me, okay?"

"Yeah," Kevin says as he nods back.

The two go upstairs, and Kevin goes into his room while Krista knocks on Klause's door. "Klause?" she yells on the hallway side of the closed door. "I'm going to the coffee shop to study, so I'll be home later!"

"Okay!" Klause shouts back through the door.

Unbeknownst to his brother and sister, Klause has been pacing around his room since they got home. His strange experiences from last night are still ringing in his mind. Above all, the clawing feeling in his heart and tumultuous wrenching in his gut have been intensifying since then. *Is this a heart attack?* he thinks to himself, then dismisses the thought. *No, I'm too young for that. Maybe a panic attack?*

Klause stops pacing and looks at the floor-length mirror hanging by his door. Studying himself in the mirror, he looks intently at his eyes, watching to see if they change again. He recalls the saying that the eyes are the windows to the soul and thinks that if he can force his eyes to change, maybe he can look through them into the soul that seems to be darkening on its own.

Down the hall, Kevin is also looking in his bedroom mirror. Fixing his hair and shifting his weight back and forth, he analyzes his appearance. Bella is coming over, and now that it's out in the open that they both like each other, he feels the need to look his very best when she gets here.

A few minutes after Krista drives off, the doorbell rings. Kevin calls out, "I'll get it!" as he rushes downstairs.

Opening the door, he sees Bella, still dressed in the black skinny jeans and red top from school. "Hey," she says with a coy smile as she sweeps her hand through her hair, brushing it behind her ear and out of her face.

"Hey," Kevin smiles back. "Oh! I accidentally took this earlier. Here . . ." he says as he pulls her watercolor pen from his back pocket.

"Oh, thank you," Bella says as she places the pen in her own back pocket. "So what do you want to do?"

"I was thinking of just sitting out here and doing some more artwork?" Kevin asks with a shrug, wondering if Bella might be hoping for something more.

"How about we do that later? Let's just go for a walk and talk."

"Yeah, that sounds good," Kevin says as his heart skips a beat, worried that she thinks he's lame now for having limited date ideas.

"C'mon," Bella says happily as she grabs his hand, leading him off the front steps and onto the sidewalk.

CHAPTER 24

A FEW MILES AWAY, KRISTA ARRIVES AT the Mirror Valley Coffee House and walks inside. *First things first: coffee!* she tells herself as she goes up to the counter to order. "Large coffee please." Then she looks up and catches the barista's eye.

"Any cream or sweetener?" the barista asks.

Krista just stares, momentarily lost in the deep brown eyes of the girl, which seem to glimmer impossibly in the faint light of the coffee shop.

"Cream or sweetener?" the girl repeats.

"Oh!" Krista blinks. "No, thank you."

"Wow, you're stronger than I am," the barista says as she punches in the order.

Krista laughs. "Yeah, I've got a big test tomorrow, and I could definitely use all the caffeine I can get."

"High school or college?" the girl inquires.

"Oh, high school. Almost in college! Just one more year."

"That's awesome. Mirror Valley High?"

"Of course!" Krista grins.

"I graduated from there a few years ago. Is Mr. Haney still there?"

"Yes, he's my brother's history teacher this year. I had him sophomore year myself," Krista says and cocks her head to the side. "Interesting character."

"Ugh," the barista grunts. "He was so frustrating. Worst teacher ever. I mean, his tests were fairly easy as long as you read the textbook, but the tangents he'd go off on were so annoying!"

"Yep," Krista chuckles. "As I said, interesting character."

The two girls laugh together, and Krista's heart skips a beat, but she doesn't know why. *I must become friends with this girl. She's so funny.*

"Let me grab your coffee," the barista says as she turns around to pour plain black coffee into a large cup.

Suddenly, Krista hears her name behind her in a man's gentle voice.

She turns around to see a familiar face standing behind her. "Oh, hi, Rick! Fancy seeing you here."

"Indeed," he replies. "Come here a lot?"

"Actually, no. I drink a lot of coffee, but I usually make it at home. I wanted to try something new and study here for a change."

"Mr. Pippin!" the barista exclaims when she turns around to hand Krista her coffee.

"Oh, hi, um . . ." Rick pauses, looking between the girls, searching for . . . what, Krista doesn't know. "Right, um, you look different!" he finishes.

The barista chuckles as she waves her hand at him. "I'm so offended you don't remember me," she says, then she smiles. "It's okay; you don't have to pretend to remember me. It has been a few years, and I was just a low-level journalist for two years during high school."

"You were on the news team?" Krista chimes in.

"Yeah. I'm actually in my senior year studying broadcast journalism in college now."

"That's so exciting! You think I could pick your brain sometime? I want to go into international journalism myself."

"Yeah, for sure," the girl says. "Hey, set up your stuff over there." She points to the coffee bar beside the counter. "During slow periods, I can more easily chat with you there. I'm Sheri, by the way," the barista says as she reaches out her hand.

"Krista." She takes Sheri's offered hand in hers, feeling her soft skin and warm touch, and shakes it. "Nice to meet you." Krista turns to Rick. "Are you staying, too?"

Rick blinks before answering. "Oh . . . no, I have to get going." He quickly gives Sheri his order, and Krista moves to the counter to find a seat.

Sablo had been staring at Sheri during her exchange with Krista. The young Hispanic woman with her light-brown skin and medium-length brown hair up in a bun reminds him of his sister, Zuriel, especially when combined with Sheri's kind and upbeat attitude with hints of sarcasm and sass. He chuckles to himself as he thinks about how his sister would have had some kind of jab about his bumbling response to Sheri.

Sheri hands Rick his coffee, and he turns to leave. He stops at the door and looks back at Sheri as she continues to chat with Krista, whose eyes are locked on Sheri's even as she sets up her books and laptop at the bar. In seeing Sheri one more time, an idea crosses his mind.

CHAPTER 25

B ACK IN THE ATWOODS' NEIGHBORHOOD,
Kevin and Bella continue on their walk, still holding
hands as their conversation gets heavy.

"Yeah, my dad didn't really want me, so it was easy for my
mom to get custody," Bella says, her eyes sad. "I must have
disappointed him at some point in my life, and I guess he
kinda stopped trusting me at that point."

"But you would have been so young," Kevin objects. "How
could he expect so much?"

After blinking several times, Bella replies, "Um, yeah, I
don't know." She pulls her hand out of Kevin's and crosses
her arms.

"I'm sorry," Kevin says softly.

"It's okay, I really am over—" Bella stops mid-sentence
and gasps as she looks out ahead of them.

Just a few dozen feet away on the sidewalk are the two
bullies that picked on them yesterday.

Kevin and Bella stop in their tracks and begin to walk backward as inconspicuously as possible, but it's too late. The boys spot them, and Kevin and Bella can hear them say, "Look, it's those two punks that got us in trouble yesterday."

When the two bullies start trotting toward Kevin and Bella, Bella turns to Kevin and yells, "Run!"

When they turn and dash away, the bullies break into a run after them.

"Where do we go? Home?" Kevin asks Bella, his voice shaking.

"No! We don't want them to know where we live."

"What, then? I don't think I'd win in a game of endurance with those two," he pants.

Bella's expression changes abruptly. "I've got an idea," she replies. "Follow me!"

She pulls Kevin across the street, toward the forest. As she bounds across the sidewalk and onto the dirt of the forest, however, Kevin suddenly hesitates. The strange feeling he got when he woke in the middle of the night last night comes over him once again. It's a sense that something dark is happening—or is about to happen.

"What are you doing?" she pleads. "Come on!"

"I . . . I . . . I can't, I have a bad feeling."

"What do you mean?"

"I don't know. I can't explain it." Kevin's eyebrows pinch together. During the summer he went there all the time to draw the trees, and he never felt that way. So what's up now?

Looking past Kevin's shoulder, Bella sees the two bullies gaining on them. "Please, Kevin, trust me. I think we can lose them in the forest." She reaches out her hand.

He looks into the anxious eyes of the girl he really likes then down at her hand. He hesitates just a moment longer, then, shaking off the bad feelings, takes her outstretched hand and lets her lead him into the woods.

Weaving their way through the trees, they run as fast as they can without tripping and falling, looking left and right for a hidden clearing away from the path. The adrenaline pumping through their systems, fueling their energy, is starting to fade away.

"I can't . . . run . . . much longer . . ." Bella says, panting heavily. "We need . . . to find . . . a spot . . . to . . . rest."

Thinking about all the times he used to walk around the forest sketching, Kevin suddenly has an idea. "I know where to go. Follow me!"

Jumping over rocks, running through underbrush, and ducking under low-hanging limbs, Kevin finally arrives at a large boulder that sits atop some risen ground. With so many trees and foliage around it, the boulder is shielded from obvious view. Kevin finds a small gap in the branches and leads Bella through this makeshift secret passage to get to the boulder.

When they get there, they work their way around its base until they find a few small bushes that are perfect to hide behind. Kevin grabs Bella's hand and pulls her close, their bodies forming a protective ball.

In the distance, they hear the stamping of feet and the snapping of twigs. "I think I saw them go this way!" one bully shouts, his voice closer than they expected.

Kevin and Bella hold their breath until the voices start to fade. They wait and listen intently, and finally there are no more sounds at all in the forest.

"I think they're gone," Bella whispers.

"Yeah . . . I . . . think so, too," Kevin says as his adrenaline dissipates completely, and his body goes limp.

Bella looks up at him. "Thank you for trusting me and coming into the forest."

Although Kevin's bad feeling about going into the forest remains strong, when he looks back at Bella, he is able to shut out his uneasiness and embrace his trust in her. "You were right—the forest was a good escape plan. And I do trust you."

Smiling, Bella pushes her body up and embraces Kevin in a hug, then places her head on his chest. He's certain she can hear his heartbeat slow down as they sit together, looking out into the sinewy branches of the forest.

CHAPTER 26

MELLOW CLASSICAL MUSIC FILLS THE Atwood dining room. Its low volume is just loud enough to drown out the immutable silence between the Atwood siblings but not so loud that it could interfere with conversation—though there isn't much conversing happening anyway. Like elevator music, the songs fill the ears of the three but don't penetrate deep into their minds. Their minds are already far away.

Kevin shakes his leg back and forth under the table, as if anxiously waiting for something to happen or for someone to speak up. It's been three days since the bullies first attacked him and Bella, two days since they were chased into the woods, and he can't shake the feeling that something sinister is happening in those woods, a darkness only he can feel. Even Klause's episode the other night has him on edge.

He wonders if the woods, once a place of comfort and escape for him just this summer, has now been invaded with a darkness somewhere deep within.

Klause reaches for his third slice of pizza and gnaws on it, thinking too about that night in the woods. When Kevin had found him wandering outside, he didn't have control of his own body—it was as if someone, or some*thing* was calling him to those woods, beckoning him inside.

And, though it scares him a little, Klause felt strength and safety within him as he ventured closer to the woods, as if the forest was calling him home. And he didn't even fight it. The dark feeling scratching at his heart as he neared the trees—the same feeling he'd had after that incident with his coach—had grabbed hold of him and wouldn't let go.

It's probably only a matter of time until the darkness wins, until he follows in his siblings' footsteps and loses complete control over this mystical new power. As he swallows down the last of his pizza, his stomach gets queasy at the question he can't seem to ignore: How long would it be until he killed someone, too?

At the head of the table, Krista pokes at her salad and ponders what her life and her family are turning into. Just a few weeks ago, her biggest worry was whether or not she would become Editor in Chief. Now that concern seems so trivial with all the things happening not only to her, but also to the two young men she cherishes most in life.

She senses they haven't been entirely honest with her—had anything else power-related happened with them? How could she take care of them, protect them like she promised their mother two years ago, if they wouldn't tell her what was going on?

If they're not sharing, neither will she. But she still wishes she could talk to them about this, wishes she could tell them what she'd found this week researching karma. Although just about everything online talks about the traditional Indian belief of karma as a principle of cause and effect, she's found several interpretations of this belief that lead to saying things like: *Karma is a bitch, she'll give you what you deserve.*

An idea pops into her head and Krista freezes, her fork poised over her plate. *Where are these ideas of karma being a woman coming from? Is karma actually a person?* Figuring that's as good a theory as any, she shrugs then stabs a piece of lettuce with her fork and brings it to her mouth. She glances quickly around the table at her two brothers as she chews, the soft drone of classical music continuing in the background.

After a long call with their mom and dinner cleanup, the Atwood children proceed upstairs to get ready for bed. After brushing their teeth and changing into their pajamas with barely two words to each other, they settle themselves in bed.

Sleep overtakes them immediately, and their lives intertwine once again within the deep recesses of their dreams.

CHAPTER 27

K RISTA OPENS HER EYES TO SEE THAT she's standing in the middle of a city street. Though it's dark around her, the full moon above her lights the surrounding area. Looking around at the tall buildings, the scattered street lamps, and the lit windows dispersed sparingly around her, she recognizes her surroundings. She's in downtown Mirror Valley. Although the city is usually still buzzing at night, for some reason, she doesn't hear anything or see anyone. Only the sound of her own breathing reaches her ears. As she looks around, one building in particular catches her attention, and she walks closer to it. It seems familiar to her, but she can't put her finger on why.

A door swings open in front of her, and a man comes walking out, talking on the phone. "Do you need anything from the store? I can stop on the way."

Krista's eyes widen, and she takes a sudden breath. "Dad?" she whispers, bringing a trembling hand to her mouth.

"I miss you, too—see you soon. 'Bye, Babe," the man continues.

"Dad!" Krista calls out, running toward her father. As she approaches him, she quickly realizes that he can't hear her, and this observation is confirmed when she reaches out to touch him. Her fingertips go straight through his body as if trying to touch a wisp of fog.

Though she knows he can't hear or see her, she can't help but stare up at his face, walking next to him as he starts down the sidewalk toward his car.

Krista's senses are so overwhelmed at seeing her father again that she doesn't even notice that they're not alone until a dirty old man grabs at her father's arm. "Please! Help me," he begs.

Krista hears her father yell back at the homeless man. "Get your hand off me, you miscreant! Help yourself, and get a job!"

She frowns at hearing her father say that to the poor old man. She's always been taught to treat people with respect and hearing her father so rudely refuse to help catches her off guard. She is confused at this entire scene. The man she knew as her father would never have said that.

Her confusion only continues to rise as the cityscape suddenly spins in a circle around her, blurring in every direction. The spinning lasts only a second—as it fades away, she finds herself sitting next to her dad as he's driving home.

"Dad?" she tries again, having to shout through the blaring music coming through the car stereo. Nothing.

Taking a deep breath, she tries to figure out what's happening. Then it hits her: she's dreaming. She's had dreams of him before, but they were never like this. Never in a way that she couldn't interact with him.

This must be lucid dreaming, she tells herself, remembering something she learned last year in psychology class. *But wait—if it is, aren't I supposed to be able to control the dream? Why can't I touch him? What does that mean?*

Her thoughts continue to swirl in her mind, but she doesn't let them consume her, happy to just be able to see her father and feel so close to him once again.

The car rolls to a stop at a red light. Krista's eyes follow her father's as he looks at the clock on the car's dashboard: 11:24.

Krista briefly looks around, not seeing anyone in sight on the dark road. A green light illuminates her and her father, piercing through the darkness and shining brightly onto the front of the car and through the windshield. As she feels the car pull forward, she sees another light appear out of the corner of her eye, getting bigger. She realizes that the lights are getting closer much too quickly, and, in a split second, she screams as she sees a truck barreling toward them. Krista hears a loud bang as she shuts her eyes tightly, blocking out the lights and immersing herself in darkness.

Klause's dream begins similarly to his sister's as he opens his eyes to a dark setting, and he finds himself standing in a dense forest at night. His eyes quickly adjust to the darkness with the full moon peeking through the tops of the trees, giving faint light to his immediate surroundings.

After briefly looking around, he ventures forward through the woods. He hears no bugs chirping or branches swaying in the breeze, only the twigs breaking under his feet as he walks.

After walking aimlessly for some time, he begins to hear whispers. But the whispers aren't coming from any specific direction; rather, they seem to be directly in his ears, urging him forward.

He recalls the whispers he heard the other night and how they seemed to urge him toward the forest. Well, he's in the forest now, but what is this pull that he is still feeling? It's the same pull that he felt the other night, a pull toward somewhere his heart belongs, to a place of safety.

But as he continues forward, despite that feeling of safety, he can't help his heart racing, his eyes incessantly scanning the woods, his mind on full alert. This is one of the spookiest dreams he's ever had; and, given the similarities, it just has to be connected to his sleepwalking the other night. That can't be a good thing.

Klause steps out into a clearing in the forest, a beaten path now at his feet. Looking left and right, he starts down the path, but something stops him, something deep inside himself. He feels the scratching at his heart once again, and he turns to see a large boulder through some dense foliage. It sits on the top of a small hill, and Klause notices that the entire forest seems to converge at the rock.

Hearing the indistinguishable voices again, he makes his way to the towering, large stone. Upon his arrival, he looks up at the stone. The voices immediately get louder. Klause narrows his eyes as he surveys the top. The boulder could only be like ten feet high, right? He decides to climb it. A part of him is hoping to be able to see his surroundings better at the top, but another part of him wants to climb it because he believes that doing so will give the voices what they want.

With Klause's athletic build, he easily reaches the top in no time, only misplacing a small rock that chips off the top edge of the boulder, clicking down the stone and landing in the dirt at the base of the boulder. As he stands up fully, he grins. An unexplainable energy is flowing through his veins, making him feel like he could take on anything.

He stands there, breathing in the cool air, when suddenly a girl's scream pierces through the silence.

While his siblings are experiencing dreams of darkness, Kevin opens his eyes to a luscious garden. Surrounding him are dozens of trees, bushes, vines, and every kind of fruit imaginable. Vibrant colors of red, orange, yellow, and green abound around him. A pleasant, peaceful feeling fills his heart as he smells the sweet citrus of the nearby trees and feels the warm breeze flowing through his shaggy hair.

He looks forward into the spectacular garden stretching as far as he can see, but when he turns around, he's met with a sight unlike anything he's ever experienced in his small town of Mirror Valley. His eyes widen, and his jaw drops at the sight of a marvelous castle atop a steep hill. The white, crystal-like palace glistens in the sunlight.

Kevin begins to step forward, eyeing a staircase a small distance ahead that slithers up through the bright green lawn until it reaches the base of the castle.

"Isn't it beautiful?"

Kevin jumps at the sudden sound of a girl coming up behind him and stopping at his side.

His heart skips a beat, and he takes a step back at the sight of her eyes. Her left eye is white and her right is black, just like he saw Krista's eyes turn at the homecoming dance.

The girl smiles at him as her eyes squint as if confused by his reaction. She doesn't say anything, but, in continuing to look upon the young girl, Kevin's fear slowly fades.

The young girl couldn't have been older than Krista, and the resemblance to her is almost uncanny, like that of a sister. Wavy light-brown hair cascades down her head, and when she smiles at him, Kevin is overrun with a sense of love, comfort, and care.

"Ekthesia is truly a wonderful kingdom," the young girl continues, her voice light and soothing.

"Ekthesia?" Kevin asks, frowning.

"My home," the girl replies with a smile. "Come, I'll show you," she says as she holds out her hand for Kevin to take.

Kevin's eyes unfix from her face. As his eyes slowly lower to her outstretched hand, he notices that her pearly white dress, adorned with crystals and diamonds, almost matches the stunning appearance of the castle.

He looks back up at her, and, even though her eyes seemed terrifying at first, now all he sees is goodness and honesty. He feels like he can trust her, and, without any further hesitation, he takes her hand. Upon grasping it, he feels the warmth of her touch and realizes that this dream is unlike any other—he is completely present in this beautiful world.

CHAPTER 28

AFTER EXPERIENCING THE CAR WRECK that took her father's life first-hand, the darkness that Krista became immersed in fades away. Now she's standing in a dark forest, and, despite the moonlit night, she can barely make out the leafy branches around her.

She ventures forward, careful not to hit her head on low-hanging branches and cautiously stepping over rocks and fallen limbs. As she steps out onto a worn path in a small clearing, she looks around. The place looks familiar, but she can't quite pinpoint it.

An abrupt *thud* breaks the quiet surrounding her, and she jumps, the too-loud, too-close sound resounding in her head. *What was that?* She ducks behind a tree then starts surveying the forest.

Looking ahead through the dense foliage, she sees a large rock at the crest of a small hill. But that's not what catches her eye.

"Klause?" she whispers as she sees her brother standing atop the massive boulder. He doesn't seem to hear her. But just as she's about to call out more loudly, the trees blur around her, just like the buildings did in the city. She lets out a long, terrified scream, her world suddenly spinning. She can barely stay upright as she struggles to keep her balance.

Eventually—not soon enough—the blur swirling around her fades away, and she's left standing in a different part of the forest.

Krista blinks her eyes hard, trying to orient herself again, panting heavily. This time, she's not in complete silence. She hears hushed tones coming from a distance ahead. She thinks about calling out to them, but something in her heart tells her not to. She begins to slowly creep toward the voices, careful not to break even a twig beneath her feet as she silently proceeds. As she gets closer, the voices get louder until she's right next to them.

Standing behind a tree and looking through the branches, Krista sees six figures, appearing like shadows in the moonlit night, standing in a circle. In the darkness of the forest, she's only able to make out their shapes.

"I'm surprised at the events of that meeting. Our good siblings rarely vote on our side," a woman's melodic voice says from within the circle.

"They know that there must be balance," a man's scratchy voice replies.

"She's going to be furious," a woman's raspy voice chimes in. "What if she refuses to proceed with her duty like her mother did?"

"That's why she'll never know the truth," a deep voice echoes through the forest. "We'll need to make his death look like an accident so that no suspicion is aroused."

"Can I kill the husband, Brother?" a third woman speaks up, her voice whiny and high-pitched. "I have just the idea."

"Yes, Lillith," the echoing voice replies. "But remember, the other side of the council only agreed to his death if we give him one final test to see if he possesses the good to be willing to sacrifice for another."

"I'll do that," another man's hoarse voice speaks up.

"Very well, Lahash," the deep voice replies. "Lillith, how will you do it?"

"A car crash should do the trick." The woman cackles.

Krista sees the six spirits erupt in maniacal laughter over their discussions of murder, but before she can do or even think anything, the forest spins again, and the dark blur of trees whirling around her resumes.

What was that? Klause scrambles down from the rock and starts to head back into the thick foliage to investigate the scream he'd just heard echoing through the forest.

But he's only able to take a few steps before the forest spins around him. His head starts swimming as the trees rush around him in a circle, creating a blur of gray darkness.

Then the spinning stops, and he looks around but is still unable to pinpoint where the scream came from. So he circles the rock, hoping to find something familiar, but to little avail.

The voices resume, and his heart starts to ache as he feels the scratching begin again.

"Who are you?" Klause cries out.

The whispers only continue as they were, remaining indistinguishable but getting louder and more aggressive.

"What do you want?" he yells out as his head begins to throb from the constant barrage of voices in his ears.

Again, the only answer is the continuous jabbering of the voices in his head, still getting louder. He clutches his head as he squeezes his eyes shut, hoping to alleviate his misery.

"Please! Stop this!" he pleads as his eyes begin to well up. He falls to his knees.

Suddenly, a new darkness begins to stretch out across the rock, expanding into a black hole of emptiness behind him. The vortex sucks Klause into the darkness it provides.

It happens so fast that Klause is barely able to even scream.

Kevin makes his way to the sprawling staircase with the young girl at his side.

"Where am I?" Kevin asks, still trying to figure out this strange dream.

"I told you," the girl chuckles innocently. "This is my home, Ekthesia."

Kevin just stares, so she smiles. "My father rules up there. He is kind but also just and keeps our kingdom in harmony."

"So, like a king?" Kevin inquires.

"Yes, like a king," the girl laughs again.

Only now does Kevin see a silver tiara sitting atop her head. "Does that make you a princess?"

"Yeah, it did." The girl stops in her tracks and drops her head. "I don't know why I'm disappointed. My father gave me an amazing gift, a power that he bestowed upon me after his brothers and sisters failed him. Which is wonderful, but it might force me to leave this place, my home, and not be able to spend as much time with my family as I would have," she continues as she puts her hand on her chest, tears welling in her eyes.

Kevin frowns at the girl's story. If he couldn't see his family all the time, he doesn't know what he'd do. It would be miserable.

He looks back at the girl, just now noticing the dazzling and elaborate necklace that she's wearing as she places her hand on it and looks at the center stone. He takes a peek at the centerpiece and smiles at the beauty of the shimmering white stone with black veins permeating through it like marble. "What's that?" he asks, thinking it must be important to the girl, given the way she's holding it close.

"My mother and I found this stone at the edge of the garden, underneath an apple tree. It was a perfect stone, with no rough edges, and it was beautiful. She picked it up, kissed it, and put it in my hand, saying that she'd always be with me. I was only a small child at the time, so I didn't think much of it, but a few months later, she died," she confides, sniffling as tears stream down her face. "As the years have passed, things of hers have come and gone, but the only things that remain for me to connect with her are this necklace and this kingdom, my home."

Kevin places his hand on her shoulder. "Then show me your kingdom and experience it to its fullest while you're still here, in honor of your mother."

The girl smiles at him and sniffles again, nodding her head. The two start up the staircase, a comfortable silence between them on the hike up.

When they arrive at the top of the stairs, Kevin gasps at the sight of the shining crystal castle towering over the city a few miles ahead of them. Hundreds of people swarm around the palace, each doing their own tasks but seeming to work together in harmony.

In the garden, Kevin could only see the palace in the distance and didn't even notice the bustling village around it until now.

The villagers are clothed in browns, grays, and whites in the form of loose clothing draped elegantly over their bodies. Their skin colors range from the whitest white to the darkest black with zero animosity or prejudice existing within them. Kevin imagines their hearts being open to all and to everything that this kingdom has to offer.

"Come," the girl speaks up. "I'll take you to meet my father," she says as she holds out her hand once again.

Kevin takes it without hesitation.

"Hold on tight!" the girl shouts.

"Wait, wh—" Kevin can't even finish before the girl's body lifts off the ground, taking his along with her.

Kevin screams and takes a deep breath as the two soar through the sky like birds, witnessing the village beneath them.

"Don't make me have to pull your weight!" the girl shouts at him through the strong gusts of wind generated in the high altitude. "You can do it, too—just embrace who you are!"

Kevin's eyebrows scrunch together. What does she mean—he could do it, too? Do what? *Fly?!* She can't be serious.

"Oh no," the girl's voice breaks into his thoughts.

Kevin follows her gaze and looks up at the dark storm clouds suddenly forming over them, blocking out most of the light. Suddenly, a bolt of lightning streaks down from the angry sky and strikes the pair's hands, causing them to let go.

Kevin screams as he begins to plummet toward the ground.

Because he's looking up at the girl who's trying to fly down and catch him, he doesn't see the large black hole forming over a stone monument in the village. He sees only the wide-eyed face of the girl as she watches him fall.

Before he can even register what's happening, the vortex sucks him in, and Kevin's surroundings turn to pitch-black darkness.

CHAPTER 29

K RISTA STARES AS HER INDISTINCT
surroundings change from scattered foliage to
scattered lights. Then the disorienting, circling
blur finally slows down, stopping to leave her back on the
streets of downtown Mirror Valley. Looking around, she
realizes she is back in the same place she was at the beginning
of this chaotic dream.

"Do you need anything from the store? I can stop on the
way."

Krista quickly turns to face her father stepping out onto the
street after work. He's talking on the phone, same as before.

"Dad?" she whispers to herself, walking toward her father.
*Wait, something else is going on here. What were those figures
talking about? Car crash . . .* Krista gasps suddenly as the
pieces start to fall into place. *They were going to cause a car
crash to make someone's death look like an accident.*

"Get your hand off me, you miscreant! Help yourself, and get a job!"

Krista breathes in sharply as she realizes that the figures were talking about her dad and helping the homeless man was his final test. It was a test to see if he would act selflessly and help the old man. A test he failed.

Krista rushes up to her father, hoping at first to stop him, but quickly remembering that it's only a dream, and he can't see her.

Wait, Krista stops herself. *If this is my dream, I should be able to control what I see. Maybe this time will be different—maybe this time I can see what* really *happened.*

"Please! Help!" the old man cries out a final time as Krista's father walks away.

Rather than follow him, Krista decides to stay behind and watch the homeless man. She confirms that there is indeed something sinister going on: as she watches with wide eyes, the man's eyes change to pitch black with no whites in sight. They appear empty and soulless, and her hair stands on end at the chilling sight. But worst of all, when she looks into his eyes, Krista is overcome with immense sadness and grief she just can't shake.

Suddenly the city spins around her again, and she's left sitting in the passenger side of the car next to her father, speeding down the road once again.

No, I don't want to be here again, she tells herself as they approach the red stoplight and come to a full stop. The time once again lights up the dashboard: 11:24. *I'm in control. I can be in control*, she repeats to herself as she closes her eyes and concentrates.

A breeze whips through her hair, and she opens her eyes to find herself standing at the corner of the intersection, outside the car. She looks in the direction the truck had come from last time but sees nothing.

The light turns green. Suddenly she sees a black pickup truck materialize out of thin air right in front of her. Concentrating again, Krista holds her hands out, palms facing the truck, and yells one word: "Wait!"

Both vehicles and time stops.

She looks at the truck, then she closes her eyes and concentrates on moving locations once again. After feeling the now-familiar gust of wind, she opens her eyes. She's now in the passenger seat of the pickup truck.

To her horror, she gazes upon a revolting vision of a witch-like woman. Her nose is pointy, teeth jagged, and, rather than warts, her dead, white skin is covered with black scars. Both of her wrinkled hands are wrapped around the steering wheel, putting her long, talon-like nails on full display.

Krista freezes, losing her focus. Time resumes, but only for the last remaining seconds of that terrifying crash. Krista is pushed back into the seat from the sudden acceleration, and she lives through the car crash once again, this time in the phantom pickup truck. As sounds of skidding and crunching metal reach her ears, Krista just breaks down and cries.

As Krista's dream takes her back to the city, Klause emerges from the black hole in a different part of the forest. Before he can even open his eyes, Klause is bombarded with the voices once again. But this time, he makes out two words: "Turn around."

The whispers get louder, more insistent, and Klause notices that they seem to be a mixture of male and female voices. "Turn around," they repeat again and again in discord, one voice starting before another finishes.

Klause obeys and turns to find a young girl curled up in a ball next to a nearby tree. Klause notices that she's panting heavily, trying to catch a breath between her sobs. He approaches cautiously, carefully, but the sight of him towering over her shoots her wide eyes to his as she leaps to her feet and tries to run away.

"Stop her," the array of voices tell Klause.

"Wait!" he says as he grabs her arm.

"No! Please!" the girl begs as she falls to her knees in front of him. "Please!" she screams.

"Kill her!" the voices yell at Klause. "Kill her . . . kill her . . . kill her . . ." the voices echo, getting louder and deeper into the recesses of his mind.

As if in a trance, Klause's shaky hand reaches toward her and grabs her neck, dragging her to her feet.

"Please!" the girl gurgles, trying to cry out as she fights to breathe.

"Kill her . . . kill her . . . kill her!" The voices now scream in Klause's ears.

As he begins to tighten his grip, Klause's eyes change to the contrasting colors of black and white, but his body doesn't stop its transformation. As he watches her struggling for air, he sees black veins begin to permeate through the layers of his skin, down his arm, all the way to his outstretched hand.

When Klause notices black tendrils emerge from his fingertips and wrap around the girl's neck, the trance the voices seemed to put him under breaks. He lets go of the girl, his eyes and skin returning to normal.

"Ah!" the girl gasps as she tries to regain the oxygen she'd lost.

Klause backs away from her, eyes wide, knowing full well what he just did but unable to believe that he would even be capable of such a horrible act.

"I'm . . . I'm sorry," he tries to apologize, his voice shaky.

The girl doesn't respond, but instead looks up at him once again, gets up, and runs away.

In the moonlit darkness, Klause watches the girl run from him, getting further and further away.

With each step the girl takes, the voices in his head get more violent. "Kill her . . . kill her . . . kill her!" they continue to scream.

Tears stream down Klause's face as he clutches his head, dropping to his knees, overwhelmed by the voices terrorizing his mind.

"Kill her . . . kill her . . . KILL HER!" they continue.

"STOP!" Klause yells at the top of his lungs, his eyes changing back to the black and white orbs for a second as he looks at the girl running away, as if screaming at both the voices and the girl.

Suddenly, in the distance, Klause sees the girl trip and fall.

The voices stop completely, leaving Klause in complete silence and standing fifty feet away from the girl in the dark forest.

Klause rushes to check on the girl, but there's nothing he can do. He looks down on the teenaged girl sprawled out on the ground, blood pooling under her head, her eyes and mouth open, frozen in a gaze of death.

Kevin drops from the black hole that swallowed him, landing on his back on the hard ground.

Kevin gasps for air, unable to breathe, the wind knocked completely out of him. Looking up, he watches as the black hole shrinks to nothing, and he finds himself gazing up at a full moon peeking through leafy branches.

After taking a few breaths, he slowly stumbles to his feet and looks around. He appears to be in a forest.

A girl's scream pierces the darkness. Kevin runs forward, listening, hoping to find the girl who'd screamed. She sounded like she could use his help.

Kevin runs through the forest, trying not to get lost, ducking under branches and dodging trees and bushes.

With his adrenaline pumping hard, Kevin's eyes adjust quickly to the dark setting. He starts to run faster than ever before, eager to get to the girl and help her in any way he can.

Kevin stops in a small clearing to listen for another clue when something moving through the trees catches his attention. He sees a brief flash of a girl running through the woods, but quickly loses sight of her.

Just as he starts to run after her, somebody stops him.

"Kevin!" a girl's voice says behind him, grabbing his arm.

Turning around, Kevin sees the girl from Ekthesia standing with him, her white dress and silver tiara sparkling in the moon's light.

"Come with me, Kevin," she pleads, her eyebrows furrowing. "We must get back before they get to you, too."

"But—" Kevin tries to object.

The girl closes her eyes and sighs. "There's nothing you can do for her now. Please, we must go."

Kevin reluctantly takes her hand, and she turns and starts running in the opposite direction.

"Where are we going?" he asks as the two speed through the woods.

"We must get back to Kathrepta!" the girl shouts. "I can open the veil for a moment, long enough to get back."

Kevin doesn't understand, but, as they continue to run, he decides to trust her and wait until they're safe for further questions. He doesn't know what they are running from, but the girl is certainly afraid of whatever it is.

The two climb a shallow hill, dodging dense foliage, and arrive at a large boulder at the top. Kevin recognizes the place, but, before he can say anything, the girl commands his immediate attention.

"Anixeh!" she shouts as she reaches out her hand and pushes her fingers through the rock as if it were a ghost. Then, as she slides her fingers through the stone, a black emptiness appears—almost as if she is lifting up a curtain to a dark space. "Let's go!" she yells as she ducks under the open curtain of stone, pulling Kevin in with her.

Kevin gasps for air as he emerges from the pitch-black darkness just as he did after falling from the black hole. This time, he finds himself back in Ekthesia, surrounded by light. He turns around, facing where he just came from. In front of him, a massive stone structure towers over him and stretches out a hundred feet in every direction. The ginormous formation is plain with just one word etched into the stone in large block letters.

"Kathrepta," the girl says as she looks at the expression on Kevin's face. "The portal between the mirrored realms of the two worlds."

Kevin turns to face the girl once again, feeling himself start to fall apart. "Who are you?!" he screams, his voice shaky as tears roll down his face.

The girl looks at him, her eyes soft. In a calm voice, she replies simply, "Princess Karma."

CHAPTER 30

THE MOMENT KRISTA EXPERIENCES THE crash for the second time, Klause sees the dead body, and Kevin learns the name of the girl, all three suddenly awake from their dreams, gasping.

Krista gets up immediately, hurrying to the bathroom to splash some cold water on her face. She stares at herself in the mirror, droplets of water clinging to her skin. *What was that?* she ponders. It had to have been something more than just a dream, especially with everything that's been happening in the last few weeks.

She tries to think of a correlation between the six dark figures she saw in the forest and the five shadows she saw out her window the other night. Why were there more this time? Are they the same things or something completely different? And what's the connection to her father?

She shudders at this thought, thinking about her dad's death. Everything she was ever told about his death in the two years since is that a drunk driver hit his car. But if her dream really was more than just a dream, then the drunk driver story isn't the truth. Something much more sinister might be behind his death.

Thinking of the words exchanged between the six figures in the forest, she ponders on their conversation about making his death look like an accident. Krista straightens up as another memory dawns on her. *Who else were they talking about? Who is the woman that would be too upset by his death and end up forsaking her duty like her mother? Wouldn't it be someone close to my father . . . ?*

She jumps at a sudden knock on the bathroom door. "Krista? Are you okay?"

"Kevin?" Krista inquires, opening the door.

"Were you talking to someone last . . ." Kevin's question trails off as he sees the sweat forming on his sister's brow and notices her eyes quivering. "What's going on?" he says as he pulls Krista into a caring embrace.

"I don't know!" she cries on his shoulder. "My dream last night was freaky. It was terrifying and I . . . I don't know . . . just so crazy. Then combine this with all that's been going on with the strange accidents and my eyes changing colors, and I'm just so confused. There are too many questions. What's happening to me?"

"You mean, 'What's happening to *us*?'" Kevin replies sullenly.

"What?" Krista lets go of her brother to look in his eyes.

"I had a freaky dream, too, but it didn't feel like just a dream. It felt real."

"Mine did, too," Krista says. "Mine was about Dad—or at least most of it was. I also saw these things in the forest . . ."

"Wait, the forest?" Kevin interrupts. "A part of my dream was in the forest, too, and it gave me really creepy vibes."

"Same!" Krista shouts. "We need to tell each other about our dreams. Ugh, there are just so many questions and no real answers!"

"Well, mine might have provided some answers," Kevin says hesitantly. "That is, if we can trust them as answers."

Krista leads Kevin downstairs, and the two of them sit on the living room couch facing each other. Kevin goes first, sharing his strange night, starting at the beginning.

While the two discuss the strange occurrences of their lucid dreams, Klause is still lying in bed.

Looking up at the ceiling and covering his body up to his chin with his sheets, he thinks about his dream—or, rather, his nightmare. The voices haunt his conscious thought, with "kill her . . . kill her . . . kill her . . ." reverberating in his mind. He can still hear the girl's blood-curdling screams piercing through the darkness. He gulps as he remembers the terror in the girl's eyes as she looked at him, then her hollow eyes staring at him from beyond the grave. He feels a pit forming in his stomach as he recalls the black veins snaking up his arm, turning it darker than night, wrapping unrelentingly around the girl's neck.

Though glimpses of these horrific scenes invade his mind, the things that haunt him most are the feelings of comfort and safety. *It felt so real,* he thinks to himself, wondering how a dream could have been so immersive. His cheeks raise a sliver, forming a faint grin on his face as he thinks about his superior powers and ponders their dark potential.

Though he's happy he didn't actually kill anyone, he can't shake the feeling of relief that cascaded through his body when he gave in to the voices in his head. *Maybe the voices are extensions of me,* he theorizes to himself, contemplating his true nature, wondering who he really is deep down in his soul.

≪○≫

In the living room, Krista and Kevin continue to talk about their dreams.

"So you went through the stone when you transported worlds? I wonder why mine just spun around," Krista muses. "The difference must mean something."

"Yeah," Kevin confirms. "And I just now figured out why the stone looked so familiar. It's the boulder in the center of the forest by our house."

Krista takes a deep breath as if trying to absorb the influx of information from her brother. "My dream was mainly about Dad, but yours was about something totally different."

"Princess Karma . . ." Kevin audibly ponders. "She looked so much like you. And she acted like she knew me. Could we be related?"

"I've been researching karma lately," Krista answers. "Most of what I've found is about the religious belief of cause and effect, but other places refer to karma as a woman.

Following that, karma *could* be a woman. Maybe we're somehow related to her, and that's why we seem to possess these powers."

Kevin takes his own deep breath, contemplating all the questions and unclear answers swirling in the room. "We'll have to research more," Kevin announces. "And we should look into the stone and the forest. We've lived here our whole lives, and we know the unique layout of the town and how it surrounds the forest, but why does it do that? Other cities aren't like that, right?"

"That's right," Krista sighs. "The forest must be connected to these powers of karma somehow. Why else would it be so prominent in both of our dreams?"

Kevin nods his head in agreement and opens his mouth to say something, but he stops himself at the sound of Klause coming down the stairs. "Should we tell him?" Kevin whispers to Krista.

"Let's wait for him to come to us," Krista responds in a hushed tone. "I feel like he still thinks all of this is too crazy."

"What's up, guys?" Klause shouts as he heads to the kitchen in just his sweatpants. He pours himself a glass of orange juice, trying to act as nonchalant as he can. "Whatcha guys talkin' 'bout?"

Krista and Kevin exchange glances before Krista speaks up for the pair. "The weird dreams we had last night."

"Hmm," Klause grunts. He had planned not to tell them about his nightmare, anticipating the annoyance their barrage of worry would cause. But after hearing the topic of conversation, he begins to wonder if they had crazy dreams, too. Closing his eyes, he takes a deep breath in, about to tell them about his night, but is interrupted by the sudden ring of the doorbell.

"That must be the Sunday paper," Krista says after a brief pause.

"I'll get it," Klause replies as he walks over to the door.

Klause opens the door and leans down to snatch up the paper. As he picks it up, his eyes widen, and his glass of orange juice slips from his hand.

Looking down at the front page picture, he recognizes the face staring back at him, though the expression is drastically different from the one still haunting him. The headline reads, *"Young Girl Found Dead in Woods."*

Klause barely hears the glass shattering at his feet as he freezes at the sight of the girl from his dream, realizing that it felt real because it actually was.

CHAPTER 31

J ACK-O'-LANTERNS ARE OUT ON PORCHES, orange and black streamers hang on railings and wrap around street lamps, and houses are decked out with scattered skeletons and tombstones. Holidays in the small town of Mirror Valley can't help but be a cause for great festivities among its residents, an excuse to decorate the town and come together as a community. Mirror Valley's adults are busy planning the town's annual Halloween Horror Night, while most of its youth are busy trying to figure out what to wear.

Krista, however, has been trying to keep herself busy and occupy her mind with school and yearbook, but she has been failing horribly at it. After hearing about Kevin's dream three weeks ago, she's been having a hard time focusing on anything other than the questions that have arisen, taking any answers from the dream with a grain of salt.

A few days ago, she thought about calling her mom and asking her about her father's car wreck but was worried about opening old wounds. Krista was the rock in her family when her dad died, as she was the one person her mother felt comfortable crying around, so she was worried that mentioning his crash would distress her mother once again.

But after sitting on her thoughts about his crash for three weeks, she decides that today she will finally start doing her own research. Everything she had been told about his death revolved around the culprit being a drunk driver, but if it was indeed an intentional murder carried out by one of those dark beings in the forest, then who really was the driver? And where is he or she—or, rather, *it*? Krista sits in the newsroom thinking about all of this, barely comprehending Rick's voice droning on in the background.

"Krista?"

Rick's voice finally breaks through, and Krista blinks and looks up. "Sir?"

"I said, do you have any news updates on the Halloween Horror Night coming up?" Rick repeats. "You have connections with the planning committee, right?"

Krista exhales. "Yes, while they are still planning on having the regular haunted house and carnival-style games and rides, this year the committee is trying to work out the logistics of setting up a haunted maze in the town square, one leading into the forest," Krista replies. "Actually, I think they want to do it in the forest itself, but they're having trouble figuring out exactly how."

"Wow!" Rick exclaims. "That would be fun."

The newsroom erupts in approving head nods and excited whispers.

"Well," Rick continues, "stay updated with the planning, and write up an article as soon you know for sure. I want the newsletter to go out in three days—on Halloween—so that students can see what they have to look forward to that night."

"Yes, Sir." Krista nods her head.

"Alright everyone," Rick announces to the class. "That will do it for today."

Students rush to put their laptops and notebooks away so they can get home for the day. Krista follows suit but is stopped before she walks out.

"Krista," Rick calls out to her, "stay for a moment. I want to talk to you."

Krista jolts slightly at the request. "Oh, um, I really can't. My brothers will be waiting on me."

"Sit down, Krista," Rick's voice becomes more stern. "They can wait a few minutes."

A lump forms in Krista's throat as she worries she might be in trouble. "Is everything okay?" she asks.

"I don't know, is it?" Rick counters.

"What do you mean?"

"Krista, I've noticed you've been a little absent-minded lately. Which isn't like you. What's going on?"

"Nothing," Krista lies, still unwilling to share her deep, dark secrets with anyone other than her siblings.

"What's on your mind?" Rick continues to pry.

Krista's heart starts to beat faster as she tries to quickly come up with an excuse that he'll believe. "It's just . . ." her voice trails off. She acts like she's deciding if she should share the thing that's bothering her when really she's just stalling for time, hoping to think of *something.*

"What?"

"It's just . . ." she says again before finally coming up with a good response. "My mother has been gone a while, and I really miss her. And . . ." She trails off again, realizing that the best lies have elements of the truth. "And I'm just feeling really overwhelmed right now. I feel like, with everything going on, I'm failing at taking care of my brothers, my family."

"With what going on?"

Krista blinks hard as she realizes that she let something more than what she wanted to reveal slip from her tongue.

"Oh, um, just with senior year stuff," Krista brushes off, flipping her hair behind her back.

"I see." Rick takes a deep breath. "I can ease up on your editor in chief duties, or maybe we could give the position to someone else."

"No!" Krista yelps then catches herself. "I mean, no, that's okay." She swallows once. "I like the job. I just have a lot of unanswered questions that are bogging down my brain."

"What questions?" Rick asks. "Maybe I can help."

"No, that's okay," Krista responds softly, slinging her backpack over her shoulder. "I'm going to do some research later and figure some stuff out on my own. Thank you, though."

Rick nods his head. "Anytime," he says as he watches her head toward the exit. "Oh, Krista!"

Krista turns around to face her favorite teacher, one hand holding the door halfway open. "Yes?"

"While things may not always be as they seem, the world isn't all black and white. Vibrant colors and radiant light abound around us, especially for genuinely good people like yourself. Knowledge is important, but life is a much more powerful force."

Krista smiles, her face lighting up with a brief glimpse of hope for the first time in months, before she closes the door behind her to make her way to the front of the school.

Upon her departure, Rick's eyes glow white, and Sablo, who is still inside him, calls out to his brother. "Abraxos!"

A gust of wind sweeps the room and Abraxos materializes, his bleached-blond hair settling down on his muscular shoulders. "Yes, Brother?" he asks calmly.

"Something has been going on with Krista," Sablo expresses his concern.

"Well, she is experiencing her powers of karma early. It's probably a lot for her to handle."

"Okay . . ." Sablo responds sullenly. "But she said that she has a lot of unanswered questions and that she's going to look into them later. Should we be concerned? Should we tell her what's going on?"

"You're attaching yourself to her too much, Brother. Remember our mission. We're trying to turn her to only goodness. If we tell her—or let her mother tell her—what's going on, she'll never be accepting of only good karma and will want to act like the thousands of Karmas before her. We need to take the power of the Council to spread goodness in the world, and she and her siblings could be the key to that. She'll figure it out in her own time. The situation is too fragile to force anything."

Outside the school, Krista meets up with Kevin, who's been hanging out with Bella in their usual spot.

"Klause not out yet?" Krista asks her little brother.

"Do you really think that he would voluntarily walk up and hang out with only me and Bella?"

"Good point!" Krista snaps her fingers, then taps her foot as she pulls out her phone to call Klause.

"Hey!" she says into the phone after he picks up. "Where are you? Kevin and I are ready to go."

"Oh, I'm going to hang out with Tyler for a little bit," Klause says on the other line. "I'll be home later tonight."

"Okay." Krista sighs. "We'll see you later then. Stay safe. 'Bye."

Krista hangs up the phone and shrugs her shoulders. "Well, I guess we're riding solo then. Bella, do you need a ride home?"

"Yeah, that would be great!" Bella says as she smiles at Kevin. "Thank you."

"I'm just going to drop you two off at the houses," Krista remarks. "I'm gonna go to the coffee shop to study."

Klause, who is standing around the corner of the school building, watches the three walk away, toward the car. He waits for them to get in and drive away before he comes out of hiding—he needs to check some things out for himself and needs time away from his family and friends to do it. He slings his backpack over his shoulder and starts to head toward the forest.

On his way to the woods at the center of town, he reflects on his experiences over the last couple of months.

First, there was the incident with Jessica. He had wished bad thoughts on her new nose, and, soon after, she broke it. Then there was his opponent at the homecoming game and his broken leg. He didn't intend for either of those things to actually happen; he didn't even know he *had* the power, say nothing of actually controlling it.

His first time purposely activating his power was on his coach, and he remembers that powerful feeling of superiority when he did it—especially since he didn't kill anyone like his siblings had.

Klause smirks at the thought, but his smile quickly fades as he thinks of the more mysterious happenings surrounding this new power of his.

He calls to mind his incident with his sister. *My eyes changed after I thought badly of Krista, so I activated my power for something. But it didn't actually do anything. It even backfired. Why did that happen? Is that what it even was? Did it really backfire, or could I just not control it?*

Klause makes it to the edge of the forest before he stops himself. He looks up at the great trees in front of him, taking a step back. He peers through the dense foliage. Even though it's still daytime, the woods are dark, somehow absorbing the light of the sun. Klause remains where he stands for a moment and shivers as a gust of wind whips through the air, hitting him straight in the front of his body as if coming from deep within the woods itself.

As he stands there, he thinks about the last strange incident that happened, when he thought he was dreaming. When it was actually reality.

A single tear rolls down his cheek. He cringes as he recalls the loud and violent voices in his head and the dead silence that permeated around him the moment the girl died.

Klause thinks about turning back as he gazes into the shade of the forest, a level of eeriness in the air, but he knows that he needs to find some answers. Taking a deep breath, he steps forward into the unknown, holding on to the hope that he will figure out what is really happening to him.

CHAPTER 32

FRESHLY BREWED COFFEE, SCATTERED conversation, and every kind of person fill the small coffee shop, but Krista takes little heed of her surroundings, concentrating solely on the computer screen in front of her. The only thing she hears is the tapping of her own fingers on the keyboard. Krista sits at the coffee bar with a full view of Sheri and the other baristas working on new drink orders, but she doesn't look away from the screen. She's too engrossed in her research.

Victim was a middle-aged, Caucasian male. Cause of death was blunt force trauma to the head and body, the result of severe impact on the left side of the body due to a motor vehicle accident, she reads to herself.

It took awhile to dig up the autopsy report of her father's death; she had to find a source in the town morgue willing to feed her the information. Looking at the document, she shakes her head and lets out a deep breath. *Ugh, I already knew this,* she anguishes.

With no new information from this source, she continues to dig, now searching the Mirror Valley Police Department's website.

"Whatcha doin'?" Sheri says in a curious tone, leaning over the other side of the counter right in front of Krista.

Krista chuckles, lowering the screen of the laptop to get a full view of the four-foot-six Latina girl standing on the other side of the bar. "Just doing some research."

"On what?"

Krista shrugs. "Just some family stuff."

"Ooo, like a family tree?" Sheri asks excitedly. "I did that one time. Apparently my great-great-great"—she counts the number of greats on her hand—"great-grandmother, on my dad's side, was a witch in Salem!"

"Dang!" Krista exclaims.

"I know, right?" Sheri responds. "Oh yeah, and my mom's side is from Mexico. Who knew?" she says sarcastically.

"Fun fact," Krista perks up. "I don't look it, but my great-grandfather on my mom's side was Mexican, too," Krista giggles before continuing. "No, I'm actually looking into my dad's car wreck. I feel like I didn't get the full story about how he died."

Sheri's expression quickly changes, her eyebrows pulling together. "Krista," she says softly. "Do you really think that's a good idea? It's not healthy opening old wounds."

"I have to," Krista chokes up. "I have this weird feeling that there's more to the story. There are too many unanswered questions."

"Like what?" Sheri asks.

"Like, who killed him? What happened to the driver of the truck? What was it?"

"What was what?" Sheri counters.

"I mean . . ." Krista's voice trails off, and she averts her gaze for just a moment. "I mean, who was he? Or she?"

Sheri takes a deep breath. "It was a drunk driving accident, wasn't it? I'm sure whoever did it is in prison for manslaughter or something."

"But there was never a trial or anything! Wouldn't there have been a trial? I just remember he died a-and . . ." Krista stutters, tears welling in her eyes, "and we held his funeral . . . and that's . . . and that's it. There was no other closure!"

"Maybe the driver died, too," Sheri suggests then sighs. "Krista, I don't think you should be doing this. It's hurting you and learning more isn't going to bring your dad back." Sheri reaches out to grab Krista's now-trembling hand. "What happened, happened. It sucks, I know. But you can't change the past."

"But . . . but . . ." Krista sniffles, gasping for air, tears now streaming down her cheeks.

"Krista, I know this is really hard, and I wish I could take your pain away." Sheri squeezes her hand. "Look, I believe that everything happens for a reason, and, while these things may not seem good or fair on the surface, it always leads to something new, something great, creating a new balance, a new harmony. This was a trauma, and it will always be a trauma—you'll never forget it. But because you've experienced this, you've changed, you've grown, and I'm confident that your kindness and humanity will only flourish more as you live your life, filling your life with love and happiness."

Krista tries to control her breathing as she wipes her tears away with the sleeve of her sweater. Sheri remains in front of Krista with a warm smile on her face, still holding her hand, ignoring the fact that new coffee orders are pouring in behind her.

"Krista?"

Krista sniffles one more time and takes a deep meditative breath. *In and out*, she thinks as she exhales. Composing herself, she looks at Sheri, her heart warming at the sight of love and care on her face, and she lets her lips form a small smile. "Thank you."

Though Sheri returns to work, Krista keeps watching her. Sheri's high bun bounces as she walks around, and Krista can't help but smile at her. Something about her makes Krista feel comfortable and safe.

After a few moments, Krista opens her laptop again to continue her research. Staring at the screen, she takes a few more breaths, and her eyes light up at something Sheri said, about how the driver could be dead. If the driver did die, then she'd be able to use her source at the town morgue to dig up the report. She shoots off a quick email.

While waiting for a response, another idea pops into her head. *Hang on, I'm approaching this wrong,* she says to herself. *Instead of trying to figure out what happened during the wreck, I should be researching what happened* after. *Mom got the call from the hospital . . . and I remember seeing her with some cops. What was their procedure? How did the cops process the scene? Was there evidence collected? Who was present at the scene? I could talk to them.*

Just then, a Mirror Valley police officer walks into the coffee shop. She recognizes him as the father of her friend, Heather, from yearbook. Krista jumps up and hurries to the cash register, handing the cashier her debit card just as the officer is about to pay, hoping that her generous act will earn her a conversation with him.

"Let me get that for you, to thank you for your service."

"Why, thank you. I really appreciate it," the officer responds. "Do I know you? You look familiar."

"Oh, your name is Dallas, right? Heather's dad," Krista asks, reaching for any familiarity she can conjure up.

"Yes . . ." his voice trails off into a lower tone, one eyebrow raising.

"Hi, I'm Krista," she says as she reaches out her hand. "I'm Editor in Chief at the high school. I'm friends with Heather."

"Ah, yes. I remember you from that fundraising event last year," Dallas says, shaking her hand. "You're quite the hard worker. I still can't believe you organized that whole thing."

Krista blushes at the compliment. "I just have a lot of connections," she responds with a sweet smile. "Speaking of connections, I would love to connect with you more. I'll be going to school for journalism, and a knowledge of crime procedures and things like that would probably help me know how to approach those kinds of assignments."

"Absolutely," Dallas says, eyes sparkling. "This world needs more educated young women like you who are familiar with law and justice."

"*Dallas!*" one of the baristas calls out.

"Look, I'm actually on duty so I have to get going, but feel free to email me or call me at home. My email address can be found on the department's website."

"Fantastic! Thank you so much," Krista responds enthusiastically. "Can I just ask you one quick question before you go?"

"Sure."

"I'm working on a school project, and I need access to a case file." Krista stretches the truth. "How would I go about getting that?"

"You would have to put in a request with the department, and it has to be a closed case. We can't divulge any information on an ongoing case."

"Oh, okay," Krista says. "Well, thank you again. I'll definitely be getting in contact with you."

Dallas smiles and gives her a big thumbs-up as he turns around to leave.

Krista returns to her laptop and immediately saves his contact information, then she works to submit a request for the case file, eager to finally find some answers.

Just as she sends the request email to the department, she feels something that compels her to look up from her laptop. To her left, peeking back at her over the tops of the espresso machines, are the eyes of an absolutely *gorgeous* guy.

He can't be much older than her, but something about him feels like he's had a full life, experienced things that have shaped him. Krista can see his deep blue eyes, even at this distance, staring right back at hers.

Krista's heart skips a beat at the sight of the handsome young man who looks like he came right out of "Grease" with his black hair brushed back in a pompadour, and his white v-neck shirt stretching tightly across his chest under his fitted black leather jacket.

The side of his mouth curves upward ever so slightly into a side smile, and Krista takes in a quick breath just before he picks up his coffee and turns to walk away.

Krista thinks about calling out to him but refuses to stoop to that level and instead watches him walk out of the shop and never look back.

Krista lets her inhale release as she rolls her eyes. *Ugh, come on, Krista. Why are you acting like you've never seen a cute guy before? You don't need to be sidetracked by boys. Not now. Not with everything going on.*

"I think that guy was checking you out," Sheri leans over to tell Krista.

"Don't remind me," Krista scoffs.

"What?" Sheri questions. "You don't like hot guys?"

"I don't like bad boys," Krista defends herself. "I mean, come on—you didn't feel the darkness in him? That 'I can do anything I want' attitude?"

"A little," Sheri allows. "But maybe he's had a troubled past or something."

"Whatever. I don't need to be focusing on boys right now. So what if he has gorgeous eyes, and a great body . . . and . . . and hair I just wanna run my fingers through . . ." Krista's tone gets softer, and her eyes drift upward toward the ceiling.

"Mm-hm," Sheri nods her head. "Yeah, you're *definitely* not into him."

Krista looks down and stares at the screen in front of her without really seeing it, instead thinking about that guy and wondering if she'll ever see him again.

CHAPTER 33

WITH ONLY TWO DAYS UNTIL Halloween, students are finalizing their plans for the big night and discussing with their friends which after-party will be worth attending. For the small town of Mirror Valley, holiday festivals are such a big deal that nobody dares miss them. Even if there's nothing fun for the teens to do, they can still watch the adults of the town make a fool of themselves, dressing in costumes and trying to act scary.

In class, Kevin exchanges a side glance with Bella every time they see a student pass a note to each other, and they chuckle to themselves. The two recently discovered they both enjoy people-watching and sometimes even find themselves watching the same person without realizing it.

RRINNG!! With class over, Kevin and Bella turn to each other.

"So that Halloween Festival is a pretty big deal, huh?" Bella queries.

"Yeah!" Kevin exclaims, grinning. "Everyone goes to it. You're probably more of a social pariah if you *don't* go."

"Do you dress up?"

"You can. It's not mandatory, but I think it's pretty fun. Do you wanna dress up?"

Bella chuckles. "I will if you do."

"Cool. Maybe we can go shop for a costume after school."

"I can't today." Bella's face falls. "My mom wants to hang out with me, and I've got a lot of homework I need to catch up on. I need to get ahead so I can stay out late on Halloween."

"That's a pretty good idea. Homework doesn't rest for Halloween. And neither do the spirits," Kevin adds.

"Spirits?" Bella freezes, her eyes wide.

"You know, like ghosts and stuff." Kevin laughs. "It was a joke."

"Oh," Bella snorts, bursting into a nervous laughter. She mumbles something under her breath.

"What was that?" Kevin asks.

"Oh, nothing. Just talking to myself." Bella smiles.

The two head to their lockers to retrieve the books for their last class, discussing today's people-watching experiences along the way.

"So what are you thinking of dressing up as?" Bella asks.

"I don't know." Kevin shrugs his shoulders. "I'll probably just look around and see what the costume shop has."

"You're not going to DIY any of it and save some money?"

"I don't think I'd be too good at that."

"What?" Bella asks. "You mean Kevin Atwood, the most amazing artist I've ever met, doesn't think he'd be able to design a costume?"

Kevin laughs. "Drawing and designing an outfit are two very different things. What about you?"

"Hmm," Bella ponders the question. "I have a black dress my mom made me buy for a funeral last year. I could dress as a witch."

"Wow, that sounds both incredibly morbid and incredibly cliché all at the same time."

"I think it's just morbid and cliché enough for Halloween." Bella chuckles. "Oh! How about Morticia Addams? I love her finesse and nonchalant attitude—basically qualities I aspire to have."

"I like it! Much more original."

"Perfect! Then I won't have to buy a witch hat, maybe just some crazy makeup to complete the look," Bella starts talking faster and almost starts bouncing in place. "And you could be the Gomez to my Morticia! All you would need to do is slick back your hair, wear a black suit, and get a little fake mustache." Bella reaches up and smooths his hair back, tilting her head and narrowing her eyes at him. Then she giggles. "Oh my gosh, now I'm picturing you with a mustache."

Kevin grins back, closing his locker. "Sounds like a pla—" He turns around quickly to head to class . . . and crashes into another student, his books spilling all over the tiled floor.

"Oh no!" shouts the student as he bends down to help Kevin pick up his books.

"No worries," Kevin responds. "I think this is my own little curse. I drop my books at least once a week."

The other student chuckles. "Are you okay?" he asks.

"Yeah, I'm good," Kevin says as he stands up with his books once again in hand.

"I've had a lot of things on my mind lately with school and family, and now I'm nervous about what part I'm going to get in the school play," the student says quickly, quietly. "Obviously I want the lead, but that's probably not going to happen. If this is how my day is going so far, I wouldn't be surprised if my misfortune triggers an even worse domino effect," he mumbles before walking away.

"What a jerk—he didn't even say 'sorry,'" snaps Bella after he walks away. "He just made excuses. I wouldn't doubt it if his misfortune *did* continue."

Kevin shrugs his shoulders. "He seemed nice to me. At least he helped me with my books and didn't just walk away."

Bella shrugs.

The pair make their way to class, and, just before entering the classroom, Kevin looks off toward the student who is walking down the hall, his head lowered. He smiles and hopes that things will turn around for him and get better. As he thinks this, he turns his head to face the door and faintly sees his reflection in the small glass window. His eyes change, just like Krista's did at the homecoming dance, one eye black and the other white.

Kevin jumps back, almost losing hold of his books once again, but Bella catches him by the elbow.

"Are you okay? What's wrong?"

"I saw . . ." Kevin shakes his head. "My eyes . . ."

"What about your eyes?"

Kevin blinks and looks back at his reflection. His eyes have returned to their natural brown color. Then he looks back down the hall, watching the student in the distance as worry strikes him. Did he just inadvertently hurt him? He hadn't been angry at him.

Kevin doesn't answer Bella and heads into the classroom. Taking a deep breath in, Bella looks down the hall at the student, then breathes out and follows Kevin inside.

Class seems to go by slower than usual as Kevin stares forward at the teacher, not paying attention. Instead, he's thinking about the boy who ran into him and how, at the thought of him, his eyes changed. Kevin thinks about Princess Karma and her white and black eyes, then about his sister at the homecoming dance. Whatever happened to them is now happening with him.

As he ponders the meaning of the eyes, it suddenly hits him. *Our eyes change whenever our powers of karma activate. It must be that! Whether Princess Karma was real or not, maybe she was a representation of karma. Maybe the dream was meant for me to put this all together? Maybe we* do *possess this power of karma?*

Kevin sighs, then his eyes widen. *But what about that guy? I wasn't thinking bad thoughts about him like I was with the guy in the parking lot, so what's going to happen to him?*

RRINNG!! sounds the bell, interrupting Kevin's train of thought. He and Bella gather their belongings and head out of class.

"Kevin, are you okay? What happened earlier?" Bella tries as soon as they're out in the hallway.

"It was nothing," he says as he shakes his head. "I just need to talk to my sister about something. Family stuff."

The two walk down the hall to the front of the school, but, before they get there, Kevin stops in his tracks. The student he ran into earlier is standing at the bulletin board just ahead of him.

Kevin's heart beats faster, and his face becomes pale as he watches him, but he tilts his head to the side, eyebrows scrunched together, as he sees the student jumping up and down, hugging everyone around him. Kevin takes a few steps toward the student to see what the commotion is really about.

"I can't believe it!" the student shouts in excitement. "I can't believe I got the lead roll! This is amazing!" he cries out as tears begin to well in his eyes.

Kevin watches the celebration as he and Bella saunter by and head out the school's front doors where Krista is waiting for them.

"Hey, guys," Krista calls to them. "I'm going to do some field research today on Halloween Horror Night instead of the regular yearbook meeting. So I'm just going to drop you off at home and go from there. Klause said he was going to hang out at the gym after practice and come home later tonight, so it's just us again. Shall we go?"

"Actually, it will just be you two," Bella replies. "I have to take care of some stuff here, and my mom is going to pick me up later. Thank you for the offer, though, as always. I'll see you tomorrow, Kevin!"

Kevin and Bella hug, and Bella turns to walk back into the school.

"I need to talk to you about something," Kevin tells his sister upon getting in the car. "I saw my eyes change colors, just like yours did at the dance. One eye was pitch black and the other was solid white."

"What?" Krista's eyes shoot to his. "What happened? Who got hurt?"

"That's the crazy part. No one did."

"You mean, not yet?"

"I don't know for sure, of course, but I don't think anything bad will happen," Kevin replies. "So another student ran into me in the hall today, and I dropped my books. Although he didn't apologize, he was really nice. He helped me pick up my books and told me about how he had a lot on his mind, including how nervous he was about what part in the school play he would get. Then shortly after, when I was looking at him and wishing him better luck in the future, I saw my eyes change colors. Don't you see? I didn't wish harm on him, I just wished him good fortune. Then, just now, when I was leaving school, I saw him yelling. He had gotten the lead role in the play!"

"Wait, did you give him *good* fortune?"

"Yeah," Kevin responds. "I think so! And another thing: I think the Princess Karma in my dreams might be a representation of karma and our abilities. Her eyes were black and white, too, so maybe our eyes change colors when our powers are activated."

"Hold on," Krista says as she pulls into their driveway. "Karma! It's karma!"

"Yeah, I think that's what I was saying . . ."

"No, I mean . . ." Krista puts the car in park then turns to Kevin. "Remember our research? There's good and bad karma. If we *do* possess this power of karma, then maybe we can do more than just hurt people. We were hurting people by wishing bad thoughts on bad people; in other words, bad karma. But if we wish good thoughts on good people, we can give them good karma!"

"Woah," Kevin says. "So this ability can be used for good, too! We can actually help people with it!"

Krista reaches over the middle console and hugs Kevin, holding him for a few moments before backing away. Her face lights up, and her eyes sparkle. "Now we just need to figure out how to control it."

CHAPTER 34

WHILE KIDS ARE HANGING OUT WITH friends, doing homework, or having dinner with their family, Krista is out in the field. As she walks through the crowd of volunteers, working away in the town square, she feels the brisk wind of the fall air on her cheeks and pulls her scarf up a little higher.

Her pocket notepad and voice recorder in hand, she explores the events around her. Some adults are setting up booths, some are decorating, and others are coordinating the efforts.

She tries her best to get into her journalistic mindset. With the good news from Kevin that they might be able to help people now, her spirits are lifted for the first time in weeks. Finally, she has hope again. Hope that this new ability will be more than a curse, perhaps actually a gift.

Wandering through the crowd, she spots a woman who seems to be the one in charge. She takes a deep breath then heads over to her.

"Hi, I'm Krista, Editor in Chief at Mirror Valley High." She reaches out her hand to shake the woman's. "I'm guessing you're the one in charge here?"

"That's correct."

"I don't believe I've met you before," Krista says as she looks up at the woman who is much taller than she expected when she saw her in the distance. Krista briefly admires her bright green eyes and copper red hair before looking away so she doesn't get caught staring. "I usually communicate with Diane Beslinger. She usually directs the town's festivals."

"Ah, yes. Diane had to go to rehab," the woman scoffs before looking around and proceeding in a whisper. "Apparently dancing naked on top of a bar downtown was finally enough for her to realize she has a problem." She chuckles. "Anyway, I'll be leading the festival coordination instead. My name is Hertha. Hertha Auber."

"Nice to meet you . . . M-Mrs . . . Auber . . ." Krista stutters as she grimaces from the woman's strongly grasped handshake.

"No need for formalities. We're going to be working together for the foreseeable future. Call me Hertha."

Krista breathes in deeply as if gasping for air after Hertha lets her hand go. "So what are the plans for Halloween Horror Night? What booths will be open? What activities will there be? I want the works. Students would love to see what's to come in the Halloween issue of the newsletter."

"Of course. Follow me, and I'll show you around."

The two make their way through the festival grounds. Hertha points out everything going on, from the snack carts and drink stands to the carnival games and Halloween-themed activities, needing to shout at times over the hectic noise of drilling or hammering and shouts of directions from various volunteers.

Krista takes careful note of everything she sees and hears, listening intently to everything Hertha says about what's yet to come and taking copious notes.

"I was told that the festival committee was thinking about adding a maze this year," Krista asks toward the end of the tour. "Are you doing that after all?"

"Yes!" Hertha exclaims. "We're all very excited about the maze. I would hate to ruin the surprise by showing it to you before it's completed, but I'll just tell you—it's shaping up to be pretty impressive. The walls of the maze will be ten feet tall and a mix of wooden posts, brick walls, and hay bales. We also may or may not have some actors in costume spread throughout the maze to give it a more haunted theme. But I can't confirm that on the record, of course."

"Wow, that sounds really cool," Krista gushes. "I totally understand wanting to keep it a surprise—I can't wait."

"Me neither!" says Hertha. "Well, that's going to conclude the tour. Is there anything else I can answer or help you with?"

"No, that will be it." Krista smiles. "I would like to talk to you the night of the festival and get some insider insight into the turnout and how you think it went. My photographer, Marsha Thornberry, will be coming around and taking pictures of the event as well, so just a heads-up on that." She pauses, looking around. "Would it be alright if I sit at a picnic table nearby and get to work on my article? I would like to be able to write while I'm still here in case I forgot something."

"Absolutely, that all sounds great. There's a table right over there," Hertha says as she points to a wooden picnic table on the outskirts of the town square. "You're welcome to stay as long as you need. Just let me know if you need anything else. I must get back to work now. It was fantastic to finally meet you in person."

"You, too!" Krista replies before something hits her. "Wait—'finally meet me'? You knew who I was?"

Hertha stops in her tracks and slowly turns around to face Krista once again. "Oh, uh . . . yes, of course . . . um, Diane told me about you and that you might stop by. Honestly, I wasn't expecting you until Halloween night, though." Hertha chuckles.

"Oh, okay. Well, as I said, students will read about what's going to be at the festival in the school newsletter. It helps them get pumped about the festivities."

"Ah, yes. That makes sense!" Hertha nods her head before turning to walk away. "Well, I'll see you in a couple of days. Have fun writing your article!" she calls out from afar.

Krista heads to the picnic table and takes a seat on the bench. She sets her bag beside her then pulls her laptop out. She starts typing as soon as it powers up.

Every once in a while, she looks up from the screen to take in her surroundings: the hustle and bustle of the volunteers, the sounds of shouting and hammering, the feeling of the autumn air whipping through her hair, and the sights of trees with red and orange leaves swaying in the wind. Then she goes back to her article, writing away, hoping to finish before she goes home so she can do homework the rest of the night and work on edits tomorrow.

Then she stops—the conclusion is always the hardest for her. She likes ending with a compelling sentence that evokes emotion and makes the reader want to take action, but she can't seem to find just the right words. Taking one last mental break, she looks up from her laptop. And someone catches her eye.

From across the town square, she spies the guy from the coffee shop yesterday. His black leather jacket is off, and he's instead wearing a sleeveless black shirt, his toned arms flexing as he lifts a hay bale onto the bed of a truck. His black hair is still holding up strong—with incredible volume, if she's being honest—despite his attempts to wipe the sweat off his forehead.

Krista's heart starts racing as he starts walking toward her, and she tries to look away. But then he turns to grab a drink of water from the water coolers near her, and she exhales, her shoulders relaxing. The young man chugs the cup of water—then, after taking off his black sunglasses, he gets another and proceeds to pour it on his head. He fills another cup and starts to walk back to the hay bales when his eyes find Krista's. He freezes in place.

He stops to gaze at her. His deep blue eyes focus in on hers and seem to pierce through the fall air. His chest heaves up and down as he catches his breath. Krista's heart beats faster and faster the longer she looks at him. His expression is unreadable except for the fire in his eyes—one Krista recognizes but hasn't seen directed at her in, like, *ever*—but there's something more to his emotions, something she can't quite pinpoint, only adding to his mysterious allure.

After what seems like forever, he slowly puts his dark sunglasses back on. And somehow, in an instant, his smoldering look becomes even more entrancing, blocking the cool, icy stare from his blue eyes and shielding the world from his inner emotions. Krista takes a deep breath as she watches the handsome young man smile at her, just as subtle and small as yesterday, before he turns around and gets back to work.

Krista shivers as a strong gust of wind hits her face, and she looks down at her keyboard. She chuckles, smiling and showing off her pearly-white teeth. She brushes her hair away from her face and behind her ear then smirks again, her heart still beating faster than ever as she finally admits to herself what Sheri already pointed out: she is incredibly attracted to the mysterious new kid in town.

Klause stands at the edge of the forest, ready to head in. After lying to Krista once again about what he was doing, he's determined to make this trip into the forest more fruitful than yesterday. After wandering the forest for hours yesterday with nothing to show for it, he's eager to get back in there, hoping to find answers. He doesn't know what he's looking for specifically, but he's confident he'll know when he sees it.

Stepping through the dense foliage, he makes his way through the woods, avoiding the path. Just as he was in his dream, his real life experience, or whatever it was that really happened the other night. Which is one of the many reasons why he needs answers. *Maybe if I find where the girl died, I can find some evidence of me being there, or at least see if it looks familiar*, he thinks to himself as he makes his way through the forest.

As he slowly moves through the woods, a gust of wind blows through the trees, and he shivers. After wandering the woods for two hours, it seems that he isn't going to find anything once again, and he turns around to make his way home.

"Klause . . ."

Klause spins around as he suddenly hears his name. "Is anyone there?" he cries out.

No answer, only the rustling of fallen leaves on the ground.

He turns again to go home, and, as another breeze shifts the pile of leaves by his feet, he hears the voice again. "Klause..."

His heart starts pounding as he whips around again, expecting to see something. Again, nothing, so Klause decides in that moment to try a different approach.

Since the first time he heard the voices, he felt something strange leading him to the places the voices wanted him to go, so he decides to trust his instincts. Closing his eyes, he takes a deep breath and whispers both to himself and to anyone who's listening: "Help me. Guide me. I can't do this alone. Tell me where I should go."

"Ath—" he hears faintly, and he opens his eyes. Another gust of wind blows the leaves forward then shifts them toward the right. Squinting his eyes, he sees a makeshift path ahead of him and follows it.

Klause walks for several minutes, allowing the wind to be his guide, when he suddenly hears his name whispered again. But this time, it's a little louder, as if he's closer now.

"Klause . . ." he hears again as he steps through the dense foliage and finds himself at the large boulder, the same one from his dream. The stone towers above him and is just as big as he remembers.

"The veil . . ." the whisper says in Klause's ear as he looks upon the boulder.

Klause shakes his head at the whisper's new words. "The veil . . ." he hears again.

Klause slowly approaches the rock and reaches out his hand. Just as he places his fingertips on the cold stone, he hears his name once again. But this time, the loud, deep voice startles him, and he jumps back, blinking hard, heart racing.

He hears the rustling of leaves again and spins around, coming face-to-face with a black, shadowed, soulless figure, like the angel of death himself. Klause shrieks at the terrifying thing in front of him, but, in the blink of an eye, the shadow disappears back into the forest.

As the dark figure speeds away, Klause finds himself once again alone in the forest, his heart palpitating faster than ever before and his jaw dropped as he thinks about what he just saw. He wasn't able to make out any features other than what appeared to be massive wings flowing behind it as the dark figure ran—or flew—away.

CHAPTER 35

"AIT," MARSHA GROWLS. "YOU met a hot guy, and I'm just now hearing about it? I thought we were best friends!"

Krista shrugs her shoulders, fighting to hide her smile as they approach their lockers. "Because we *haven't* met. I just saw him at the coffee shop and then again helping out at the festival. We haven't said one word to each other."

"So? I still wanna know about him. What's he like?" Marsha asks as she puts her books away.

"As I said, we haven't officially met yet." Krista sighs. "We just keep making eye contact. He stares at me with his deep blue eyes, and I stare back. I don't even know how I feel about him. He seems like a bad boy, which, you know, isn't my type. But something about him is so alluring."

"Yeah, he's alluring because he's hot. Don't try to make it more than it is." Marsha laughs.

"You would have to see him in order to understand what I'm talking . . . about . . ." Krista's voice trails off as her jaw drops.

Walking down the hall toward them is the mysterious boy in question. His black combat boots make subtle thuds on the tile floor, and he brushes his fingers through his voluminous black hair as he approaches.

He turns his head as he slows his pace to catch a glimpse of Krista. Their eyes lock, and he tilts his chin up, nodding his head as he smiles. "Hey," he says to her, his voice hoarse and casual. He continues to walk forward, passing them in the hall, adjusting his black backpack on his shoulder.

Krista and Marsha watch him walk away until Krista shivers out of her trance and turns back to her locker.

"Okay, wow." Marsha breaks the silence. "Girl, if you don't talk to him, I will."

Krista's cheeks blush.

"I'm serious, girl. You really need to talk to him. And I get that bad-boy vibe, but that smile was too handsome for him to be a total bad boy—plus, you said you saw him helping out at the festival setup. I get your vibe, but you'll never really know until you talk to him and get to know who he really is."

"You're right," Krista sighs. "I should give him a chance. But I just freeze up like that. He said 'hey,' and I couldn't even mutter a single word back."

"Well," Marsha reasons. "This is the first time you've had a crush on a boy. Granted, you're extremely late to the party. But still."

Krista sniggers.

"Look, just talk to him. You have the advantage that he at least knows you exist. Most girls with hardcore crushes aren't even that lucky. You owe it to yourself to explore the connection. At the very least, you get to network with someone, and I know how much you love networking!"

Krista rolls her eyes, but Marsha hit her in her weak spot. She does love networking.

"Fine . . ." Krista mumbles. "Next time I see him, I'll talk to him. But I'm not going to seek him out!"

"Yay!" Marsha shrieks as she jumps up and down, clapping her hands.

"Let's just get to yearbook," Krista says as she rolls her eyes again at her best friend. "We still have a lot of work to do before the Halloween issue of the newsletter comes out tomorrow."

The two make their way across the school when suddenly the sweeping melody of a dark, ethereal voice singing a long and unwavering pitch rings out in the now-quiet hallway.

Krista shuffles through her purse to find her phone.

"That's new," Marsha remarks.

"It kind of spoke to me after I saw that guy in the coffee shop," Krista mutters before glancing down at the caller ID. "Go on in, I'll be right there."

Marsha nods as Krista answers the phone. "Hello."

"Hi, is this Krista Atwood?"

"Yes, this is she."

"Good afternoon, Krista. This is Juliet from Town Hall. I'm calling in regard to your request for files on the car wreck of . . ." her voice trails off for a second before continuing, "a Michael Atwood."

"Yes!" Krista exclaims. "That's right."

"Right. Well, I can't seem to find the files related to the accident."

Krista's smile fades away. "Wait—like, there's no record of the car accident? Did it not happen in the town limits of Mirror Valley?"

"No. Actually, you see, I have the record of the car accident in question. If it took place in another city, we wouldn't even have that. But it seems that the records surrounding what happened *after* the wreck have disappeared."

"What?" Krista nearly shouts.

"Unfortunately, stuff like this happens sometimes. Clerical error, usually. Perhaps they were just filed under the wrong category. I will keep digging, but that could take some time. Just wanted to give you an update."

"Oh, o-okay, uh . . ." Krista stutters. Since Kevin's and her revelation about good karma, she thought that, with this phone call, the good news would continue, and she could finally get to the bottom of what happened to her dad. But now, she's not sure what to do next.

"I understand," she says into the phone, though she really doesn't. "Yes, please keep digging. Thank you. Let me know if I can do anything to help."

"Of course. You'll know as soon as I find anything. And you can bet I'll have something to say to the idiot who filed it wrong, too."

Krista chuckles. "I really appreciate it. Talk to you soon."

She sighs as she hangs up the phone and drops it back in her purse. Thoughts about what may have actually happened to the file crosses her mind. *What if the shadows hid the documents? What if it's all one big conspiracy to hide the truth? What if the town's officials were in on the cover-up?*

Her thoughts are interrupted when the newsroom door opens and Rick pops his head out. "You coming in?"

Krista shakes her head and forces a smile. "Yes, coming!"

Outside, Kevin and Bella sit silently at their usual spot under the big tree. School books litter the space around them as they work on their homework.

"I need a break," Bella announces, looking up from her papers.

"Okay," Kevin replies, more than happy to agree. "What did you have in mind?"

"Something to shift the focus from the left side of my brain to the right."

Kevin pulls out his sketchbook from his backpack in response.

"Oh! I know!" Bella interjects. "We should design our costumes for tomorrow. We can use your sketchbook to get all our thoughts and ideas out. We're still doing Morticia and Gomez Addams, right?"

"Yeah, I liked that idea."

"Great!" Bella perks up. "We can sketch out our ideas and try to think of all the things we already own that we can use in the costumes. That way we can go to the Halloween shop later today and work on our costumes tonight. Do you think your sister would mind stopping by the store on the way home?"

"Probably not," Kevin replies. "She may want to dress up, too—I don't know. But yeah, I'm sure she wouldn't mind stopping by there. As long as we keep it brief."

"Perfect! Well, that's where designing it now will come in handy—we'll be able to decide exactly what we'll need from the store so we can be in and out."

"Sounds good," Kevin responds with a smile as he grabs one of his pencils and gets started.

Meanwhile, at the edge of the forest, Klause stands ready to explore once again. His nerves keep him from walking in. After seeing the dark, winged figure yesterday, he's unsure if he even wants to continue his search for answers.

No, I need to figure this out, he reminds himself. *That figure was directly related to the voices I've been hearing. I need to know who or what it is and why they keep calling out to me.*

Taking a deep breath, he takes his first step into the unknown once again and makes his way through the trees, dodging low-hanging limbs and walking toward the center of the forest to find the large rock once again.

Krista stays in the newsroom a little later than usual, finalizing tomorrow's newsletter so she can send it to the printers tonight.

She feels the desk vibrate and glances down at her phone. A text from Kevin lights up her screen. *Is everything ok?*

Crap. Krista hurriedly glances over the newsletter one last time, hits submit, and shuts down her computer. She picks up her phone to reply. *Yeah, on my way out.*

She meets Kevin and Bella by her car. "Sorry about that," Krista apologizes. "I needed to make sure everything was ready for tomorrow's newsletter."

"No worries," Kevin responds. "Hey, do you think you can do Bella and me a favor?"

"Yeah, what's up?"

"Could you stop by the Halloween shop on our way home? Bella and I want to work on our costumes tonight, and we just need a couple of things from there."

"Yeah, of course. I should probably get a little something to wear, too," Krista muses. "I don't think I'll go all out like in previous years. I need to remain somewhat professional since I'm the editor in chief now and I'll be conducting interviews."

The three load the car and hop in.

"No Klause again today?" Kevin asks his sister.

"No, he messaged me earlier. Staying back to workout with Tyler again," Krista responds as she puts her car in drive and heads out of the school parking lot.

Back in the forest, Klause finds his way to the large boulder atop the small hill in the center of the woods. He paces around for what feels like an hour, trying to figure out its significance and both hoping and fretting that he'll see the dark figure again.

He stops his pacing and turns to face the rock. Just like yesterday, he reaches out his hand to touch it. But this time, he holds his hand there for a few moments, sliding it across the cold stone, feeling the rough texture scrape across his palm.

"Why are you so important?" he says under his breath as if he's talking to the object of his thoughts. He doesn't expect a response, so he's surprised when he gets one.

"Klause . . ." the deep voice whispers in his ear again.

A cool wind whips around him, and he turns to face the dark figure once again. Klause locks eyes with it, staring into the pitch-black orbs glaring down at him. The monstrous figure towers over him, its black wings resting on its back.

"The veil." The deep voice echoes around him as the figure points his long black finger at the rock behind Klause.

"W-what?" Klause stutters. His eyes are wide and his mouth open as he keeps staring at the creature.

The figure breathes loudly and turns to run—or fly—away. "Wait!" Klause shouts, grabbing the creature's arm and pulling him back. "Tell me what's going on. Now!"

The shadowy figure nods its head and takes a step back before speaking. "You are a powerful and magnificent being, young Klause."

"What?" Klause asks as he shakes his head, his eyes beginning to tear up.

"One day, you'll bring about a change that will ultimately better the world. You just have to have faith in us," the dark figure announces in its deep, entrancing voice.

Before Klause can respond, a gust of wind sweeps around them, and the figure disappears from view, leaving Klause wide-eyed with a pit in his stomach.

CHAPTER 36

I
T'S FRIDAY, HALLOWEEN DAY, AND THE
town bustles around the Atwood children as they each
prepare for the evening, each thinking about their own
thing.

Krista worries about the town's records of her father's car
wreck while trying to focus on the newly released school
newsletter about the Halloween Horror Night festival
happening tonight.

Klause ponders what happened last night and what the dark
figure said to him while struggling to decide if he should tell
his siblings about the event or not.

Kevin is the only one in his family excited about tonight,
but inside, his heart is racing. His matching "couples costume"
with Bella will be the first relationship-type thing they've ever

done, the first time they've done anything even resembling a date. He thinks he might throw up.

The three siblings impatiently wait for school to let out for the weekend so they can take their minds off everything and just have fun at the festival.

"So, what are you going to wear tonight?" Marsha asks her best friend as they walk toward the front doors of the school.

"Well, last night I went to the Halloween shop with Kevin and Bella and found a cool black costume corset, so I'm going to dress in a Victorian-style outfit and pair the corset with my maroon dress. I might pop in some small fangs and go as a vampire, or maybe I'll go with a masquerade vibe. I haven't quite decided yet."

"Oh, that sounds sexy—are you going to ask that guy to join you?" Marsha teases.

"I told you," Krista shoots back, rolling her eyes, "I'll talk to him when I see him, but I haven't seen him yet. I don't know when I will," Krista shrugs.

"Well, now's your chance," Marsha announces. "There he is by the bulletin board."

Krista freezes, and her heart begins to pump harder. "Fine," she snaps back, flipping her hair toward Marsha and taking a few steps. Then she quickly turns around and heads back to Marsha, wiping her sweaty palms on her jeans. "I can't," she panics.

"I'm going to take a page right out of your book," Marsha whispers as she puts her hand on Krista's shoulder. "Just breathe. In and out, in and out. Now turn around, march over there, and talk to him."

"But what do I say?" Krista says, her voice shaking.

"Say 'Hi,'" Marsha rolls her eyes as she grabs her friend's shoulders and turns her around, then shoves her toward the boy.

Krista glances back over her shoulder to see her friend staring at her with wide eyes, waving her forward. Turning around, she takes a deep breath and walks up to him.

"Hi." She cringes as her voice cracks.

The boy stops looking up at the bulletin board and turns around to face her. His deep blue eyes immediately seem to penetrate her soul as she stares at him, noticing his chiseled jawline and black horseshoe septum piercing now that she's close enough to see more of his features.

"Hey," the boy nods back as his lips curl up into a smug smile.

"Um . . ." Krista freezes, not sure what to say. "I'm Krista." *Wow, so original,* she thinks to herself before remembering to paste on a smile.

"Hi, I'm Chad. Chad Hellker."

"Oh, that's a unique name."

"Yeah, I guess." He chuckles. "My dad's side has an affinity to the devil."

Krista blinks hard, not knowing how to respond. *He worships the devil? Run away Krista, run away.*

"I'm kidding." Chad laughs when he sees the blank look on her face. "With a name like Hellker, I've gotten that comment a lot. So a few years ago I started coming up with random origin stories about my name just to freak people out."

"Oh!" Krista chuckles nervously. "Sorry, I don't get that comment with *my* last name."

"Well, what's your last name?" He tilts his head to one side.

"Atwood."

"So people don't ask you if you live in the forest?"

"Huh?"

"Oh, that's just what came to my mind." Chad shrugs. "You know, *At-wood*, like 'at the woods.' I don't know," he chuckles nervously as he rubs the back of his neck.

"Oh!" Krista laughs, finally getting the joke. "No, although I do live across the street from it, which is pretty cool." Then it hits her. "Wow. I never knew how fitting that was."

The two chuckle together, and Krista shifts her weight. She has no clue what to say next.

"Wait—Krista Atwood," Chad says, scratching his head. "I know that name." Reaching into his backpack, he pulls out a crumpled sheet of paper and straightens it out. "Did you write this?" he asks, pointing at the article about Halloween Horror Night in the school newsletter.

"Yeah!" Krista perks up, eager to start actually talking about *something*. "I'm the editor in chief of the yearbook."

"Yearbook?" Chad queries. "But this is a newsletter."

"Oh." Krista offers a half-smile. "Yeah, our news team and yearbook team are the same thing. We just call it yearbook because our small town school is so tiny that it focuses more on the yearbook than on the news of the town. After all, nothing usually happens here. But we go all out on the yearbook, so yeah. We just call it yearbook. But we publish the newsletter every week, too."

"Oh, okay! Gotcha." Chad nods. "I wouldn't call this cool festival thing nothing though."

"Well, since we're a small town, we tend to go all out for holidays." Krista grins. "So it's special this week. But normally we're fishing for stories."

"Nice," Chad comments, smirking. "Hey, is that what you were doing there a few days ago? Writing your article?"

"Uh, yeah, it is." Krista blinks at him. "I saw you helping out there. How did that happen? Usually just the adults of the town help set it up."

"Oh, yeah, well, my uncle and I just moved here, and he really wanted to get into the community, so he signed us up to help out."

So he is *new to town! I'm not crazy!* Krista thinks to herself. "Oh, okay! That's cool. Where did you move from?"

"Paris." He stands taller, smiling.

"Wait—like, Paris, France?" Krista asks. "*That* Paris?"

"Ha ha, yeah," he chuckles to himself.

"You've got to be kidding!"

"*Pas le moins du monde, mon amour,*" he says as he bows down and takes her hand to give it a kiss.

Krista's stomach flutters at the sound of his French. "Okay, I caught on to the fact that you just said 'my love,' but what was the other part?"

"'Not in the slightest,'" he responds and raises one side of his mouth in a crooked smile. Krista's heart leaps at the sight of it. "I wasn't kidding. We lived there for a few years, but I'm originally from California."

"Wow, that's awesome." Krista's eyes widen. "Why the move to France originally?"

Chad slumps his shoulders and looks down at the floor. "Uh, after my parents died, I had to move in with my last remaining family, my uncle who lived in Paris at the time. But after some drama over there, we both wanted to get back to the States and just start over, you know?"

"Oh, I'm so sorry to hear that." Krista frowns, her mind yelling at her. *Way to go, Krista. Only you could make this already awkward conversation come screeching to a halt.*

"It's okay," Chad smiles weakly at her, his eyes beginning to well up. "Starting over, remember?"

"Right!" Krista can tell she needs to move on. "Well, as Editor in Chief at Mirror Valley High School, and the one who knows this town inside and out, I would like to officially welcome you to Mirror Valley and propose that I show you what our little town has to offer."

Chad looks at her for a second before he blinks the tears away. Then he grins, showing off his straight white teeth. "That would be awesome."

"Great!" Krista replies, finally feeling almost like herself again, before the nerves made their embarrassing appearance. "Well, since you already know about Halloween Horror Night"—she points at the newsletter still in his hands—"you wanna go with me to that?"

"Yeah, that sounds like fun," he replies, and Krista swears he sounds excited.

"People usually dress up—as I said, our small town likes to go all out on holidays. But you don't have to. I know it's late notice."

"Are you dressing up?"

"Yeah." She nods her head.

"Then I'm sure I can scrounge something up." He smirks again, and Krista's breath catches. "Meet you there?"

"Yeah, sounds good," Krista says as she turns to leave the school. "Oh, wait." She twirls around. "Meet me at the candy corn stand. It's a classic every year, and that way we can find each other easier."

"You got it," he says, and Krista quickly whips back around to head back to a giggling Marsha, feeling like giggling herself.

≪○≫

On the other side of the school, Kevin packs up the remainder of his things from his locker and makes his way to the front to meet up with Bella and his siblings.

"Hey, Kevin," a woman's voice sounds behind him.

He turns around to witness Miss Lavers carefully jogging up to him, her high heels making clicking noises every time they land on the tile floor.

"Hi, Miss Lavers," Kevin says, frowning. "Is everything okay?"

"Oh, yeah, I just wanted to talk to you," she says calmly. "I just wanted to check in with you. I know you had been dealing with some stuff at the beginning of the school year, but lately, you seem to be happier. What changed?"

"Well a lot, actually," he smiles. "I met Bella, and we've been spending a lot of time together. She's really awesome, and we've been getting closer—which is definitely new to me—but it's still pretty cool. And—" He stops himself as he tries to figure out how he can talk about the good parts of his newfound power without actually talking about his power.

"That's so great," Miss Lavers says in her characteristically soft, melodic voice. "I've noticed that you two have been getting really close. Love is a powerful thing; I'm so happy for you."

"Oh." Kevin panics, eyes wide. "I wouldn't say it's love. At least not yet. We haven't even talked about if we're a couple or just friends."

"Of course." Miss Lavers nods. "My apologies if I made you feel uncomfortable. In general, though, my statement remains true. Love is a very powerful and special thing. And I'm fully confident that when it comes down to it, you would choose love over anything else." She smiles. "And what else were you going to say?"

Kevin smiles as his teacher's words spark an idea about how to tell her the other part of his good news. "I was just going to say that, um, I found out that something about me that I feared would only hurt others is actually capable of doing good. That made me really relieved."

"Oh, really?" she asks.

"Yeah, sorry—that probably didn't make much sense, but I don't really know how else to describe it."

"Oh, don't worry about it," she says as she waves her hand in front of her. "In the end, it's not about me; it's about you. And I'm happy that you've figured some things out and realized the goodness and love within you. And that you're happy now, too."

"Thanks," Kevin smiles. "I have to go. Bella and my siblings will be waiting for me. We're all going to the festival together."

"No problem," Miss Lavers responds kindly. "Maybe I'll see you there. It's my first Halloween Horror Night, so I'm eager to experience this town's tradition."

"You'll love it," Kevin replies with a grin. "And yeah, maybe! If we do, I'll show you around the highlights of the festival."

"Sounds wonderful."

Kevin smiles at his favorite teacher once more before adjusting his backpack on his shoulder and turning to head out to the school courtyard.

After a quick and easy pasta dinner, the Atwood siblings, along with Bella, hurry to get ready for Halloween Horror Night.

"Hey, Kevin? Can you help me with my corset?" Krista calls out to her little brother as she runs down the stairs.

Kevin and Bella are already standing by the door. Kevin is dressed in a black tuxedo, wears a fake mustache on his upper lip, and has his hair slicked back.

Bella looks perfectly in place next to him. Her long-sleeved, floor-length dress hugs her slender body, and her straight black hair frames the excessive makeup covering her face. The makeup makes her skin look ghostly and pale, with the exception of the pop of red lipstick on her lips.

"Of course," he replies before looking at the back of the corset, his forehead creasing.

"Here, let me do it." Bella nudges him over and begins to tie up the back. "Let me know if it's too tight."

"That's good," Krista says as she flips her hair to flow down her back. "I can breathe so that's all I wanted," she says half to herself and half to Bella. She turns to face them, then gasps. "Aw! Don't you two look cute."

Kevin and Bella blush, their rosy cheeks peeking through their deathly makeup.

"Klause! Are you almost ready?" Krista shouts up the stairs, where Klause is finishing up with his costume.

"Coming!" he calls back as he quickly grabs his cowboy hat and trots down the stairs.

"Really?" Krista looks him up and down. He's wearing brown cowboy boots and blue jeans, a red bandana around his neck, and only a brown suede vest around his shirtless torso, showing off his abs and toned arms. "You had to dress sexy?"

"Ew," Klause makes a face at her. "Don't ever say 'sexy' to your little brother again."

Krista rolls her eyes at him, and he just smirks back.

"Well," Klause remarks as he puts his cowboy hat on for the finishing touch. "Let's getter goin' y'all," he tries to say with a forced country accent.

Krista rolls her eyes again before grabbing her black leather clutch and opening the door to usher her family out to the car.

CHAPTER 37

U PON ARRIVING AT THE HALLOWEEN Horror Night festival, the four exit the car, nod to each other, and go their separate ways.

After putting on her black, lace, masquerade-style mask, Krista's mind becomes focused fully on Chad as she wanders through the festival grounds, looking for the candy corn booth. Kids of all ages rush around her, laughing and screaming as hired actors pop out from hiding places and scare them. She barely notices the attractions around her and the scent of carnival food wafting through the air; her eyes are searching intently for the boy her heart is aching to see.

Through the crowded festival, she catches sight of the booth, its huge triangular sign hard to miss over the tops of everyone's heads. She smiles as her heart begins to race, and she wipes her sweating palms on her cotton dress despite the fact that she's a little chilly in the brisk fall air. Approaching the stand, her smile fades as she only sees excited kids jumping up and down next to their parents. She walks to the end of the line and sighs. *Maybe he'll be here later on*, she tries to reassure herself.

After about ten minutes, her hope to see him begins to fade. *Who was I kidding? A handsome guy like him was probably asked out by a dozen other girls at school.*

As she stands there, beginning to sway to the faint sound of music coming from the stage, she hears a deep voice whisper in her ear. "'It seems she hangs upon the cheek of night . . . beauty too rich for use, for earth too dear.'"

Krista's heart flutters at the romantic quote, knowing full well where it came from—it's from one of her favorite Shakespeare plays. While still looking straight ahead, she whispers back the best response she can think of. "'What man art thou that, thus bescreened in night, so stumblest on my counsel?'"

Krista turns to face a young man, half of his face covered with a white mask, and a black cape draped over his maroon vest and black tuxedo. He smiles at her, and, through his mask, she looks into his blue eyes. In this darkness, they seem happier and warmer than she's experienced so far.

"I swear I didn't plan this," he comments, breaking the air of mystery. "But we're practically matching."

"No kidding," Krista chuckles as she traces her fingers across his chest, pointing to the maroon vest. "It's like we planned on treating tonight like a masquerade ball. Though, with music this subtle, we're a far cry from a ball."

"We can make our own ball," he responds slyly and takes Krista's hand in his, twirling her around in a fanciful dance.

Krista giggles, allowing her white teeth to make an appearance. "We can dance later, but right now I need to show you around."

"Sounds like a plan," he says enthusiastically as he reaches down for her hand once again and slips his fingers between hers. "You're cold."

"I don't have as many layers as you," she remarks.

"You tease now, but just wait for fancy summer events when you get to wear a light, sleeveless dress, and I'll have to wear a three-piece suit. Then *I'll* be the jealous one."

"True," Krista sighs, her heart skipping a beat at the prospect of him thinking they'll still be together in the summer. Then she lets out a laugh. "On that note, let's go," she says as she pulls her hand from his grasp and leads him forward into the festival. *It's our first time hanging out—I'm not letting him hold my hand quite yet. Although, I will say, his Romeo and Juliet quote was quite impressive.*

The pair make their way through the festival, and Krista points out some of the more traditional attractions like the carnival games, food stands, costume runway show, and live band.

"Oh, let's go to the haunted house," Krista announces. "It's always a coin toss. Sometimes it's epic, but sometimes it's really cheesy."

Chad just nods, so they make their way to the haunted house, but the smell of coffee stops Krista in her tracks.

"Oh my gosh, coffee!" she shouts. "I need!" she says and jogs over to the coffee stand, Chad trailing behind her.

"Krista!" cries out a girl on the other side of the stand.

"Sheri!"

The two shriek, and Sheri comes around the booth and hugs Krista.

"You look gorgeous," Sheri says as she looks Krista up and down.

"Thanks!" Krista chuckles as she blushes, then she looks at Sheri's costume. "Love the zebra onesie. And whoa! That hair!" she exclaims after she sees that Sheri replaced her characteristic bun with a giant mohawk of her own hair, teased straight up.

Sheri laughs, then she rubs her hands together. "Well, it's cool out here, and I can't move around much. I'm working the coffee stand this year, and it's been crazy. The adults are loving the hot decaf coffee so they can still go to sleep tonight, and the youth are loving the iced caffeinated drinks so they can stay up all night." Then Sheri notices the strapping young man standing next to Krista. "And who's this?"

"Sheri, this is Chad," Krista introduces them.

"Oh, you're the blue-eyed bad boy from the coffee shop!" Sheri recalls as Chad chuckles. "You know, you really made Krista—"

Krista coughs, and Sheri moves on.

"Two hot, black coffees, no cream, no sugar," Sheri says as she points to the pair in front of her. "Right?"

"Definitely!" Krista says. "You know me so well."

"How could I not?" Sheri smiles and subtly winks at her. "Okay, I'll grab those for you and let you skip the line."

"She seems cool," Chad whispers to his date as Sheri pours the coffee for them.

"Yeah," Krista smiles, still gazing at Sheri. "She's really sweet."

"Are you two . . . ?" Chad trails off as he points his finger back and forth between them. "You know . . ." he says before making a small gesture with his hips.

Krista squints her eyes at him before it hits her. Her eyes widen. "Oh! No!" she exclaims. "She's just a friend. She's studying journalism like I want to, and we have a lot in common."

"Ah, sorry," Chad tries to apologize. "I just saw the way you looked at each other and wondered if you'd rather be here with her than with me."

"Nonsense," Krista looks up into his eyes and grazes his bicep with her fingertips. "I wanna be here with you."

Sheri returns from behind the stand, coffee in hand. She hands the first cup to Krista then extends the second cup to Chad. As he reaches for it, their hands briefly touch. The two of them gasp, and Sheri drops the coffee, letting it spill at their feet.

"Oh my gosh!" Krista shouts. "Is everything okay?"

The two stare at each other for a moment before laughing. "Yeah, that was weird. Static electricity shocked us or something," Sheri theorizes. "I'm so sorry, let me grab you another."

"Don't worry about it," Chad interjects. "Besides, it was my fault. I thought I had fully grabbed it."

"Are you sure?"

"Yeah, it's cool." Chad waves his hand. "I'm good."

Sheri smiles and says farewell to the two of them, and the pair departs to make their way to the haunted house.

Somewhere else on the festival grounds stands Klause, throwing some balls at the bottle game, trying to knock them off, and, of course, succeeding, thanks to his football training.

"Wow, you're good at that," says a girl's voice off to his side.

Klause turns and comes face-to-face with his costume counterpart. She's dressed as a cowgirl, but something about her outfit makes it almost seem natural for her. Wavy red hair cascades down her head, bringing Klause's eyes to her bright green ones and slightly freckled face. His gaze gravitates toward her cleavage, but he tries not to stay there long. He instead lets his eyes wander down to her bare midriff, her tight blue jeans hugging her hips and muscular thighs. Klause gapes at the beautiful girl in front of him for a moment but shakes it off and turns on his charm.

"Thank you." He grins widely. "Hey, you look familiar."

"I'm Bailey," the girl says in a southern twang that sounds natural, especially compared to Klause's forced attempt back at the house. "I go to Mirror Valley High. I'm a cheerleader there—"

"Impossible," Klause interrupts. "I know all the cheerleaders."

"Well, if you were to let me finish," she scoffs, "I just became a cheerleader. My dad is in the Army, and we travel around a lot, so we just moved here. Well, we actually moved here during the summer, but I wanted to adjust to the new school before I got involved in any clubs or sports. So you may have seen me around school."

"And the country accent is part of your costume?"

"Genuine," Bailey shrugs. "I grew up in Texas before we started moving around a lot."

"Nice!" Klause exclaims. "You're lucky. I've never been outside of Mirror Valley, but that's the dream."

"It's not as glamorous as it seems." Bailey sighs. "Yeah, you get to see a ton of cool places, but you lose all your connections every time you leave a place. Then you have to start all over again and again."

"Have you made any new connections here?"

"A few." Bailey shrugs. "But I just met this one guy who seems really cool. His abs are great, but his attitude is still a little questionable."

"Oh, really?" Klause smirks. "And how do you feel about him?"

"I don't know," she replies. "Too soon to tell." She places her hands in her back pockets. "Especially since I don't even know his name yet."

Klause shifts his weight before replying. "I think I know who you're talking about. His name is Klause. He's the star player on the football team. And while he may seem like an arrogant prick on the outside, on the inside he has a heart of gold and a lot of respect for others, especially the beautiful ones."

"Is that so?" One corner of her mouth turns up. "I'd love to get to know him then. Do you think he'd like to escort me around the festival and be a strong man I can bury my face in when I get scared?"

"He definitely wouldn't object," he says, extending his open palm between them.

Bailey stares at his hand for just a second before placing her hand in his, and the two walk together into the heart of the festival.

"Thanks for winning this teddy bear for me!" Bella exclaims.

"Absolutely!" Kevin smiles. "It only took ten tries," he says under his breath.

But she hears him. "Eight," she corrects, chuckling to herself and swaying back and forth, hugging her new enormous stuffed bear. "Which is half the amount it would have taken for me."

The two laugh together as they continue to make their way through the festival.

"Is that Miss Lavers?" Bella asks, nodding toward a young woman in the distance in a sparkling blue dress with a tiara atop her head.

"I think so," Kevin agrees as he squints in that direction. "Miss Lavers!" he calls out, waving.

Turning away from the cotton candy stand, Miss Lavers faces the pair, and a smile lights up her face. "Hey, guys!" she says. "Don't you two look cute. Let me guess—Morticia and Gomez Addams?"

"Yes, ma'am!" Kevin and Bella say in unison before looking at each other and bursting into laughter at the same time. A genuine smile spreads on Miss Lavers' face.

"And you're . . ." Bella starts after their laughter dies down, scratching her chin. "Cinderella?"

"Yep." Miss Lavers laughs. "Though I had to settle for plastic shoes because no one makes actual glass slippers."

"Well, if they did, I feel like a lot of girls would be walking around with their feet all cut up from breaking them," Bella offers.

"You're probably right," Miss Lavers stage-whispers to her, then addresses them both. "What have you two been up to?"

"Well, we went through the haunted house, rode a couple of rides, and have just been looking around at all the unique booths," Kevin offers.

"And he won me this teddy bear at the balloon-popping game!" Bella interjects, holding out her prize for Miss Lavers to see.

"I see that." Miss Lavers nods her head. "Well, I was about to do the haunted maze. It looks really cool. Do you two want to join me?"

"You read our minds!" Kevin says with a grin. "We were just about to go there ourselves."

Klause and Bailey get off the spinning teacup ride and lean on each other for support as they stumble through the grounds, heads swimming.

Klause laughs at their antics and stands up straight to collect himself then stares into Bailey's eyes, admiring their beauty. She stares right back.

Then he hears a whisper coming from behind Bailey. "Klause . . ."

Klause's heart begins to race as he recognizes the now-familiar voice. Looking over Bailey's shoulder, he sees the dark, sinister figure from yesterday, peeking its head around a scarecrow. Klause holds his breath as he thinks about what it could mean. *Can other people see it? What does it want?*

The figure gestures for Klause to follow, turns around, then glides toward the entrance to the maze, followed by two other dark shadows.

"Um," Klause says, looking around. "Hey, I'll be right back," he says calmly to Bailey. "I need to go to the bathroom. Wait for me by the haunted house?"

"Yeah, sure." Bailey nods her head, smiling at Klause before walking away.

Once he's sure she's not looking back, Klause takes a deep breath and follows the three figures into the maze.

Exiting the haunted house, Krista and Chad laugh about how lame it was.

"That one guy who jumped out to scare us and tripped over his own costume had me in tears," Krista laughed.

"Ha ha, yeah," Chad agrees. "And that hallway where they just grabbed at our ankles was hilarious, too. I thought for sure I would trip and fall into you."

"Thank goodness you di—" The sound of her phone ringing cuts her off.

Chad turns to her as she hurries to silence it. "Hm," he says, rubbing his chin as he listens to the ethereal sound of the familiar song's long and haunting melody. "Don't you have to be a little dark to enjoy that?"

"I think we all have a little darkness in us, don't you?" Krista smirks.

"Definitely." Chad smirks back. "You just have to decide whether to embrace the darkness or not."

"Do you embrace it?"

"I try not to." He shrugs. "But sometimes it slips through."

"I think we're more alike than I originally thought," Krista says as she gazes up at her date's deep blue eyes. She takes a deep breath. "So what—" Krista cuts off again, freezing at the sight in the distance. Three shadow-like figures glide through the crowd unnoticed, heading into the maze.

Krista gasps as she recognizes the strange, shadowy figures she saw outside her house a few weeks ago.

"Um," she starts, trying to think of an excuse to leave Chad and go investigate. "Hey, I almost forgot that I need to do some reporting for the yearbook and talk to the festival coordinator. I just saw her go into the maze so I'm going to go catch up to her. Do you mind waiting here? I won't be long."

"No problem." Chad shrugs. "I'm a little hungry anyway. Meet at the picnic tables by the main stage?"

"Yeah, sounds great," she whispers back as she affectionately grazes her hand across the side of his face. "See you again soon," she says before running toward the maze to chase down the shadows.

Once inside, Krista scours the maze, trying to find the shadowed figures. She wanders through aimlessly, her adrenaline pumping harder and her speed increasing with every step. *They have to be here somewhere,* she muses. *Right?*

Meanwhile, at the heart of the maze, Klause has already found them. The three figures tower over him and slowly materialize into their true forms.

One of them looks like a humanoid dragon with black scales across his skin and wings.

Another materializes into what seems like a rock formation, his skin a charcoal gray like molten rock, and his head adorned with rocky spikes forming a crown. He smiles and his jagged gray teeth appear to be like sharpened stones.

And lastly, the third shadow materializes to reveal an emaciated, bony figure with dead, white skin and black scars across her body. She cackles maniacally at the sight of Klause and rubs her talon-like hands together.

All three figures have one thing in common—solid-black eyes in their sockets.

Klause gasps at the sight of them, and he feels like his heart has stopped. He catches his breath before staring up at the figures and addressing them in a shaky voice. "What do you want?"

The one in the middle, the one he recognizes from yesterday, speaks first. "We need your help, O Great and Powerful One," he says with a deep voice that seems to echo around them. He reaches his solid-black hand out to Klause.

Klause stares back into his eyes but has to look away when a shiver creeps up his spine. "What do you need?" he asks as he reaches out to grab the hand of the creature before him.

At their sudden touch, black tendrils snake from the dark figure and turn the veins in Klause's arm black. In an instant, the image of the girl he saw in the woods flashes through his mind as he recalls the feeling of gripping her neck and the sight of his arm ejecting black tendrils from it. He gasps and pulls away from the creature's grasp.

"I can't," he mutters, pushing past the three figures and running away.

"Wait!" the witch-like one shrieks, and the three figures begin to chase him. Klause speeds up.

≪O≫

Klause turns a corner and runs straight into Krista, knocking both her and himself to the ground. They make eye contact, and Krista sees the sheer terror in his eyes before he gets up and yells at her to run.

Krista gets up but freezes in her tracks as her eyes widen. Heading straight toward her are three monstrous figures, their eyes solid black. With a fierce glare in her eyes, she pushes aside all fear and stands her ground to defend herself and save her brother.

When the three figures come within reaching distance, almost instinctively Krista's eyes change into the contrasting colors of white and black. She screams as a burst of light shoots from her hands, powerfully driving the creatures away from her.

The three figures fall to the ground, and Krista's tear-soaked eyes make contact with Kevin's. He, along with Bella and Miss Lavers, stand across from her, staring with eyes wide after watching Krista ward off the demonic creatures.

Bella screams, and Kevin stands frozen as the monsters get up and rush toward them. Miss Lavers acts quickly and pushes the pair away and into the side of a hay bale wall.

The figures rush toward her, and Krista jumps into action again, pouncing onto one of the figure's backs and digging her nails into the creature's eyes. Light emerges from her hands again, black, snake-like beams permeating through it. The emaciated one screams as the light blinds her, and she dematerializes into thin air, the other two following suit immediately after.

Krista pants heavily and falls to her hands and knees. Klause shakily stands up as he comes out of the ball he made himself into behind her. Kevin and Bella stumble to their feet, rubbing their heads after being pushed into the maze wall.

"Is everyone o-okay?" Kevin stutters before being answered by Bella's terrified scream.

The three siblings turn to follow Bella's gaze.

Splayed out on the ground, Miss Lavers' body lies still, her eyes open and glossed over in a deathly stare, and her skin pale—as if the life was sucked right out of her.

CHAPTER 38

SPARSE SNOWFLAKES DRIFT TO THE ground and come to a halt on the yard already blanketed in white. The cold winter breeze whips through the air, shaking the limbs of the trees. Krista watches from her window, gazing into the darkness and the unknown that the forest by her house has come to represent.

Tears well up in her eyes as she recalls Halloween night. Though it was almost two months ago now, she still doesn't know what to think.

After the incident, Klause told her and Kevin about the shadow in the woods and what it said to him. She shivers as she remembers the creature's face and his solid black eyes staring back at her.

It's winter break, and school is out. But rather than feeling relief and relaxation, she's more burdened than ever before as the weight of everything that's happened this past semester bears down on her shoulders.

Her trance breaks at the sound of a knock on her door.

"Hey," Kevin whispers as he peeks his head into her room.
"Hey."

Kevin sees the pain on her face so he opens the door fully and steps forward to hug his sister.

The two hold their embrace for a moment, leaning on each other.

"Thinking about Halloween again?" Kevin inquires.

Krista slowly nods her head, her eyes sad. "It's been almost two months, and it's still so hard. It's hard thinking about what I did and what I am. It's hard thinking about those creatures that attacked us. It's hard keeping up with this horrible lie and keeping this dark secret from everyone around us, including my best friend and my boyfriend. You're so lucky. You have Bella, who was thrust into this craziness with us, but I have no one."

Kevin shakes his head. "Don't say that. You have me. You have Klause—"

"Klause," she interrupts in a harsh tone. "If he had just told us what was happening from the start, maybe all of this wouldn't be happening. Maybe . . ." she chokes up. "Maybe Miss Lavers would still be alive."

"You can't say that for sure," Kevin offers. "Hey, look on the bright side. We're finally going to see Mom again after who knows how long."

"You're right." She nods her head. "I've missed her so much." Krista sniffles, then she cries out. "Oh, gosh! We're going to have to lie to her! If our damn phone calls to her had connected back in November—instead of just our texts—and she had come home, maybe we could have told her the truth. But now we're caught up in this web of lies surrounding the night and everything else that's been going on. How can we tell her now?"

Kevin sighs then looks to the side to see Klause stepping into the room.

"As much as it pains me to see you like this—and as much as I want to tell my girlfriend, too—we can't say anything," Klause says solemnly. "If we were to tell the truth about even just one of the crazy things that has happened around us, we'd either get institutionalized or all the blame would fall on us."

"Klause is right," Kevin agrees. "We can't say anything. At least not until we have this all figured out. I mean, we just figured out that we possess the power of karma, but now we know that there's way more to it. Like what those creatures were and what they wanted. And then, of course"—he looks over at Krista—"we can't forget about that black and white light that streamed from your hands."

"Plus, there's the death of Miss Lavers," Klause interjects. "The authorities don't know how she died. There were no physical wounds on her. It was like the life was drained out of her body."

Kevin whimpers at the memory of his favorite teacher lying dead in front of him.

"As much as I hate to admit it, you're right." Krista stands up, wiping the tears from her cheeks with her purple knit sweater. "Even if we were to tell a partial truth of what happened to Miss Lavers, we still wouldn't even be able to say how she died without mentioning the creatures. There's no logical explanation for how it happened. We're lucky that Bella went along with our lie about coming across her body instead of witnessing her death."

Kevin nods his head. "Yeah, she's pretty special."

"I'm so sorry I didn't tell you guys," Klause says as he stares at the ground. "I didn't know how to tell you, what to say. I was scared. I was deceitful. I was a coward. And I'm so, so sorry."

"It's okay." Krista sighs. "We can't change the past. All we can do now is hold on to the hope that we'll figure this all out before anyone else gets hurt."

Skidding on the icy road, Karmasha slows her pace as she heads home. She's eager to finally see her kids after being gone for the last three months. The Council has kept her so busy that she hasn't had time to return home and see them. She sighs. She hasn't heard their voices in almost a quarter of a year, having to rely on text because they just kept missing each other's calls.

While still keeping her eyes on the road, she sees a white mist materialize in the seat next to her out of the corner of her eye.

"Go away, Abraxos," she says sternly.

"But we need you to investigate something in the next state over," he tries to reason.

"I'll do it later." She sighs. "I miss my children too much to go another day without seeing them."

"But you're neglecting your duties as Karma," he argues.

"Screw the duties for one day!" she snaps back.

Abraxos gasps.

"Oh, relax," Karmasha shoots back, rolling her eyes. "I'll check in with the Council tonight. I just want to have a quiet dinner with my family without having all of your voices swirling in my head. So spread the word to back off tonight. If I sense any of the spirits' presence, even in the slightest, I'll unleash a world of hurt on all of you."

"You wouldn't dare," Abraxos growls.

"Try me," she whispers fiercely to him. "Now go."

"Fine. I'll spread the word, but you'd better check in with us tonight."

"I will." She frowns. "Now leave me alone!"

Abraxos sighs once more before dematerializing into the air.

≪○≫

Abraxos materializes in the In Between and joins the brothers and sisters present, both the light and the dark combined.

"We have a problem."

"Maybe *you* do," Lillith cackles before being quickly silenced by her older brother, Bernael.

"What do you mean?" Bernael's voice echoes.

"Look, I know we each have our own agendas for the children, and may the best side win there. But I think we can all agree that no matter what our respective side's mission is, we don't want Karma to know that her children have received the power of karma, too. That's why we've been collectively keeping her from them, isn't it?"

"Wait," Bernael interjects. "Backtrack—how do you know that we know?"

"One of yours killed the human body of one of mine!" Abraxos snaps. "That's how!"

"I knew it!" Lillith shrieks, pointing a finger at Dina.

"Oh, shut up!" they all say in unison to their youngest sister, who hisses in response.

"You have our attention," Lahash speaks up.

"Well, despite my best efforts, Karma is on her way home to see them."

"What?" they all shout at once.

"I'll keep an eye on her and run interference if I see that they're about to say something to her," Lahash announces. "Though I think, based on what we've all observed of the children, they seem to want to keep their secret from their loved ones."

"No," Abraxos interrupts. "She said that if she senses any of us near them tonight, she'll unleash her powers on us."

"She wouldn't dare," Bernael growls.

"My words exactly." Abraxos shrugs. "But she wants a quiet dinner with them and will do anything to have it. She did say, though, that she'll check in with us tonight when she goes to bed. So we just have to hope that the children keep their secret from her until then."

Back at the house, Krista, Klause, and Kevin get a text from their mom saying she's almost there, so they hurry to finish cleaning up the house.

"Hey, Kevin, can you help me with this 'Welcome Home' sign?" Krista asks her little brother, holding a long piece of plastic between them.

"Sure," he nods, grabbing one end and taping it to the pillar beside the staircase.

"Thanks," she says when they finish, smiling. "I'm going to go ahead and start cooking the garlic bread and boiling the water. That way it'll be almost ready when she gets here."

Krista gets to work on dinner while Klause puts the cleaning supplies away. Kevin does a walk-through, making sure the house looks perfect for their mother's arrival.

All three of them stop what they're doing when they see a light pass by the window overlooking their front yard. The three rush to the window and peek through the falling snow to see if it's her. Sure enough, they see their mother's car pull into the driveway. Krista rushes to the door and opens it, the cold winter air immediately stinging her face, but she doesn't care.

"Mom!" she calls out as her mother is running to the front door, duffle bag in hand.

"Krista!" she exclaims, dropping her duffle inside and shutting the door behind her before she wraps her arms around her only daughter. "Oh, I missed you so much!"

"I missed you, too!"

"Klause! Kevin!" Karmasha calls out before making her rounds, pulling Klause in for a long embrace first. "Ugh, it's only been three months, but it feels like it's been years. I'm so happy to see you all and be with you again." She releases Klause and reaches for her youngest child.

"How long will you be here for?" Kevin asks, his arms squeezing her tight.

"I don't know." Karmasha sighs as she pulls away to look at all of them. "Work has been crazy. They keep sending me around every which way. I'm actually supposed to be on an assignment right now, but I told my company that I absolutely had to see my family. It's been way too long."

"Aw." Kevin sighs. "Well, stay as long as you can. We missed you being here."

"Kevin, I will do everything in my power to do just that," Karmasha assures him. "But let's not talk about work tonight." She takes a deep breath. "Mmm, something smells good."

"I'm making us pasta and garlic bread," Krista announces as she heads to the kitchen and starts to plate the food. "Go ahead and take a seat at the table. I'll bring it all out to everyone."

When she arrives with the food, her family is seated at the table, Karmasha at the head of it.

"So," Karmasha starts as the kids dig in, "update me. Tell me about the last three months. How was the semester? How was football, Klause? How's Editor in Chief going, Krista? How's the high school adjustment been, Kevin? Are there any new people in your lives you want me to know about? Oh! Tell me about your special someones. You each are seeing someone, right?"

The three children exchange smiles, relieved that they can actually answer all of her questions without flat-out lying about anything—maybe just hiding the whole truth here and there.

Krista starts, telling her about Chad Hellker and how, though she originally saw him as a bad boy, he's actually very intelligent and likes the same literature and music as her.

Klause tells her about Bailey Jones and how they've become one of Mirror Valley High's all-star couples. He talks about their mutual interest in sports and traveling and brags about how awesome her country accent is.

Then it's Kevin's turn, and he talks about Bella and how they made it official the day after Halloween after realizing that they completely trusted and needed each other.

The family laughs together, telling each other funny stories about the semester, and Karmasha telling them funny stories about her clients.

≪○≫

"So, Christmas is coming up." Karmasha changes the subject. "I told my company that I *have* to be home for Christmas, so, whether they like it or not, I'll be here. What do you all want for Christmas?"

"Ooo! A new tab—" Klause feels a kick to his shins under the table. He glares at Krista, knowing immediately who it was.

"Klause." Krista admonishes. "Mom, just having you home for Christmas would be enough of a gift."

Their mother smiles, blushing. "That's so sweet, but I'm getting you all someth—"

She's interrupted by the sound of a revving engine outside and a disruptive pattering hitting the front of the house. The four stand up and make their way to the window to see what's going on and spy three boys throwing snowballs at the house.

Klause growls. "They won't be laughing when I'm through with them," he says as he reaches for his coat.

"Klause, don't worry about it." His mother stops him with a hand on his arm. "They'll move on. It's just a few young pranksters."

"But they're disrupting our nice dinner," he whines, staring out the window at them, his temper starting to flare, his breath coming more quickly.

"It's okay." Karmasha shrugs. "They'll go away eventually."

As the heat builds inside him, Klause barely hears his sister's warning. "Klause," she whispers. He ignores her.

At once he feels his eyes change colors, one eye white and the other black. Seconds later, the three boys slip and fall on the icy ground, one falling hard on his arm, another twisting his ankle, and the third face-planting in the street.

His eyes already back to normal, Klause lets out a small smile and turns to face the dining room to see his mother staring back at him. Her eyes are wide, and her jaw is dropped. She stands there speechless, gaping at her son.

Then, as if gasping for air, she whispers under her breath. "You have the power of karma."

CHAPTER 39

"WHAT . . ." KRISTA WHISPERS AT HER mother's words, her voice strangled. The entire room stands frozen.

"What . . ." Krista whispers again, a little louder this time.

"What did you say?" Klause whispers to his mother.

"You have the power of karma," she says again, just as breathy as before.

"What?" Krista asks, her voice almost at a normal speaking level.

"How do you know about that?" Klause inquires.

"Your eyes changed colors, just like mine do," Karmasha mutters. "One eye white and the other black."

"What?" Krista says again, voice getting louder still, nearly yelling.

"Wait, like you?" Kevin interjects.

"How is this possible?" Karmasha asks, still staring blankly at Klause.

"What?!" Krista cries out at the top of her lungs.

"Krista!" the three shout at her in unison.

She takes a deep breath, followed by Klause, then Kevin, then lastly, Karmasha. They slowly inch their way back to the table and sit down, trying to calm themselves as best they can. After a long silence, Karmasha finally speaks up, tears welling in her eyes and trying to escape.

"My given name is Karmasha, but my name, by birthright, is Karma. I possess the power of issuing out good and bad karma to deserving parties and keeping the balance between good and evil. I inherited the power and responsibility from my mother when she died. And she inherited it from her father when he died, and he from his father when he died, and so on since the beginning of time. But I'm confused. You weren't supposed to possess the power until I died. So how can you have it now?"

"We don't know," Klause whimpers.

"We?" Karmasha says intently.

"Yeah," Kevin speaks up. "We all have the power."

"What?" she whispers. "That's impossible."

"Speaking of impossible," Krista finally chimes in. "Mom, what is this power, and why do we have it?"

"Karma has been around since the beginning of time, but the truth behind what, or rather who it is has been muddled over the years," Karmasha explains. "My mother used to tell me stories about its origins. The Fair King ruled over a kingdom named Ekthesia. He was called the Fair King because he ruled with a just hand. He possessed the power to give good fortune to those who did good and bad fortune to those who did evil.

"Eventually, he got tired of the power and gave it to his twelve brothers and sisters, which went well for a few thousand years, but then they became corrupted by the power. Six of them wanted to only give good fortune while the other six only wanted to give out bad fortune, no matter what you did. The kingdom fell into war and so the Fair King stripped the power from his younger siblings and bestowed it instead on his only daughter, Princess Karma. He made her mortal, which was fairly easy as her mother was human, too. Princess Karma had half the blood of a human and half the blood of a spirit. She became mortal, and, when she died, that same bloodline passed down to every Karma after her."

"Princess Karma became human?" Kevin interjects. "That's why she had to leave her home in Ekthesia."

"You speak as if you knew her," Karmasha chuckles.

"She visited me in a dream," Kevin replies.

"You've met her?" Karmasha chokes up. "That's so amazing. I've never met Princess Karma. I've only seen glimpses of her in flashbacks of the past lives of Karma," she says, looking down at her necklace. "This stone belonged to her and has been passed down from generation to generation. It possesses no power, other than allowing the current Karma to call upon the wisdom of every previous Karma before him or her, including Princess Karma herself."

"That's amazing," Klause responds.

Karmasha frowns, and tears stream down her face. "I was going to tell you about all of this one day." She sighs. "But I kept pushing it off because I hoped that it would be many years before I died and left you with the powers. And I didn't want to burden you all with it until you were adults." She smiles sadly. "I also had a smidge of hope that none of you would possess it and it would end with me. Traditionally, the bloodline has only passed to a single person at a time because each Karma before me has each only had one child. But when I had three, I hoped that it was because the power would end with me and not be passed down to any of you. Clearly, I was wrong, and you all possessed it early instead. How long have you all known?"

"We only just settled on the idea of it being karma about two months ago," Kevin replies. "But things have been happening since the beginning of the school year."

"What kinds of things?" Karmasha asks. "Start from the beginning."

Krista starts first, telling her about the bully at school whose head cracked open. Then Kevin explains the guy in the parking lot with his girlfriend. Krista brings up the homecoming dance—and Klause interjects that the dance is when they first noticed their eyes changing. Then he talks about his own incidents, how none of them ended in death, keeping the girl in the forest to himself. Kevin talks about how they discovered that they could pass out good karma, too, and the siblings share their karmic dreams with their mother.

Then Klause brings up the shadows, how they keep trying to lure him into the forest, about the incident in the maze, how they killed Miss Lavers. Krista mentions the light that shot from her hands, the white light with black tendrils that she used to ward off the creatures.

At that, Karmasha gasps. "Pandora."

"Pandora?" Krista inquires.

"It's a battle-slash-protection power that all Karmas possess. It emits both good and bad karma out into a concentrated stream of light and releases it all into the world. Did you feel weak after it?"

"Yeah." Krista nods her head.

"That's because all of that power comes from inside of you. It was meant as a line of defense to protect yourself in dire threats. But because all of that power is being released through you, it takes up a lot of your karmic energy, which can make you very weak if it's used too much."

"Wow," Krista remarks.

"Wow, indeed," Karmasha says. "Luckily, you don't have to release so much karmic energy from yourself all the time. You don't even have to use it in day-to-day life for the most part, unless you're doing investigations. The Council takes care of all the little things."

"The Council? Investigations?" Kevin queries.

"Ah, yes, the Council is made up of the twelve brothers and sisters that previously possessed the power before it was bestowed on Princess Karma. Because of their years of experience, the Fair King didn't want to totally exile them. So he made them into the Council of Twelve. The six good spirits were to give out good karma to deserving individuals, while the six evil spirits were to give out bad karma to those who did wrong, taking that burden away from Karma. But the active, serving Karma must do investigations per the Council's request. These investigations are needed when the two sides of the Council disagree about what an individual deserves.

Usually, these are cases where someone does something good but with bad intentions, and vice versa."

The three siblings nod their heads, trying to process all that has been said.

"This is certainly a lot to handle, and I'm sure this is information overload for all of you. ButI've gotta say," Karmasha smiles, "even though I'm sad that you all have to deal with this now, I'm so excited that I'll be able to teach you. And you won't have to go through it alone and scared like I did. Oh! And now I don't have to lie to you about what I do." She chuckles. "Yeah, now that you know, I should probably tell you: I'm not a pharmaceutical sales rep. That's just a cover. The Council has me traveling a lot for investigations."

"Wow." Klause speaks up. "After everything I've heard, my mother admitting to lying about her job is probably the least shocking thing I've heard all night."

"I'm sure it is." Karmasha laughs. "How about we continue tomorrow? It's getting late. Let's all go to sleep—I'll explain some more in the morning."

The children nod and each give their mother a long goodnight hug before heading upstairs to bed.

Upon closing her eyes, Karmasha allows her spirit to materialize in the In Between. She stands before the twelve thrones in the white room with its cloudy wisps of fog at her feet.

"Council of Twelve," Karmasha announces, "I have some very strange news to report." She takes a breath before continuing. "Somehow, my three children, Krista, Klause, and Kevin, have inherited the power of karma early. I don't know how this is possible—and why they have it before I died—but apparently they've possessed the power for about three months."

The council remains silent, all gazing at Karmasha with contempt in their eyes.

"What's going on?" Karmasha inquires, eyes sweeping over each council member.

Abraxos makes eye contact with Bernael, who is sitting next to him, and he nods. Then he looks to his left at Lahash, signaling him with a nod as well.

In an instant, Lahash dematerializes as a black wisp of fog surrounds him, and he disappears from view.

"Where did he go?" Karmasha asks, pointing at the now-empty chair.

The remaining eleven spirits sit in silence, though Karmasha notices that the six good spirits seem to bow their heads in shame.

"What's going on?" she shouts. Then suddenly she gasps for air, holding her neck as if an invisible force is choking her. She struggles to stay upright as she feels like someone is pulling and tugging at her body. She wisps away from the In Between, her spirit returning to her body.

≪O≫

A heart-wrenching scream fills the house, and the three children are instantly awake. They rush out of their bedrooms and meet each other in the hallway, each looking at the others with wide eyes.

Then the scream erupts again, and they realize it's coming from downstairs. They race to the origin of the scream and see one of the monsters from Halloween night dragging their mother out the door. They witness the pure terror in her eyes as the stone-like creature drags her by the hair. She kicks and twists around, trying to escape.

"Mom!" they shout in unison. They chase after the creature, out the door and into the harsh winter night. The figure seems to hover over the ground while the children trudge through the foot-deep snow as fast as they can.

The chase continues across the street and into the forest. While the children don't have to worry about the snow being as deep here, now they're having to dodge snow-covered tree limbs to continue forward. Meanwhile, just ahead of them, the monster becomes like a shadow and goes through the limbs like they aren't there. And poor Karmasha, who is still kicking and screaming, finds herself getting cut up and bruised by being dragged through the branches.

"Stop! Mom! Stop!" the children continue to shout at the monstrous predator.

The three run as fast as they can, Klause slightly ahead of Krista and Kevin due to his athleticism. They quickly traverse the mile and a half of the forest that leads to the center, where, just ahead of them, they see the large boulder atop the small hill.

The three children dodge the low-hanging branches and climb the small hill until they find themselves in a little clearing surrounding the massive stone. Just ten feet ahead of them, they see their mother being dragged into a black hole on the side of the rock. Her screams come to a deafening halt as the portal closes up just before the children make it to the boulder.

"No!" Krista screams as she slams her hand against the now-solid stone, tears streaming down her face.

Kevin and Klause follow suit, screaming and crying as they beat the rock with their hands, trying to open the portal but to no avail.

CHAPTER 40

A FTER WHAT SEEMS LIKE HOURS OF lashing out at the bare stone, the children fall to the ground, exhausted. The cold air whips through the trees, freezing their faces and bare hands, making them shiver uncontrollably.

"We need to get back to the house," Kevin speaks up.

"But Mom!" Krista protests.

"We'll be of no help to Mom if we freeze to death out here," Kevin reasons. "We need to get back to the house and warm ourselves, then figure out what to do."

Krista nods her head reluctantly, and the three siblings trudge back through the snow to their home.

The air in the house seems still and lifeless as they enter. Though it instantly begins to warm them, they walk around aimlessly, pacing back and forth as they try to calm themselves down and think of something.

"This is useless," Klause mutters. "Five hours ago, we found out that our mother is Karma and that we've inherited this crazy power from her!" he shouts. "Now she's gone, and with her goes any chance we have of even figuring out what to do or how to open the portal. We need her to save her!"

"I remember going through a portal in the rock when I dreamed about Princess Karma and Ekthesia," Kevin chimes in. "Maybe I can find a way to see her again . . ." He freezes. "The necklace!" he shouts. "Didn't mom say it could be used to call upon the wisdom of past Karmas?"

"Mom was wearing it," Krista grumbles as she slumps down onto the couch with her arms crossed.

"Well," Kevin sighs, "she came to me in a dream originally. So maybe I can concentrate when I dream tonight and see if she comes to me again?"

"Wait," Krista interjects. "You're actually proposing going to sleep? How can you go to sleep right now when our mom has been taken to who knows where and is probably getting killed or tortured or something?"

"I don't want to," Kevin argues with her, "but it's all I can think of right now. And the sooner I get to sleep and at least try, the sooner I'll know if we have to come up with something else."

"I agree with Kevin," Klause speaks up. "I think it's worth a try. I'll try, too. Maybe both of us calling out to her will be a force strong enough to get her attention."

Kevin nods his head in reply, and the two make their way upstairs. "Are you coming?" he calls down to his sister.

"I can't sleep right now." Krista shakes her head. "You guys go and try your way," she says as she opens her laptop. "I'll try my own research."

"What are you even going to research?" Kevin asks. "There's not a logical explanation to any of this."

"I don't know!" Krista shrieks. "But our mom was just dragged out of her bed and taken through a black hole before our very eyes! There's no way I could sleep right now!"

Kevin nods sullenly. He knows that his sister is in anguish; after all, he is, too. But he also knows that arguing with her won't get anywhere and will only make her more upset, so he lets it go and proceeds to his room to go to sleep.

Kevin's eyes open, and he looks around to find himself standing on a beach. The white sand seeps between his toes, and warm light beats down on his face. Behind him there's a tropical forest—filled with every vibrant color imaginable—with colorful birds flying around, chirping their beautiful songs. Ahead of him, a vast ocean goes on for as far as the eye can see. Its clear, blue waters lap gracefully on the sand near his feet.

As he looks out onto the horizon, something catches his eye.

Rising out of the ocean, a female figure floats gracefully over the water, her long, white dress flowing with the gentle breeze.

She glides over the water, and, as she comes closer, Kevin's eyes widen. He recognizes the lovely blonde woman in front of him.

"Miss Lavers?" he whispers as she lands on the beach next to him. Everything is the same about her except one thing: her loving blue eyes have been replaced by glowing white orbs.

"Yes," she says softly, her voice just as sweet and melodic as ever. "But my actual name is Dina, the Spirit of Learning."

"What?" His voice cracks.

"I was sent to watch over you in your world and steer you toward goodness and love."

"What do you mean?" Kevin asks.

"I am a good spirit of karma. Five of my brothers and sisters join me in the light. We wanted to help guide you toward the light so that you can help us bring peace to this world. Well, we wanted to help guide you and all your siblings, but there's definitely something about you that we admire most. Whenever you activated your power and sent bad karma, you ate yourself up inside, because you value love over hate more than anyone we know."

Kevin chokes up and blushes at the compliment, though he's still confused about what he's hearing.

"The duty of Karma is to embrace both the light and the dark, so why do you think there's still war and hate in this world? If we were to eradicate the darkness and hate, we could bring about peace and utopia. But we can't do it without the help of a Karma. With three potential Karmas, we thought this was the perfect opportunity to bring at least one of you to the light. Then maybe, together, we could stop the hate and fill this world with love."

"That sounds amazing," Kevin says as a smile lights up his face before quickly turning to a frown once again. "But that's not what I'm looking for right now. I'm looking for my mom. She was taken."

"Yes." Dina nods her head. "My evil brothers and sisters, spirits of the dark, did that. They want to separate her from all of you so that they can corrupt each of you to join their side." She chokes up. "Even a few of my own good brothers and sisters, spirits of the light, agree with them because they want to guide you to our side without her interference. But I think that's wrong. I want peace and happiness in this world, but a mother should never be ripped away from her children like that. I brought you here to the light realm of the spirit world to help you, against the wishes of my family, because a young man like you needs his mother."

"Thank you." He smiles at her. "How do we find her?"

"You must go through the portal at Kathrepta and go to the dark realm of the spirit world. That's where they'll be keeping her."

"But how?"

"You already possess the knowledge needed," she says softly. "Let me just help remind you of it."

Dina reaches out her hand and places it on Kevin's head, letting her thumb touch his forehead. A white light emits from her hand, and his eyes widen as memories flash before him.

He sees Princess Karma tugging at his hand, guiding him through the forest. "We must get back to Kathrepta!" she shouts. "I can open the veil for a moment, long enough to get back."

Kevin lives his dream once again and follows along as Princess Karma pulls him to the large rock at the center of the forest where he saw his mother dragged into the black hole.

"Anixeh!" she shouts as she reaches out her hand and pushes her fingers through the rock. The portal opens into a black hole, and the two dive in.

Kevin gasps as the image flashes away, and he's back on the beach with Dina. "I know what to do!"

Klause quickly drifts off to sleep, his mind focused on finding answers, and he wakes up in a lucid dream state.

He's in what seems to be a white room, but one with no walls. Wisps of fog swirl around his feet, reaching up to his knees. Ahead of him, atop a short altar, stands twelve thrones arched in a semicircle. The chairs look like they're made of black leather, with ornamental designs surrounding the borders of the cushions. But his eyes quickly lose focus on the thrones as he hears whispers coming from his right. He whips his head toward the sound.

There he sees the black figure that appeared to him in the forest and in the maze. Its skin is made up of black scales, dragon-like wings protrude from its back, and a pair of long, curved horns come out of its skull like that of a ram's.

The figure is talking to another muscular being that looks much more human. His wavy blond hair cascades down his head, and solid white eyes fill his sockets. He stands tall, his chest bulging out powerfully.

"You!" Klause growls from across the room.

Upon seeing him, the human-like one disappears from view, and the solid-black figure turns to face the middle sibling.

"Klause," he whispers calmly, though his voice still carries loudly throughout the cloud-like room.

"You took her!" Klause shouts as he charges at the creature and begins to punch and kick him.

The monstrous figure towers over him and doesn't even flinch as each hit lands on his scales. "Please, calm down," he says as he grabs Klause's shoulders, immobilizing him. "Let me explain."

"You took her!" he cries out. "You took my mom!"

"*I* didn't take her," the figure counters.

"Yeah, *you* didn't. But your freaky counterpart who looks like a walking mountain did!" he screams as he tries to wiggle himself out of the creature's grasp.

"We had to. She would have kept you from your destiny."

"What are you talking about?" Klause yells as tears begin to well in his eyes.

"I said it to you once, and I'll say it again. You are a great and powerful being that will bring a change to this world," the dark man says confidently. "Yes, your siblings possess the powers, too—but not like you do. Why do you think you were able to handle it faster than them? Why do you think you never killed anyone when they did?"

"But I did kill someone," Klause cries out. "That girl in the woods. After you and all those other spirits whispered to do so in my ear."

The figure shakes his head. "That was merely meant as a demonstration to show you how powerful you can be. You didn't actually take her life."

"What?" Klause asks shakily.

"Listen to me," the figure says sternly, letting Klause go. "We need your help. If you choose to let the darkness in, we can finally, with your help, bring true peace to this world. We can bring those who have died back to life."

"Like Miss Lavers?" Klause gasps.

"Hmph," the creature grunts. "Miss Lavers was not who you think she was. You know that man you saw me with earlier, with the white eyes? She's one of them. They want you to embrace the light. But if you do, no change will come, and the world will fall into sadness because nothing will get done. They were trying to casually deceive you by inserting her into your life, but we tried reaching out to you as directly as we could without freaking you out. You can't trust them, but you can trust us."

"How am I supposed to trust you after what you did to my mom?" Klause counters.

"I told you." He sighs. "She would keep you from doing what's necessary. Traditionally, Karmas embrace both the light and the dark and keep it in balance. But why do you think there's so much hate and war in this world? Why do people keep dying for no reason? There's something wrong with this world, and, again—with your help—we can finally change that. Only a Karma can possess the power we need to open the veil and bring back the dead. Your siblings are too weak to do it. But you have the potential strength and power."

"But—" Klause tries to argue though he doesn't know what to say.

"Unfortunately, we had to take her. But we're not hurting her, and we're not going to kill her. We sometimes have to get our hands dirty if we're ever going to enact true change. But the spirits of the light refuse to do any dirty work, and that's why nothing would ever get done with them in power."

"I understand." Klause nods his head as he wipes away the tears from his face. Taking a deep breath, he stands up straight to look into the pitch-black eyes of the figure before him. "What do you want me to do?"

CHAPTER 41

K EVIN WAKES UP, AND HE SPRINGS TO action. He quickly jumps out of bed and calls to his siblings at the top of his lungs as he makes his way down the stairs.

"I know what to do! I know how to find Mom!"

Klause rushes downstairs to meet Kevin and his sister.

"I know how to open the portal of Kathrepta!" Kevin says, nearly jumping up and down.

"Kathrepta?" Krista asks.

"I'll explain later," Kevin counters. "Let's just get ready and get going. We have our mother to save."

The three bundle up, throwing on layers so they won't get cold again. They rush out the door and make their way through the fallen snow to the edge of the forest. The morning sun shines through the cloudy sky, peeking light through the snow-covered trees.

With their adrenaline pumping, they make quick work of the mile and a half to the center of the forest, dodging low-hanging tree limbs along the way, and find themselves at the large boulder once again.

"Now what?" Krista asks her little brother.

"Get ready to move fast," Kevin replies. "I don't know how long it will stay open."

Looking at the rock towering in front of them, Kevin reaches out his open palm and touches the cold stone. "Anixeh!" he yells as loud as he can. Suddenly, his hand sinks into the rock, and, just like he saw Princess Karma do it, he wipes his hand through the outer shell of the stone, opening it up like a curtain to reveal a solid black hole of nothing.

With a deep breath—still holding the veil open—he steps into the portal and beckons his siblings to follow.

The children emerge from the darkness and find themselves in a glittering city of crystals and white stone. Kevin squints his eyes to adjust to the light.

He immediately recognizes his surroundings. "Ekthesia?" he whispers to himself as his eyes continue to adjust.

When his vision clears, Kevin and his siblings come face to face with a girl. She's dressed in a sparkling white dress, and tears stream out of her black and white contrasting eyes.

"Princess Karma!" Kevin shouts.

"Kevin," she sobs. "I'm so sorry. I didn't know they would take her. If I had seen it coming, I would have stopped them."

"It's okay," he replies. "What's important is that you help us find her now."

"Of course," she says as she raises her head to face them, fighting back her tears. "I sensed you coming through the portal, so I brought you all here so that I could guide you to the dark realm. Kathrepta can be extremely hard to navigate for new Karmas."

"Then let's not waste any more time," Krista speaks up. "Take us."

Princess Karma nods her head. "Everyone hold hands. I don't want to lose anyone in the portal." She looks at the towering stone wall that forms the original Kathrepta, and, with a loud voice, she calls out the password. "Anixeh!"

A black hole opens up on the wall and grows into a circle wide enough for the four of them to enter. Grabbing both Princess Karma's and Krista's hand, Kevin gathers his courage and follows Princess Karma into the void.

Krista isn't able to make out anything in the solid-black atmosphere around them. She can feel herself walking, though she isn't able to see the ground below her feet. Krista tightens her grip on Klause and Kevin as they make their way through the empty void, not knowing where Princess Karma is taking them.

"How can you see anything in this?" Klause asks, breaking the silence.

"It's not about seeing," Princess Karma replies. "It's about sensing—and we're almost there."

After a few more seconds of walking, Princess Karma announces their arrival. "We're here. Get ready."

Krista takes a deep breath to try to calm her nerves. A small hole opens up in front of them. Though it appears like light at first, compared to the pitch-black darkness they've been in, as it opens up wider, Krista realizes that the other side of the hole is still dark, but more like nighttime with the light of the moon shining down. As they step out of the portal, her eyes quickly adjust, and she finds herself standing in the forest at night.

"Wait, we're back in the forest," Krista says, blinking. "Did time speed up or something? How is it already nighttime?"

"This isn't your forest in the physical realm of the mortal world," Princess Karma whispers. "This is the dark realm of the spirit world. It is permanently blanketed in night, with only the gleam of the full moon lighting the realm."

"Is our mom here?" Kevin mutters.

"Yes. I sense her presence about a mile ahead. When you return, she should be able to guide you back, but I'll help if I need to," she says as she turns around to go back into the portal.

"Wait," Kevin calls after her. "Where are you going? We need your help."

"I can't stay," she replies sternly. "As the original Karma, I watch over the Council and all of my descendants. But they don't know that, and they can't ever know. I must return to Ekthesia where I belong. But I am fully confident that if you work together, the three of you can fight off the dark spirits long enough to get away with your mother. Good luck," she whispers before stepping back into the void and letting the veil close behind her.

Krista, Klause, and Kevin watch the portal close and see it get replaced with a solid stone wall, not quite as large as in Ekthesia, but still much bigger than the boulder in the mortal world. That fact alone tells Krista they aren't back in the woods by their house.

The three turn in the direction that Princess Karma pointed, Krista in the lead. As they start the hike forward, Krista gathers every ounce of courage and strength she can muster to prepare herself to fight for their mother.

CHAPTER 42

THE CHILDREN SLOWLY MAKE THEIR WAY through the dark forest, careful not to even step on a twig and alert the dark spirits of their arrival.

"Wait," Krista whispers as she raises her hand to halt her brothers slinking behind her. "I hear something."

The siblings remain still for a moment, and Krista opens up all of her senses for any clues when suddenly she hears movement ahead of them.

Tiptoeing forward, the three peek through a shrub and see four figures talking among themselves in a small clearing. Three of the figures are the three creatures that attacked them in the maze. The fourth towers over even the black, scaly one. She stands tall and muscular like an Amazon. Her arms and thighs are as big around as Klause's waist, and her fiery-red hair is swept back in a long ponytail.

Krista spots their mom beside the circle of four, tied up, gagged, and blindfolded, lying unmoving by a small rock.

"Why aren't the others here?" the enormous woman speaks with a coarse, raspy voice.

"They remained in the mortal world to keep an eye on things in case they need to run interference with the children," the black, horned spirit replies in his deep, echoing voice. "Lahash, what are they up to?"

The one that looks to be made of stone closes his pitch-black eyes and concentrates. Then his eyes fly open. "They're not in the mortal world!" The creature gasps.

"What?" the dark one growls.

"Let me check if they're in the In Between," he says as he closes his eyes again.

"Well?"

He shakes his head vigorously. "No!"

"What about the light realm?" shrieks the white-skinned, emaciated one. "Maybe the spirits of the light got to them first?"

Lahash shakes his head once more before opening his eyes and speaking in a hushed tone. "They're here."

All four figures follow his line of sight and end up looking directly at the three children who are still watching them under the cover of the trees.

Krista's eyes widen as she realizes they've been spotted. "Run!" she calls out to her brothers.

Krista speeds into the clearing, and Klause and Kevin quickly follow suit, making a mad sprint to their mother. Halfway there, the ground begins to shake, and with a flick of Lahash's arm, rocks emerge from the earth and fly toward the children. Klause stops in his tracks while Krista and Kevin swerve to the right and left respectively.

One of the large rocks hits Krista square in the chest, thrusting her upward and pushing her back. She plummets to the ground and slides across the dirt. Groaning, she struggles to get up, feeling like she's broken at least a few bones.

Kevin, who ran to the left, screams at the sight of his sister getting hit and finds himself running into the huge body of the muscular woman, his head bouncing off her hard stomach. He falls down as he rubs his forehead then looks up at the black eyes of the monstrous figure. He tries to get up and run away but finds himself frozen at the hideous sight.

The woman stoops down and grabs his ankle. She effortlessly picks him up and flings him across the clearing, and his body slams against a tree. He sits up against it, coughing up blood as he struggles to come out of his daze.

Klause runs back into the forest, ducking behind a tree to avoid the fight.

Krista stumbles forward, gripping her stomach, wincing. She rushes to Kevin to help him up and turns to face the dark, dragon-like figure across the clearing. As she looks into his dark eyes, all she senses is hatred and pain, and she can almost hear the screams of his victims. It's like the fire deep in his black eyes is burning a hole into her terrified heart.

Krista struggles to her feet and forces herself to stand tall. Gathering up her courage and strength, she takes a deep breath. As she inhales, she draws her arms up her body, and she feels her karmic energy build. She thrusts her arms forward and unleashes pandora onto Lahash, who was standing ready with rocks orbiting around him, about to attack. The stream of white and black light catches him off guard, and he flies backward through the branches of the trees behind him.

The witch-like creature sees Krista unleash pandora on her brother, and she quickly reacts to defend him. She transforms into a ghostly shadow and flies through the air toward Krista. Coming at Krista from the side, she pushes Krista down, cackling as she interrupts her stream of light.

With his sister knocked to the ground once again, Kevin gathers his strength and reaches his arm up to defend them from the shadowy woman who is now flying toward him. Light emerges from his open palm, black tendrils permeating through it, and the light pushes the ghostly figure back. Her shadow dissipates as a blood-curdling shriek pierces the air.

Kevin falls to his knees next to his sister after releasing his karmic energy on the shadowy creature, out of breath. "Klause!" he cries out. "Help us!"

Klause peeks his head around the tree and sees his siblings huddled together, clearly in pain. Taking a deep breath, he gathers his courage and runs out to help them.

As Klause runs toward his siblings, the muscular woman calls out to her brother. "Bernael!" she shrieks.

The scaly, black-skinned figure finally moves from his solitary stance and steps forward, toward the siblings. Raising his hands, he coaxes black tendrils from the ground. The sinewy vines wrap around Klause's body and immobilize him. He gasps for air as the black tentacles tighten around his chest.

Krista looks up at the dark figure and realizes that he has to keep his focus on the vines in order for them to stay above ground. With just one other enemy standing in the way of rescuing their mother, an idea lights up her mind.

"It looks like that Bernael guy has to remain standing like that to hold Klause," she whispers to her little brother.

"So we just have that muscular giant to get through," Kevin finishes her thought.

"Exactly," Krista confirms. "I'm going to use whatever karmic energy I have left to unleash pandora on her. Do you think you can make it to mom while I hold her off?"

Kevin nods his head as he pants heavily.

"I'm going to be pretty weak after that," Krista explains. "So after you free mom, use your pandora again and attack Bernael."

"I don't think I'll have enough energy to push him back."

"That's okay," Krista says. "You just need to stun him enough to make him lose his focus and let Klause go. Then we can all run back to Kathrepta."

"Uzza," Bernael's deep voice echoes around them. "Finish them off."

Krista watches as the muscular woman stomps toward them, clenching her fists, ready to attack. "Now!" Krista shouts as she stands up and summons her remaining karmic energy, emitting the stream of light from her hands once more. Uzza doesn't fly away as easily as Lahash did, but as Krista's pandora continues to bash against her body, she slides back as she struggles to hold her footing.

Meanwhile, Kevin is already halfway to his mother. Seeing her just ahead of him, he lets his adrenaline pump hard through his veins, and he quickly arrives at her tied-up body. He rips off her blindfold, and her eyes open wide. Kevin sighs, relieved that she's not unconscious. He tears at the ropes that bind her and removes her gag, and she gasps for air.

"Kevin," she whispers as she struggles to her feet and nods in his sister's direction. With one arm wrapped around his shoulder, the two hobble over to where Krista stands, still ejecting pandora from her body.

Karmasha gathers her own strength and, with a deep breath, emits the white and black light from an outstretched hand. Krista's and her mother's pandora merge together, and their combined strength pushes Uzza off her feet, making her fly off the ground and into the trees.

The two gasp for air and slump over. "Now, Kevin!" Krista shouts, breathless.

With his remaining karmic energy, Kevin bursts out all the pandora he can gather in himself, unleashing the stream of light onto Bernael. As he theorized, it's not enough to push him back, but it *is* enough to stun him, and he falls backward, losing his focus on Klause's sinewy prison.

Klause gasps for air as he falls to his hands and knees, coughing, but he doesn't have much time to recover.

"Come on!" Krista shouts as she grabs his arm and pulls him up. The four hurry back to Kathrepta, limping, but still trying their best to go as fast as they can.

Making it to the stone wall, Kevin stretches out his hand and says the magic word. "Anixeh," he shouts as they approach. A black hole forms on the wall and quickly grows to a circle six feet across. As the four enter the dark void, their hands gripped tightly to each other's, they hear a heart-wrenching roar that echoes around them like a hundred angry predators.

Before Kevin can think of what the sound might be, the portal closes behind them, and they're left in the pitch-black darkness of Kathrepta.

CHAPTER 43

THE FAMILY OF FOUR EMERGE FROM Kathrepta and collapses to the ground. The cold December air nips at their bare skin, and light from the sun shines down on them.

The four pant heavily and moan as they stagger to their feet, their adrenaline starting to wear off. They breathe in the cool air, letting it refresh their bodies as they hobble their way home, still leaning on each other for support.

They make it home just as the sun begins to set—time must have moved differently in the spirit realm—and they collapse on the warm cushions of their furniture.

Karmasha smiles at her children. "I am so proud of all of you," she mutters as she limps around to each of them, embracing each in a long hug.

Looking at all of their bloody wounds and bruises, she staggers to the kitchen. "Let me get the first-aid kit."

She brings it back and tries to nurse everyone back to health as best she can. "We may need to go to the hospital."

"And what would we say when they ask us what happened?" Kevin chimes in.

Krista shrugs her shoulders. "Hiking accident?"

"Hey," Karmasha chuckles. "You're already getting the hang of lying about karma-related incidents."

The four laugh then quickly groan as they notice that laughing makes their bruised bodies hurt more.

"Mom," Krista whimpers, "what are we going to do when they come back? Or, perhaps more importantly, how are you going to face the Council after what happened?"

"Honestly," Karmasha sighs, "I feel like the Council will disband after tonight. They're definitely two opposing forces, and now it seems like we're a third force against them."

"Well, that's good then, right?" Kevin asks.

"I don't know," Karmasha says sullenly. "The duty of Karma is to uphold balance between the light and the dark. But with the Council disbanded, the world will slowly fall into chaos, because the balance will be ripped away." She shakes her head. "Especially with what they have planned for Kathrepta."

"What plan?" Kevin inquires.

"And what *is* Kathrepta, Mom?" Krista adds.

"Kathrepta is the portal between worlds," Karmasha replies. "There's the light and dark realms of the spirit world and the In Between of the spirit world, which is like a limbo between the two realms. Then there's the physical and spiritual realms of the mortal world. Each of those realms exist on different planes. The spirit realm of the mortal world is where souls sometimes get stuck, essentially turning them into ghosts and condemning them to walk in the mortal world without being able to be seen by the living. The spirits of the Council and Karmas are the only ones who can go back and forth between worlds and realms, either through the use of Kathrepta or through the dream state."

Karmasha stops as she chokes up. "But what I overheard them talking about in the dark realm is their plan to rip the veil of Kathrepta. If they did that, spirits of the damned, basically, those sentenced to Hell, would be able to come through the tear and into the mortal world once again, which could unleash terror and horror on the world."

"How can they do that?" Kevin asks.

"Well, they don't possess the power on their own, so they would most likely need to use the power of a Karma to help them," she says, the thought leaving a bad taste in her mouth. "So it's a good thing we're all toge—" She stops herself and looks around. "Where's Klause?"

Krista jumps up. "Wasn't he just here?" She gasps at the thought of what could happen if the spirits were to grab her brother.

Kevin leaps to his feet and runs upstairs, and Karmasha scours the rest of the downstairs. Together, the three of them frantically search the house for him, and Krista hopes they'll find him sleeping in his room or taking a warm shower to relax—but he's nowhere to be found.

"Call him!" Kevin shouts from upstairs on his way to Klause's room.

Krista snatches her phone and hurriedly jabs at the bright screen.

"No answer," she says after a few rings.

"That's because it's right here," Kevin says from the stairs as he holds out Klause's phone. "It was in his room."

"Klause!" they cry out in unison. The three rush outside, not bothering to put their coats on as they continue to call out to him.

"Klau—" Krista begins to shout until something catches her eye deep within the forest. Nudging her littlest brother, she points to the figure walking deeper into the woods. The two of them chase after it and call out once again as they reach the edge of the forest. "Klause!"

The figure stops and turns around to face them, and they see Klause's face. His eyes have changed to the eyes of Karma, but small black snake-like lines permeate through his one white eye and black veins course throughout his body, reaching from his hands to his neck and slithering across his face.

Krista and Kevin stand frozen at the horrific sight of their brother being consumed by the darkness.

Suddenly, originating from deep within the woods, a strong wind forces its way through the trees. The wind hits Krista and Kevin with the strength of a dozen hurricanes and launches them through the air, making them fly backward and land on their backs in the cushiony snow. They sit up to look again, but their brother is gone, disappeared into the darkness of the forest.

Thank You for Reading!
Please add a review on Amazon and let me know what you thought!

Amazon reviews are extremely helpful for authors, thank you for taking the time to support me and my work.

Don't forget to share your review on social media with the hashtag, #KarmasChildren, and encourage others to read the story too!

And be sure to watch out for book 2 of the trilogy, Karma's Children – The Veil of Kathrepta!

DON'T FORGET TO SIGN UP FOR THE MONTHLY NEWSLETTER

TO RECEIVE NEWS ABOUT UPCOMING RELEASES, UPDATES FROM THE AUTHOR, SPECIAL OFFERS, GIVEAWAYS, AND BONUS CONTENT:

WWW.MAVERICKMOSES.COM

ACKNOWLEDGEMENTS

To my Lord and Savior, Jesus Christ, and my patron saint, St. Francis of Assisi, thank you for all of the incredible blessings you've given me. Thank you for helping me through the ups and downs of not only this author journey, but also life. And for giving me my friends, my family, and the ability to write down and share the imaginative worlds I dream about every night.

To my papa, my dad, for supporting me in all of my pursuits. After a failed business attempt, you asked me what my greatest passion in life was, and when I answered, "Writing," you motivated me by saying, "Go for it, then." I've always dreamed about publishing a book, but I would have never gotten to this point without you in my corner.

To my mom, thank you for showing me what a mother's love should be like and comforting me whenever I was scared or stressed. Because of you and papa, and the love the two of you shared, I'm able to write loving families and realistic relationships. I think about you everyday and I know that you're looking down on me from your place in God's arms, sending your love as I continue to pursue my dreams.

To my siblings, Mareesa, Shane, and Evin, life may throw things at us, but we'll always band together as a team. It's thanks to our adventures together that I was able to write Krista, Klause, and Kevin in a way that showcased their love and support for each other, even in the midst of tragedy.

To my best friend, Rumana... to my person, Ashley... to my anthro squad, Katie and Meagan... to my cousin, Alyssa... to my oldest friends, Mari and Jamie… and to my gothic cohort, Nicky… Thanks to all of you, I've learned to embrace who I really am and not be afraid to showcase the dark and silly sides of myself. We've laughed together, we've cried together, we've thrown up together, and we've survived life together. All of you are like my family and I thank God everyday for having such amazing friends who support me in everything I do. Love y'all.

To my amazing editor, Melissa Frey, thank you for taming the seemingly jumbled mess of this crazy story and teaching me the importance of showing versus telling. I've grown as a writer thanks to your constructive feedback and I'm super excited to continue working with you in the future.

To my fantastic cover designer, Lisandra Gomez, thank you for bringing to life Krista, Klause, and Kevin, and making their Karma eyes just as creeptastic as I imagined they would be.

To my Book Fiends co-hosts, Dawn Kurtagich, Marie Ventris, and Cassandra Carpio, I can't believe how close of friends we've become just over Instagram. Thank you for joining me in the adventure of hosting a book club and for supporting my author journey every step of the way. I can't wait to meet all of you in person someday.

To my Plotter Life team members, Brittany Wang, Alexandria Johnson, Nathalie Brundell, and Cam C. Gillings, thank you for welcoming me into the group with open arms. I've learned and grown so much as an author because of our group and I'm so excited to read what all of you have in store for the world in the future.

To all of the wonderful people I've met in the writing community, especially: Holly Davis, Heather Venkat, Renee Dugan, Jessi Elliott, Kim Chance, Mandi Lynn, Bethany Atazadeh, Lenn Woolston, J. M. Ivie, Phoebe Ross, Natalia Leigh, V Renae, Destiny Murtagh, and Charity Ryan... Thank you for being such awesome cheerleaders, motivating and inspiring me to keep writing.

And last, but certainly not least, to all of YOU—to all of my beautiful, wonderful, and unique readers and fans—I wouldn't be able to continue chasing my dreams of writing without all of you and your continued support. Thank you with all of my heart. You all mean the world to me.

Maverick Moses is a Texas-based author of dark fantasy and horror novels. He is a lover of country and punk rock music, lucid dreaming, and writing all the unique dream-inspired stories he has swirling around his mind. After a sudden family tragedy, Maverick's outlook on life changed, and he started to commit his life to fulfilling his greatest passions. One of these being his dream of becoming a published author. He started a YouTube channel in 2018 where he shares his love of books and pulls from his storytelling experience to teach other writers around the world. And after making a name for himself on Instagram for his stunning photos of books, he started offering his services as a Promo Image Designer and teaching his skills to other authors. His passion for teaching others has now extended to the classroom and as of the Fall of 2019, he will be teaching English to students in Madrid, Spain. When he's not writing at his local cafe and drinking tea, filming a video for his channel, or managing his business, he can be found curled up under a blanket with a horror book and a glass of wine.

CONNECT WITH MAVERICK ON:

Website: www.maverickmoses.com
Instagram: @authormaverickm
Facebook: @authormaverickm
Twitter: @authormaverickm
Goodreads: @authormaverickm
YouTube: www.youtube.com/maverickmoses

CPSIA information can be obtained
at www.ICGtesting.com
Printed in the USA
BVHW041556040919
557355BV00038B/1596/P